THE APPEAL OF EVIL

By
Pembroke Sinclair

Booktrope Editions
Seattle WA 2014

Cover Design by Ida Jansson
Edited by Katrina M. Randall

This is a work of fiction. Names, characters, places, brands, media, and incidents are either the product of the author's imagination or are used fictitiously. Any resemblance to similarly named places or to persons living or deceased is unintentional.

Print ISBN 978-1-62015-187-7

EPUB ISBN 978-1-62015-283-6

DISCOUNTS OR CUSTOMIZED EDITIONS MAY BE AVAILABLE FOR EDUCATIONAL AND OTHER GROUPS BASED ON BULK PURCHASE. For further information please contact info@booktrope.com

Library of Congress Control Number: 2014900566

For Wendy.

Thanks for having faith in Hell Boy.

ACKNOWLEDGMENTS

Thank you, Lori and Betty, for your invaluable insight as beta readers. Thank you also to my Booktrope team. I couldn't have done it without you.

CHAPTER 1

"YOU USED TO HAVE A CRUSH ON ME, YA KNOW."

Katie stopped dribbling the tennis ball on the court and focused on the speaker. Wes stood in front of her and to the left. He crouched, his forearms resting on his knees, his tennis racket twirling in his hand. When he glanced over his shoulder at her, a sly smile covered his lips. She remembered when his hair was blonde, but recently he had dyed it black and cut it into a short spike. It made his skin look paler than normal; his thin lips looked redder. The corners of his brown eyes wrinkled as his smile widened.

She set her jaw. There were so many things she could say to him, the first and foremost that he was an idiot, but she pressed her lips into a line. Why would he bring that up at that particular moment? What did it matter? With a shake of her head, she faced forward and threw the ball in the air. Pretending it was Wes's head, she smashed her racket into it with all her might. It sailed over the net, and her opponent moved to the right to intercept it. A forehand shot sent it back toward Katie and Wes. It was beyond her court realm, so she let Wes get it. Inwardly, she kind of hoped it would hit him in the mouth, maybe swell up his lips so he couldn't speak. It didn't. He was ready and backhanded it over the net. The two teams volleyed a few more times, then the girl on the opposite side hit the ball a little too hard, knocking it out of bounds.

"Yeah!" Wes pumped his fist in the air, then approached Katie for a high five.

Reluctantly, she gave him one. The other team readied to serve, but the bell rang. Thank goodness, Katie thought. After leaving the tennis courts, she followed the rest of her class into their respective locker rooms.

Not being one to dilly-dally in the locker room and catch up on the latest gossip, it didn't take Katie long to shower and change. Being naked around other girls made her nervous. She was more developed than they were, and the way they stared and huffed at her, like she could control nature, made her uncomfortable. The sooner she could cover up her body, the happier she was. She stopped at the bathroom mirror to quickly run a comb through her hair. With her dark brown hair wet, it looked black. It touched her shoulders, so it didn't take long to get the comb through. She made sure the part in the middle was straight. Her hazel eyes caught the fluorescent lights and glittered for a moment. She leaned closer to the mirror and applied chapstick to her pouty lips. Tucking her hair behind her ears, she turned and headed out of the locker room.

As she stepped out the door and headed for the gym, someone grabbed her wrist from behind. The touch was familiar, and, if she was honest with herself, expected. Especially after what happened on the courts, an apology was in order. The action didn't surprise her, and she didn't cry out. Instead, she allowed herself to be pulled toward the storage area near the girl's locker room that held the gymnastic mats. Her wrist was released and she turned to face him, crossing her arms over her chest. Wes hopped onto a stack of mats. It was typical of him to bring her someplace private, away from prying eyes, after making a spectacle in public. Wes was good at apologizing, but he was horrible about admitting he was wrong in front of others.

"Sorry about what I said on the court, but you needed some motivation. They were creaming us. I figured the best way to get you to play better was to make you mad." He smiled.

Katie rolled her eyes and turned to walk away. She didn't make it very far. Wes wrapped his legs around her thighs and pulled her backward. He draped his arm across her left shoulder and rested his hands on her ribs, right below her breast. She shuddered. His mouth was right next to her ear; his breath tickled her lobe.

"Why don't you still have a crush on me?" he whispered. He traced his fingertip gently across her shoulder and down her arm.

Goosebumps rose on her flesh. Her stomach fluttered; a chill ran down her spine. The smell of soap and mint drifted into her nostrils. The heat from his body radiated through her, making her feel safe. It was a short-lived sensation though, and the flutter in her stomach quickly turned into a lump. She lifted her arm and dug her elbow into his side. He grunted and let go. Without a word, she stomped toward the gym.

Wes caught his breath and jumped off the mats. "Katie, come on. Come back. I'm sorry."

She turned around, her face red with anger. "Just leave me alone!"

She tried to keep her emotions in check, but the words came out louder than she expected. She spun around quickly, not wanting Wes to see how upset she was. As she did, she ran into someone. Jerking back, she opened her mouth to apologize, but the words stuck in her throat. Bright blue eyes met hers, then quickly flicked over her head. She took in the boy's short light brown hair styled with gel, the full lips that turned down in a frown. The muscles bulged beneath his shirt, and she fought back the urge to place her hands back on his chest. Josh Evers.

"Everything all right, Katie? This guy bothering you?"

Oh, my God! she thought. He knows my name. Josh Evers knows my name!

It took her a moment to find her voice. "No, I'm fine. Thank you."

The redness in her face that had been there from anger quickly turned into embarrassment. The desire to run and hide from both boys overwhelmed her.

"Hey, Josh, why don't you mind your own business? Katie and I were having a private conversation."

Katie glanced over her shoulder. Wes had placed his hands on his hips but hadn't moved forward. She looked back at Josh.

"If you ask me, it doesn't look like she wants to talk to you at all." He balled his hands into fists at his sides, a gesture that didn't go unnoticed by Wes.

"Oh, really? What are you going to do about it, Josh?" Wes spit the name out before taking a step forward.

Josh also took a step, and worry coursed through Katie's body. The tension in the air was palpable. She didn't want them fighting on her account. Although, in the back of her mind, the action flattered her. Especially coming from Josh. He had just transferred to their school at the beginning of the semester. As the captain of the baseball team, he was the desire of every girl in the school and the envy of the boys. Katie hadn't thought he knew she existed. Yet, there he was coming to her rescue and calling her by name. It was enough to make her swoon. And she would have if the situation had been different. As it was, she needed to stay alert. A teacher could come by at any moment. She didn't want them getting in trouble for her. She had no idea what she would say, but she could probably come up with something if she really needed to.

Not that she had anything to worry about from Wes. He'd never do anything to hurt her. He wasn't lying when he said she used to have a crush on him. She'd liked him since they were in kindergarten. At times, Wes even made it seem he liked her back. Then, at other times, he made it perfectly clear he didn't reciprocate her feelings. Those moments crushed her, sent her home crying on more than one occasion. But those moments of tenderness, the ones that made her believe he liked her, sustained her, kept her hoping that maybe someday something would happen between them. He had toyed with her emotions for their entire school career.

By her senior year in high school, she'd had enough. She couldn't take the roller coaster of emotion, didn't want to feel like she was being strung along. She resolved to stay away from Wes, convincing herself she could do it. Only one more year, then she'd leave for college, and she'd never have to see him again. But he showed up her in homeroom, then in her gym class. She wanted to burst into tears when he took the desk next to her. Why was he making this so difficult? Still, she wasn't going to let her resolve fail. She would ignore him, pretend he didn't exist.

When Josh showed up, he made pretending Wes wasn't there so much easier. On top of that, he was standing up for her honor, defending her against a rival. As he stood in front of her, so close to her body she felt the heat radiating from him, thoughts of wrapping her arms around his waist and kissing him ran through her mind. She imagined how firm his muscles would feel under her hands, how soft his lips would be. She inhaled deeply and the spicy tang of aftershave caressed her nostrils. It took every ounce of self-control to keep from molesting him.

Josh took another step closer to Wes. Without thinking, she placed her hands on Josh's stomach to stay him. As she suspected, the muscles were hard under her fingers. The seriousness of the situation flooded back into her mind. If she didn't say something, a fight could ensue and someone might get hurt.

"Josh, no, please. He's not worth it." She glanced over her shoulder and stared at Wes with narrowed eyes.

Wes held his hands out to his sides. Hurt crossed his face.

Without saying another word, Josh wrapped his arm around Katie's shoulders and escorted her into the gym away from Wes.

*   *   *

Katie sat in her next class replaying the scenario in her mind. Her body still shook slightly from…what? Excitement? Fear? Disbelief? She wasn't sure. Maybe a combination of all of them. Josh Evers had come to her defense. Josh freaking Evers! The coolest and hottest boy in the entire school. It was more than she could have ever dreamed of. She wasn't exactly a nobody at school; she was on the varsity volleyball team, but she wasn't as popular as Deb Lander, President of Student Council and Head Cheerleader, who also happened to be her very best friend. She couldn't wait to tell Deb what happened. Deb was going to freak! Giddiness coursed through Katie and she couldn't stop the smile. Another thought occurred to her, one that made the smile falter slightly. Maybe Josh didn't do it because of who she was. Maybe he only did it because he saw someone in trouble and wanted to help out. Yeah, that was it. He was just helping out someone in need. It could have been anyone. That's just the type of guy he was. Still, he knew her name. That had to mean something, right? Would he have helped her if Wes hadn't done what he had done?

Wes. Even in her mind she said his name with disdain. What had he been thinking? He was always doing stuff like that to her.

She never used to mind. Like the one time in third grade when he kissed her under the slide. His lips were so soft, and his breath smelled like chocolate chip cookies. Her stomach tingled at the time, causing her to giggle. They kissed a few more times before the ball rang. Katie didn't want to go in. She wanted to stay with him. To make her feel better, and to get her to go back to class, he told her he'd meet her after school and they would ride bikes. That satisfied her enough to make it through the rest of the day.

There was also that other time in junior high when she had gotten a bad grade on a test. At lunch, he pulled her into an alcove and gave her a hug, allowing her to cry into his shoulder. Again, she wanted to remain in his arms and skip the rest of her classes. His promise that he'd come over to her house and hold her hand while she broke the news to her mom got her to go back to class and made her feel like she could face anything.

The moments had been tender and wonderful. They made her believe he actually cared, that maybe they could be boyfriend and girlfriend. But then he never showed up to ride bikes, and he wasn't at the bus stop. She had to face her mom alone. For every tender action, he always followed it up with abandonment.

Even in last period when he pulled her into the storage area and wrapped his arm around her, she felt the heat of his body on her back, the caress of his breath on her ear and neck. She felt close to him, not only physically, but emotionally. There had been many instances where she told him her secrets, her fears. Always it was Katie telling Wes hers. He usually sat quietly and listened, a look of sympathy on his face. At times, she thought he wanted to tell her something too, but he never did. He always listened. Occasionally, he offered bits of profound advice. Those were the things that ran through her mind as he pulled her close, the things that made the anger boil up inside her. She wouldn't get sucked back in. She couldn't. She was grateful Josh showed up when he did. Maybe he could make her forget completely about Wes. She sighed. That would be so nice. But it was probably a fluke. Again, Josh probably wasn't interested in her; he was just helping out. Still, a girl could have her dreams.

The bell rang, pulling Katie out of her trance. She looked around the room and at the clock. Had she really spent the entire period not paying attention? Her cheeks flushed. She'd have to get the notes from someone else. Grabbing her notebooks, she hugged them against her body and ducked her head low. She tried to make herself smaller, hoping that Mr. Graham wouldn't notice her as she walked out. Mr. Graham didn't make a habit of having her stay behind, but it was possible he noticed she wasn't paying attention. She didn't want to have to explain to him what was going on. Even worse, if he asked what they had talked about during class, she wouldn't know how to answer.

Katie headed for her locker, feeling thankful she only had one more class. She wished it was Friday so she could spend the weekend getting her head on straight, but it was only Tuesday. She'd have to wait. Katie's eyes were glued to the floor as she walked down the hall. She glanced up just before reaching for her combination. Her hand stopped in midair, her eyes flicked upward. Josh stood in front of her locker. Her breath caught in her throat. He knew where her locker was. He smiled, and Katie's knees weakened.

"You doing all right?" His voice had lost the edge it had when they were in the gym, replaced with a velvet smoothness.

Katie's jaw fell open slightly, her head jerked up and down mechanically, indicating a yes.

Concern crossed Josh's face. "You sure you're all right? You don't seem able to speak."

Katie's face turned red, and she averted her gaze back to the floor. "I'm...fine," she stammered out. "Just a little surprised to see you here."

He placed his hand on her shoulder. Her skin tingled, her stomach fluttered. She thought for a moment she'd melt under his touch. Her eyes traveled back up to his face, but he wasn't looking at her, he was looking over her. Her gaze followed his. Wes stood in the hallway, staring at the two of them. Immediately, Katie set her jaw, the fluttering in her stomach turned to stone. What was he doing over here? She narrowed her eyes. Why was he trying so hard to ruin her life? Wes lowered his head and turned away. Katie watched until he was out of sight, then she turned around, closed her eyes, and took a deep breath. That guy was so irritating.

"What's his problem?" Josh's voice was quiet and laced with concern.

Katie opened her eyes. "I don't know. I guess he enjoys tormenting me."

Josh put his other hand on her shoulder. "Well, as long as I'm around, you don't have to worry about him bothering you. Get your books. I'll walk you to class." He squeezed her shoulders gently before stepping out of the way.

She couldn't contain her smile and pressed a bit deeper into her locker. She didn't want him thinking she was an idiot. Before closing the locker door, she cleared her throat and bit the inside of her bottom lip to get the giddiness under control.

"Ready." She wrapped her arms around her books, hugging them close to her body.

The two of them proceeded down the hall. Katie felt like she was floating. If it weren't for her books weighing her down, she surely would have drifted toward the ceiling. What was this feeling? Lust? Love? Enamoration? Whatever it was, Katie liked it. For too long she had only felt anger and irritation or heartache because of a boy. She'd forgotten there could be an upside to relationships, a reason to care. She didn't want the feeling to end.

"Does he bother you often?"

She shrugged her shoulder. "Depends. Sometimes he does, but most times he leaves me alone."

"Did you use to date him or something?"

"No! I used to have a crush on him, but he's never felt the same way."

Oh, crap! Why did I just tell him that? Josh didn't need to know about her feelings for another boy. She lifted her books toward her face, hoping to hide behind them.

Josh looked at her, confused. "So you don't have a crush on him anymore?"

Katie suddenly felt very uncomfortable talking to Josh about her feelings for Wes. She wanted the guy to like her, not think she was pining for someone else, but at the same time, she didn't want anything bad to happen to Wes. She didn't think Josh would beat him up or anything, but she couldn't be sure. She didn't know Josh well. Besides, she saw the look on Wes's face when he stared at them from across the hall; he genuinely looked hurt. Sad, even. It made her feel bad for him. She shook her head. That was exactly the type of thinking that kept sucking her back into his game. It was a good thing he was sad. Maybe that meant she was actually getting to him. A little heartache would do him some good.

"It's a little more complicated than that."

Did she really just say that out loud? Why didn't she tell him no? She didn't have a crush on Wes anymore; he was ancient history. The words were there, they just wouldn't come out.

"Well, maybe you can tell me about it later. Here's your class."

The two of them stopped in front of the door. Katie stared into the classroom and then back at Josh.

"Yeah, sure. I guess."

He smiled that melt-you-in-your-shoes smile. "I'll be here after class. Then, I'll give you a ride home. If you don't mind. I want to make sure you're going to be all right."

Katie's stomach flip flopped. "That would be great." The words squeaked out of her mouth.

Josh squeezed her arm before leaving to go to his class. Katie floated to her seat. She wasn't going to be able to pay attention in this class, either.

Just as he promised, Josh waited for Katie after class. Her face flushed and her ears got hot when her gaze fell on him in the hall. She couldn't look him in the eye. This much attention from a guy was new territory for her. He walked close to her, his arm occasionally brushing against her shoulder. Her grin spread from ear to ear. A giggle threatened to escape her lips, but she kept it in. As they approached her locker, the smile vanished. The giggle turned into a growl. Wes stood in front of the door. What did he want now? Couldn't he get the hint? Didn't Katie make it clear she wanted to be left alone? Didn't both Katie and Josh together make that perfectly clear?

Still, she couldn't just turn off the feelings she had for Wes, especially since she'd had them for so long. That irritated her. Why was Wes so hard to get out of her system? If she was honest with herself, she'd admit having two boys vying for her attention made her feel special and wanted, even if one of them was Wes. But she knew how the story with Wes would end. With heartache and disappointment. There was no contest who the winner of that battle would be. Josh hadn't done anything to make her not trust him. Yet. Her stomach tightened with fear. Would Josh do something to make her question his feelings? What if he turned out to be just like Wes? It was possible. Although Katie thought it highly unlikely. So far, he'd fulfilled every promise he'd made to her. It may have only been two, but that was two more than Wes had fulfilled.

Wes hadn't noticed them. His gaze focused on something down the hall. Katie slowed her approach. She really didn't want the two to get into another argument. It was possible it could escalate into a fistfight, and she didn't want either one of them getting suspended or injured. Well, she kind of wanted Wes to get suspended; then she wouldn't have to deal with him. But she knew both of them would get in trouble. Josh placed a hand on her arm, stopping her in the middle of the hall. "Wait here. I'll take care of this."

Katie opened her mouth to protest, but Josh had already taken off. Other students moved out of his way as he stomped down the hall, determination on his face. He was half way to the locker when Wes noticed him. With a scowl, he pushed himself away from the door and headed down the hall. Inwardly, Katie sighed. Josh followed him for a moment, probably to make sure he didn't hide around the corner and wait. Eventually, he turned back to her and jerked his head to the right, indicating it was now safe for her to approach. Katie nodded once before heading toward her locker.

"Persistent, isn't he?" Josh placed his back against the lockers and kept his eyes on the hall before him.

He was so close, Katie's hand brushed against his arm as she grabbed her backpack and homework out of the locker. She hardly noticed. Her mind focused on Wes and attempted to figure out what he was doing.

"He never used to be," Katie said quietly.

Josh turned his gaze on her. "What do you mean?"

She placed her backpack strap on her shoulder and closed the locker door, a little more forcefully than she intended. Several of the nearby students jerked their heads upward and stared at her intently, waiting to see what she'd do next. After a few seconds, when nothing happened, they turned back to what they were doing.

"I mean, I've known Wes for a long time. Since kindergarten, and he's never gone out of his way to hunt me down before."

Josh pushed himself away from the locker, and they headed down the hall. "So what exactly happened in gym today? Were you two having a lover's quarrel?"

"Absolutely not!" Again, she was louder than she wanted to be and turned several students' heads. She cleared her throat and lowered her voice. "He has this weird thing, I don't really know how to explain it, of keeping me on the hook." She sighed and cocked her head to the right to look at him. "Does that make sense?"

"Not really."

She pursed her lips. She didn't want to go into too much detail about her and Wes's relationship, but it looked like she didn't have a choice. How would Josh react? He had been kind enough to step in and defend her; the least she could do was let him know what he was defending. She took another breath and averted her gaze to the floor.

"See, I've had a crush on Wes since I was six. But he's never returned those feelings." The last set of words rushed out of her mouth, as if she was afraid he'd leave before she got the chance to say them. "Every time I try to get over him, he does something that sucks me back in, makes me think he might actually care for me." She glanced at him out of the corner of her eye, trying to gauge his reaction. "But since this summer, I decided I wasn't going to let him do that to me anymore. I was done with him. For good. What you saw in the gym was him trying to pull me back in and me fighting against it."

Josh nodded. "Makes sense." He stopped in front of his locker and turned the combo.

Makes sense? Was that all he was going to say? He wasn't going to comment on how he felt about it? Was he having regrets? Second thoughts? What was going on in his brain?

He finished getting his stuff out of his locker and closed it. He turned and smiled.

"You ready?"

Her worries were forgotten. Who cared what he thought? He was still interested, he was still going to take her home, and that was all that mattered.

*   *   *

Katie fumbled with her backpack strap, trying to procrastinate getting out of the car, but not trying to look like that's what she was doing. This was the first time she'd been in a car with a boy, and she didn't know the protocol. Still, she couldn't sit there forever. With each passing second, she grew more and more uncomfortable and her fake fumbling turned into real fumbling.

"Well, thanks for the ride."

Josh placed his elbow on the middle console and leaned to the side. He was inches from her. Oh, God! Was he going to try to kiss her? Katie's stomach knotted. She wasn't ready for that. It was too soon. She hardly knew him. She hadn't brushed her teeth all day. Yet, there was something intriguing about his lips. They looked soft and inviting. What would they feel like against hers?

Josh chuckled. "Not a problem. I'm glad I can be of service. Hand me your cell phone."

It wasn't what Katie expected him to say, and it took her a moment to find her voice. "My phone? Why?"

"So I can give you my number and you can call me if Wes bothers you again."

"Oh. Okay." She opened her bag and dug through her books. It took a while, but she found her phone and handed it to Josh.

"Here's mine. Put your number in there."

Katie did as he asked, then handed the phone back. As she did, his fingers brushed against her hand, sending chills up her arm, causing her breath to catch.

"You want me to pick you up tomorrow?" His voice was low, sensual.

Katie's heart skipped a beat. "Yeah. That would be great." She cleared her throat and shrugged her shoulder. Did she really sound that desperate? "I mean, if you want." Was that enough to sound nonchalant?

Josh chuckled again. "I'll be here at seven-thirty."

"Okay." Katie breathed.

She stared into his eyes for a few seconds, then fumbled for the door handle. Getting out, she tripped over the curb, but caught herself before falling on her face. She turned back to the car and peered into the window.

"Thanks again for the ride. I'll see you in the morning."

Josh smiled his wonderful smile. "See you tomorrow."

Katie took a step back and watched him drive down the street before turning to go into the house. She wanted to skip and kick her heels in the air, but she was afraid if she did, she would drift away into the clouds.

CHAPTER 2

KATIE HALF-EXPECTED Wes to show up at her house later that night. He seemed so desperate to talk to her after the gym incident, but as usual, he didn't. Katie didn't know if that relieved or saddened her. She was proud of herself for sticking to her word and not letting Wes draw her back in, but part of her also felt guilty. Whether she liked it or not, Wes knew a lot about her. When he wanted to be around, he was a great listener. He'd been there on many occasions when she needed a shoulder to cry on or advice. It would have been nice to be able to talk to him about Josh. He probably would have some great ideas on how to handle the situation, and as a boy, he could tell her what to expect or maybe what Josh was thinking. Wes could be a jerk, but he was also one of Katie's best friends. Being in his presence made her feel safe. She couldn't explain why, but when Wes was close, it made her believe nothing could hurt her. Except him. But, she reminded herself, for every moment he'd been there for her, there were twice as many when he let her down.

Still, she couldn't stop her gaze from drifting away from the TV and out the front window toward his house. She frowned. All the lights were out; the windows were dark. He wasn't home. As usual. But where did he go? Katie knew it was only him and his dad that lived in the house. She didn't have details about what happened to his mom, only that it was something really bad. Wes had told her that; then his eyes filled with tears, and he turned away before Katie saw them fall. She'd never met his dad. Once, she saw him through the open front door while she stood on the porch, but that was it. What did he do? Wes said he worked at night and slept during the day, so no one was allowed in his house, ever. That didn't really bother Katie. She and the other kids in the neighborhood made up their own stories about Wes's dad, and most of them involved murder and children disappearing. Katie never wanted to meet the man.

Katie often wondered if his dad was part of the reason Wes wasn't allowed to see her. She figured that somehow he found out about Wes and Katie and forbid his son from seeing her again. That's what she used to tell herself anyway. It made her feel like less of a loser to think someone else held Wes back. That's probably where he was now. His dad probably found out about what happened at school and took Wes to work with him to keep him out of trouble. She sighed. What did it matter? If it was Wes or his dad, there was no way they could ever have a normal relationship, so why worry about it? She turned back to the TV. But between her and Josh, anything was possible.

As if on cue, her phone rang. She picked it up off the couch. Josh's name and number were highlighted on the screen. Stifling a squeal, she hurried upstairs to her room so her mom couldn't overhear the conversation.

"Hello?"

"Hey, Katie. You all right? You sound out of breath."

Katie flopped onto her bed, her face turned red. "Yeah, I'm fine. I didn't realize I'd left my phone upstairs, so I ran to get it." She hoped he believed the lie.

"Oh, gotcha. Yeah, I hate it when I leave my phone in the other room. So, how are things going? You have a good night?"

"Sure. It was pretty typical. Nothing exciting to report."

"So no visits from Wes?"

Was that the only thing he cared about? Would he lose interest in her if Wes wasn't bothering her anymore? Should she lie and tell him he showed up?

"Nope. It's been quiet." The words came out of her mouth before she had the chance to decide if that was what she really wanted to say.

"Good. Glad to hear it. You have any plans this weekend?"

Katie's heart fluttered and she bit her bottom lip to keep from squealing. "No. I think it's wide open." Of course it was wide open.

Volleyball hadn't started yet and she hadn't heard from Deb that she wanted to do something.

"Cool. We should catch a movie."

She did a fist pump in the air and kicked her feet in rapid succession against her bed. "That sounds great."

"Nice. Well, I won't keep you. I'll see you in the morning."

"Okay. Have a good night."

"You too, Katie."

She clicked end on her phone and flung herself onto her back. In excitement and joy, she flopped around for a while, a happy dance while lying down. She was elated and a little disbelieving she actually had a date with Josh. If she had known that would happen, she would have quit pining after Wes a long time ago.

*   *   *

Katie had a hard time sleeping. She dreamt she was in a large room surrounded by darkness. She didn't know where she was, but the floor was concrete and sounds echoed eerily from a distance. Her mind told her it was a warehouse, but why would she be in a warehouse? She wasn't alone. Things were in the shadows. What kind of things, she didn't know. They scurried across the floor, their feet making scraping sounds, and they hissed. Occasionally, pinpoints of white lights shone through the blackness, looking almost like eyes. Every time Katie tried to focus on those lights, they'd blur and vanish.

Fear surged through her body. She crouched on the floor, glancing around, wondering if an attack would come. The overwhelming desire to run made her legs twitch, but she couldn't move. Her muscles wouldn't obey her commands. The darkness closed in. The creatures came with it, getting closer and closer to her. She pulled herself into a ball, hoping to fold in on herself. She wanted to scream, but no sound came out of her mouth. Soon, the darkness was on her, and with it, an unnatural chill. Goosebumps formed on her flesh, and she shivered. Something breathed on the back of her neck.

Katie jerked awake and sucked in a sharp breath. The fear from the dream lingered. The darkness still surrounded her. It took her a moment to realize she was in her room. A streak of silver light from the moon penetrated through her curtains, giving her a dull source of light to cling to. She stared at it for a long time, her hand on her forehead, as the remnants of the dream lingered in her mind. Where had that come from? It seemed so real, so vivid, but nightmares always did. She threw off the covers and headed to the bathroom.

After taking care of business and getting a drink of water, she crawled back into bed. Still, sleep didn't come easily, and visions of the nightmare remained in her brain. She rolled onto her right side and tucked her arm under her head. Just as she was about to close her eyes, she sensed something behind her. Before she could turn, a hand clamped over her mouth, stifling a scream. Katie struggled and flailed against the attacker, but the grip was too strong. It pulled her backward, right into a body. The warmth radiated through her t-shirt, an arm wrapped around her chest. Warm breath tickled her ear and neck. There was something familiar about the grasp. She stopped struggling and turned to look over her shoulder.

The fear that had consumed her body and caused her heart to pound against her rib cage subsided, replaced with anger. She grabbed the hand over her mouth and pulled it roughly away.

"Wes," she hissed. "What are you doing here?" She struggled against his grip, but he wouldn't let go. "How did you get into my room?"

"I'm sorry," he whispered in her ear.

Katie quit trying to get away from him. Even in his soft tone, she heard the sadness, sensed his desperation. What was going on?

"I didn't mean to scare you, but I've been trying to talk to you all day." His voice quaked. Was he crying?

Katie had to hold onto her resolve, her anger. Who did this guy think he was sneaking into her bedroom at 3:00 in the morning?

"Yeah, well, there is such a thing as a phone."

"Would you have answered it if you knew it was me?"

She didn't respond. He had her there. She wouldn't have picked up. Still, this was beyond creepy, even for him.

"What do you want?" She gritted her teeth and grabbed a handful of sheet. If he loosened his grip even a little, she was going to pull away from him.

He lowered his head so he nuzzled her neck. His lips were on her skin, but he wasn't kissing her. All the anger drained from her body, and her hand relaxed its grip on the sheets. The gesture should have sent warning bells off in her head, made her wonder what he was doing, made her feel like her body was in danger. Instead, all she felt was safe, comforted. She closed her eyes and relished the feel of his breath on her neck, the warmth of his chest against her back, the strength of his arm around her.

"I want you to know that I'm sorry for everything. For not being there, for making you think I don't care." His voice caught. Pools of moisture formed on her skin. She was convinced he was crying. "And I want you to stay away from Josh."

Katie's eyes flew open and anger surged back through her. So that's what this was about. It was just another ploy to pull her back in, make her care about him so he could break her heart—for the millionth time. And she almost fell for it. Her grip tightened once again around the sheet and she pulled with all her might. Wes didn't fight; he let her go. She made it to the other side of the bed and plopped onto the floor, kneeling so she faced him. He was in the same position across from her. The room was still dark, so she couldn't see him clearly, but the small sliver of light illuminated his red-rimmed eyes. If it had been anyone else, she would have felt sorry for him. On Wes, the only thought that crossed her mind was that he was getting what he deserved.

"Get out of my house." She tried to keep her voice soft; she didn't want to wake her mom.

Mom would have been a valuable asset if Wes decided to do anything, and, no doubt, her mom would have no trouble getting Wes out of the house. She kept a gun next to the bed for safety. It had been there since her dad's funeral eleven years ago. One scream would bring her mom running into the room. Yet, Katie didn't want to bring her in if she didn't have to. She could handle Wes. Besides, her mom might call the police. She didn't want the entire school talking about the incident.

"Please, Katie, hear me out."

"Hear you out? I've been 'hearing you out' since we were six. You've never told me anything. The only thing I get from you are broken promises."

Katie had had enough. Anger boiled over inside her. Jumping to her feet, she stomped around the bed and grabbed Wes by the ear. She placed her mouth inches from his head and hissed.

"I'm not going to play these games any longer. You've had years to let me hear you out." She released her grip. "Get out. I don't ever want to see you again." She folded her hands across her chest.

Slowly, Wes got to his feet. He paused for a moment in front of her and tried to touch her cheek, but she jerked away from his fingertips.

"Josh isn't who you think he is," Wes stated softly.

Katie forcefully grabbed his arms and roughly turned him toward the window, figuring that was the only way he could have gotten into her room. With slow, deliberate steps, he climbed onto the windowsill before disappearing into the night. Katie threw herself onto her bed and screamed into her pillow. She was sure she wouldn't get a wink of sleep for the rest of the night.

*   *   *

Katie's alarm screeched through the room. With a heavy hand, she hit the snooze button and moaned. Her eyes were glued shut and her head ached. For two hours after Wes left, she tossed and turned, wondering if he was going to come back into her room and thinking about all the things she wanted to say to him. She had fallen asleep for an hour, but it only felt like two minutes. It was going to be a long day.

After rubbing her eyes for several moments, she was able to open them and lifted the covers off her body. As she did, she noticed something on her sheets. It was dark brown in color and dried into the fibers. She blinked. It looked almost like blood. She pulled the covers closer to her face, attempting to get a better look. Yep. It was dried blood. But where did it come from? She pushed herself into a sitting position and looked at her t-shirt. A streak of blood went across her front. Her eyes flew open, her heart rate increased, and she flew out of bed. She stood on the side Wes had been on a few hours earlier and examined the area. The side of her bed and the floor were marked with the same brown stains. Oh, my God! Wes was covered in blood when he came into her room.

She dove across the bed and grabbed her phone. With shaking hands, she found Josh's number and pressed the call button. The phone rang on the other end. One. Two. Three times.

"C'mon!" Katie said under her breath. "Pick up."

Right before the phone went to voicemail, a groggy "Hello?" sounded in her ear.

She sighed with relief. "Josh, it's Katie. Are you all right?"

"Katie? What time is it? Yeah, I'm fine. What's going on?"

Thank God he wasn't dead! "I'll tell you about it later. Sorry to wake you."

"It's fine. You sure you don't want to talk about it now?"

"I can't. I have some things to take care of, but I'll see you when you pick me up."

"Okay."

Katie hung up the phone and turned back to her bed. She pulled the covers off and stacked them in her closet. She'd take care of them after school. Thank goodness Wes hadn't done anything to Josh. From the way Wes acted last night, it was quite conceivable he had killed Josh. At least that was the first thought that ran through her mind. Of course, she didn't really believe it. She didn't think Wes was the murdering type. She never felt threatened in his presence, ever. Not even last night. Yet, after the previous episode, she realized she knew nothing about Wes. It was completely possible he was a killer. Maybe that was why he was always gone. He was off finding victims. Or maybe his dad was a killer and forced Wes to help him with the crimes. That would explain a lot and validate her childhood fears. She shuddered.

Katie tore off her pajamas and threw them with her sheets, then high-tailed it to the bathroom to shower. She glanced at herself in the mirror, and her jaw fell open. On her face, across her lips, was a faded, bloody handprint. Wes literally must have been covered from head to toe. Where had that much blood come from? She didn't hesitate, she jumped in the shower and immediately soaped up. If her mom saw her like that, she would definitely call the police. What happened? Why was he covered in blood? And why did she feel compelled to protect him? If he was a murderer or an accomplice, she needed to call the police. He needed to pay for his crimes. Perhaps she protected him because she didn't really believe he had hurt anybody.

Oh, no! What if he was injured? What if he was dying and came into her room to tell her something important before he expired? She kicked him out. Threw him wounded into the night. How could she do that? She quickly rinsed the soap from her body and out of her hair, then threw on a towel and ran back to her room. Grabbing her phone, she dialed Wes's number. It went straight to voicemail. She contemplated leaving a message, then decided against it. She dropped her hand to her side. What was she doing? She walked to the window and looked out, just to make sure his body wasn't in the yard below. When she didn't see his corpse, she shook her head. It was another ruse, it had to be. Granted, Wes had never done anything like this before, but she'd never given him a reason to. Maybe he was crazy. Maybe he was so jealous of Josh that it led him to act like a creep. He was fine, she was sure of it. He'd be at school, and everything would return to normal. It had to. She couldn't feel guilty about kicking Wes out of her room. If he was injured, he should have said so. Yes, he would have. She was sure of it. Nodding with resolve, she placed her phone on the bed and got dressed for school.

CHAPTER 3

JOSH PICKED HER UP AT 7:30 on the dot, and she ran to his car. As she climbed into the front seat, she noticed the worry on his face.

"What's going on?" he asked. "You freaked me out when you called this morning. I almost showed up at your house five minutes later to find out what was going on."

"You're never going to believe what happened. Wes broke into my room last night at, like, three in the morning."

"Are you all right?"

"Yeah, I'm fine. He didn't hurt me."

"Did he say why he was there?"

Katie suddenly felt insecure about telling Josh the rest of the story. Wes was her friend, she'd known him for eleven years, she'd only known Josh for less than a day. For some reason she couldn't explain, she felt like she was betraying Wes. He didn't hurt her; he only wanted to tell her something, about Josh. Maybe Wes really did know something she didn't. No! He was acting crazy, being jealous. Still, would Josh hurt Wes if she told him the whole story? She didn't want anyone to get hurt.

She shook her head. "He wanted to apologize for earlier in the day."

Josh laughed. "He couldn't send you a text to do that?"

She shrugged. "I guess not."

Josh put the car in gear and they headed to school.

Katie noticed Wes's truck in the parking lot at school and that made her feel better. At least she knew he didn't die in his house or yard. Still, the mystery deepened. Whose blood was he covered in? Why did he show up at her house? Would she be able to talk to him at school? Did she want to talk to him? Confusion and anger swirled through her being. On top of that, she was exhausted. Her brain was not functioning as it should. She decided to leave it up to fate. If Wes showed up to talk to her, she would hear him out. If not, well, she'd decide what she wanted to do later.

Josh parked the car and the pair walked toward the building. He stared over her shoulder, squinting to scan the area behind her. When he found what he was looking for, a smile crossed his lips.

"Looks like your boyfriend wasn't too tired after last night's visit. He made it to school."

"He's not my boyfriend," Katie snapped.

Where did that come from? Why would Josh make that comment? He knew they weren't an item. Granted, he didn't know the extent of their relationship, but he knew enough to know they weren't together. Maybe she was reading too deeply into it. Maybe he didn't mean anything by it. She was tired, that's all. Still, that comment coupled with Wes's warning to stay away from Josh had her nerves frazzled. Maybe she should go home sick and get some rest. It might be better to approach the topic after a good nap. No. She'd never sleep. Her brain would keep replaying the scenario through her mind. She'd have to tough out the day and see what happened.

Josh escorted her to her locker. "You gonna be all right to get to class on your own?"

"Of course."

"Okay. You have my number if you need anything." He placed his hand on Katie's cheek and gave her a quick kiss on the lips. "Don't be shy about using it."

Katie was too shocked to say anything, so she just nodded. Josh turned and headed for his locker. Adrenaline surged through her. She just might make it through the day.

She made it to homeroom five minutes before the bell. Part of her expected to see Wes already at his desk, but the other part wasn't surprised he wasn't there. She took her seat and focused on the door, trying not to look desperate and worried. Student after student filed in, but not Wes. The bell rang, and his desk remained empty. Katie knew he was at school, she saw his truck, and the teacher didn't call his name during roll call, so she must have known where he was.

Katie slumped in her seat. Of course he wasn't there. It was what Wes always did. She really should have been used to it.

By second period, Katie questioned her decision to stay at school. Twice she fell asleep in class and caught herself before her head slammed into the desk. Thankfully, no one else noticed. Between classes, she went to the vending machines and got herself a Mountain Dew. She didn't think it would help, but she was desperate to try anything.

Third period wasn't much different. The pop wasn't helping at all. How could she possibly make it through the day? She still had one period and lunch before gym class, where she knew for sure she'd see Wes. She had to. He couldn't possibly avoid going to all his classes. Katie knew he was still there. The vending machines were by a window that overlooked the parking lot and his truck was still out there. She contemplated hunting him down, but thought better of it. If his actions were part of his game to reel her back in, she didn't want to give him the satisfaction of knowing it had worked. Yet, curiosity burned through her, and she wanted her questions answered. It was pretty much the only thing keeping her at school. She'd have to hold out a little longer.

She was a little disconcerted that she hadn't seen Wes in the halls. Yesterday, she couldn't lose the guy. Josh was his chivalrous self and met her after every class, escorting her to her locker or the next class. That made her feel better. At least someone cared about her well-being. And, technically, Wes wasn't acting out of the norm. However, he did have a lot of explaining to do about the night before, and she would have assumed he wanted to do that. But, if she was honest with herself, she would say she wasn't really surprised.

By the time gym came around, she was so annoyed and irritated that Wes hadn't tried to hunt her down during the day she really didn't care if she saw him or not. It all became very clear it was just another one of his stunts to keep her interested in him. Even with her sleep-deprived brain, she figured Wes killed a rabbit or other small animal and smeared it all over himself to worry her. If it was even real blood. For all she knew, he could have concocted something before climbing into her window. Ugh! That guy was so infuriating. Why did she constantly allow herself to be sucked back in? What was so damn special about Wes that she couldn't get him out of her system?

As she and Josh walked to gym, she was half-tempted to say screw it and skip class. She really didn't want to see Wes. Even more so, she really didn't want to be forced to be his tennis double again. She was so angry, she might end up beating him with her racket. Her pace slowed the closer they got to class.

"Everything all right?" Josh asked.

Katie stopped in the hall. "I don't know. I'm not sure I want to face him, you know?"

Josh put his arm around her shoulders, a gesture that made her stomach tingle and her heart skip a beat. "It'll be fine. I'm here to protect you. Besides, aren't you the least bit curious to see what he's going to do?"

If Josh had asked her that question this morning, she would have instantly said yes. At that moment, though, she honestly couldn't care less. She really didn't care if she saw him again. Katie opened her mouth to tell Josh that, and to tell him they should skip class, when Ms. Bode buzzed by them.

"C'mon, kids. Class is about to start."

Crap! No way they could ditch now. With a sigh, Katie let Josh lead her into the gym.

The bell rang as Katie slowly made her way to the locker room. She reached forward to grab the door handle when someone grabbed her from behind and lifted her up. A squeak of surprise escaped her lips, but no other sound came out. A hand covered her mouth. Really? Katie thought. Again? He's going to pay for it this time. She struggled against her attacker, but his grip was too strong. He lifted her like she weighed no more than a doll. He carried her toward the gymnastic storage area and stepped over the mats until they were in the far back corner, covered in shadow.

Wes set her down but refused to take his hand of her mouth. Katie clawed and scratched at his hand and arm and attempted to kick him. Wes calmly grabbed her wrists with his free hand and pressed his body against hers so she couldn't attack him anymore. Her face turned red and anger boiled through her veins. She screamed even though his hand was still over her mouth.

"Katie, please, calm down. I'm not going to hurt you."

In response, she struggled against his body—a futile attempt since he was so much stronger than she was.

Wes opened his mouth to speak again, but the words never came out. Instead, a familiar, "Again?" echoed through the storage space, and Wes was pulled away from Katie. Josh had him by the back of the collar and threw him onto a pile of mats. Katie took deep breaths and moved away from the wall to get a better view.

"Why can't you take a hint, Wes? The lady doesn't want anything to do with you."

Wes got to his feet and brought his fists up, ready to fight. The space was big enough that there was a few feet between the two boys, but if things escalated, Katie would be caught in the middle of the battle.

"Yeah, well, she wouldn't want you if she knew what you really were."

Josh threw his head back and laughed. "And what is that, Wes? A nice, clean cut boy who actually pays attention to her and wants to be around her?"

Wes's eyes narrowed to slits. "You know exactly what I'm talking about."

Josh clicked his tongue on the roof of his mouth. "I'm afraid I don't. I think you may be delusional."

Katie had her back pressed against the wall and slowly slid her way to the opening so she could run into the gym and get help. Josh was doing a great job of staying between her and Wes.

"Don't listen to him, Katie. He's only using you to get to me."

Katie glanced over Josh's shoulder. Wes had taken his eyes off his opponent for a second and stared at her, a pleading look in his eyes. Typical, she thought. Wes always thought things were about him. Someone needed to let him know the world didn't revolve around him. She tore her gaze from his and continued toward the exit. Wes sensed her intention and moved so he blocked the opening. He was within an arm's length of Josh.

Josh shook his head. "C'mon, Wes. That's not very nice. If Katie wants to leave, you should allow her to leave."

"No. I'm not letting you do this to her."

Josh laughed. "Do what? Show her how a real boyfriend is supposed to treat her?"

Katie stopped for a second and glanced at Josh. Did he just say what she thought he said? Boyfriend? Could it really be true? Was that how he viewed their thing? Katie wasn't exactly sure what was going on, but she was going to rethink it the next time she got the chance. If the situation hadn't been so dire, she would have let the inner smile play across her lips.

Wes's face crunched in anger, his fists balled at his sides. Without another word, he lunged forward. Wes and Josh fell to the ground, right at Katie's feet. Wes sat on Josh's chest and slammed his fist into the side of Josh's head. Katie screamed.

"Stop it! Wes! Leave him alone!"

She wanted to jump between the two to make him stop, but she was afraid of getting hit. The pupils in Wes's eyes were dilated, completely blocking out the brown that was normally there. Rage shrouded his face. Fear squeezed Katie's chest. She'd never seen him act like that before. She continued her trek toward the opening. If she couldn't stop him, Ms. Bode would have to.

Wes brought his fist up by his shoulder to smash into Josh's face again. As he brought it down, Josh grabbed it and stopped him. Katie stopped and watched the two of them. Josh stared at Wes, a smile curling his lips. Blood stained Josh's teeth.

"That all you got?" With a growl and movement almost too fast for Katie to see, Josh pushed Wes.

Wes sailed across the room, through the opening, and slammed into the wall several yards away. Katie's jaw fell open. What just happened? No one was that strong. Josh got to his feet and wiped the blood from his nose with the back of his hand. He stared at Wes, who sat on the floor, his head hanging on his chest.

Josh reached his right hand behind him, toward Katie. "C'mon. He won't bother you for a while."

Katie hesitated taking the offered hand. Her chest heaved with ragged breaths, her head swam with confusion. How did Josh throw Wes like that?

Josh looked over his shoulder at her. "You're not going to get another chance. Are you coming or what?"

Katie shook herself out of her daze and grabbed Josh's hand. The pair stepped over the mats and through the opening. They stopped in front of Wes. He looked up at them, his eyes taking a moment to focus. Katie glanced into the gym. Why wasn't anyone else coming to help them? Surely they heard the fight, her screaming.

The door to the girl's locker room opened in slow motion. Two of her classmates walked out, but their movement wasn't normal. They, too, were stuck in slow motion.

"Hey!" she called to them and tried to run up to them, but Josh had a tight grip on her hand and wouldn't let go.

"They can't do anything to help you," Josh said softly. "They don't even know what's happening."

Katie's breath caught in her throat. She turned back to Josh, eyes wide. "What is happening?" The words barely made it out of her mouth. Josh smiled.

"Let her go. I'm the one you want," Wes croaked from the floor.

Josh knelt down in front of him, inadvertently pulling Katie closer since he wouldn't let go of her hand. "You know I'm not going to do that. Besides, you never know how useful she's actually going to be."

Wes attempted to lunge for Josh, but his balance was off and he fell to one side. Josh laughed. Katie stared down the hall at the two girls as they headed to class. She reached for them, hoping they'd sense her desperation and turn around. Josh jerked on her hand, pulling her into his body. Her back was against his chest, and he wrapped his arm around her shoulders. His breath tickled her ear lobe.

"Take one last look, Katie. It might be the last time you see him."

Katie stared down at Wes. He struggled to get to his feet. Pain pinched his face, along with something else. For a moment, Katie thought it looked like sadness. He reached for her. Involuntarily, she reached for him too. Then, the world was shrouded in blackness.

CHAPTER 4

KATIE'S KNEES GAVE OUT and she collapsed to the floor. A cold, hard, concrete floor. Her head flew up and she took in her surroundings. She was in a huge warehouse, just like in her dream. Unlike her dream, however, she wasn't shrouded in darkness. Daylight streamed in through dirty broken windows. An inch-thick layer of dirt and grime covered the ground. A pile of rubble dominated the far corner. Otherwise, the place was empty. She tried to get to her feet, but an unseen force held her down. Something hissed behind her. Katie turned, and instantly wished she hadn't. A creature, the size and shape of a German shepherd, snarled at her. There was no hair on the thing's body, only thin gray skin pulled tight over bones. Katie didn't even think the animal had muscles. Drool dripped from its yellowed teeth, and its eyes glowed white. It growled and took a step toward her. She tried to recoil, but couldn't move. A scuffling sounded to her right. Three more creatures were in the room. She whimpered. Please don't let them hurt me. She wasn't exactly sure who the inner plea was directed to, she just hoped someone intervened.

"You don't have to worry about them," Josh said.

Katie looked at him. He towered over her.

"The Hell Hounds won't hurt you."

"What's going on? Why am I here? What are you doing with me?"

Josh knelt next to her. "Well, you see, Wes was kind of right. I was using you to get to him. Do you have any idea how hard it is to find a weakness in a Praesul? They shun all human contact and relationships. Mainly so we can't use it against them."

Along with fear, confusion crept into Katie's body. What in the world was Josh talking about? He must have noticed the look on her face.

"Oh, so he didn't tell you. I kind of figured. A Praesul is an ancient order of people who protect the world against demons. Hell spawn, if you will." He smiled. "Creatures like me. They've been doing it for centuries. They are incredibly secretive, and damn strong. Really, our only hope of defeating them is to take away something they love."

Katie's head spun, her mind couldn't focus. Was she dreaming?

"I see you're still having a hard time understanding this. I'm not sure how much clearer I can make it." He took a deep breath and placed his index finger on his lips, staying like that for several seconds in deep thought. "See, I'm a demon. I'm from Hell. I came to Earth to wreak some havoc. You know, kill some people and harvest some souls. I thought the best place to do that would be high school. Young souls looking for a good time are very easy to harvest. Sins flow very freely among your age group. Are you with me so far?"

Katie didn't want to admit it, but he was making sense. She nodded.

"Good. As I said, my original plan was to take a few souls and then leave at the end of the semester. Then, I discovered a Praesul. Wes. Do you have any idea how fortuitous that was?"

Katie shook her head.

"Of course not. You didn't even know they existed until a few seconds ago. Well, for a demon, finding a Praesul is like finding sunken treasure. If we can kill one, it raises us in rank. We get more power, more responsibility. I couldn't let the opportunity pass me by."

"If." Katie repeated. Her throat was dry and her voice croaked. "You said 'if you can kill one.'"

Josh scowled and nodded his head. "Yes, like I said, Praesuls are incredibly difficult to kill. The training they receive to fight demons is intense, and they are blessed. Given special powers by..." He directed his gaze upward.

"Why me? Why are you using me? Wes doesn't care about me."

Josh stroked her cheek with the back of his fingers. Katie recoiled from his touch as far as she could. "Oh, Katie. Of course he does. But he can't get too close to you. He can't let his feelings show because then I can use them against him."

Ice formed in Katie's stomach. "What are you going to do to me?"

Josh shook his head and shrugged his shoulders at the same time. "Nothing. You are going to help me."

"Help you?"

"Yeah. Why not? You said it yourself, you're trying to get away from Wes, get him to leave your life completely. You want to be free from his heartache and broken promises. Deliver him to me and I can promise he'll be gone forever."

Katie stared at Josh. Horror and disbelief surged through her veins. "You mean dead."

"It's a small technicality. You won't have to worry about him anymore, though, will you?"

Her throat tightened. "And what will happen to me?" The words came out as a whisper.

"Nothing. Well, I guess if you want, you could always stay with me. We could travel around harvesting souls together and looking for other Praesuls."

"And if I don't help you, what will happen to me?"

"I'll have to hurt you a little, just to prove a point to Wes, but you won't die. Well, hopefully, you won't die. If Wes feels about you the way I think he does, he should stop me right before I kill you."

Katie's breath caught in her throat. What was she going to do? In either scenario, someone was going to get hurt. Did she want to alleviate her pain by helping Josh fight against Wes? Josh was right: she did want Wes out of her life, but not permanently. And she didn't want to watch him die. Sure, he'd been a jerk and broken her heart for eleven years, but that didn't mean he deserved to be killed. And why would Josh want her to travel around with him? He was a demon; what could he possibly like about her? What could she possibly see in a demon? Did she have any other choices? If she protected Wes, she'd probably be right back where they started. If he didn't get close to anyone for fear of them getting hurt, he would totally abandon her after they got out of this alive. Or would he? What if he continued to play the same game, claiming he just wanted to make sure she was safe? Wes popping in and out of her life would drive her insane. It already did. If she helped Josh, she was helping evil, but he'd stayed true to his word and never let her down. Could she count the last day as him keeping his word? She thought so. Wes had never kept his word hours after giving it. What was she going to do?

"Time isn't a luxury right now." Josh interrupted her thoughts. "You need to decide."

Katie opened her mouth to speak, but before she got the chance, blue light flashed through the warehouse, temporarily blinding her. The Hell Hounds growled, and she heard Josh get to his feet. She blinked to clear her vision.

"You're not the only one who can use portals, Josh." The familiar voice hissed through the room, shrouded in anger and hatred.

"Oh, I know, Wes. I wasn't trying to get completely away from you. Just buying a little time."

Katie's vision cleared and she looked up. Josh stood on her left, Wes was on her right. They stared at each other, eyes narrowed. Wes's fists were clenched at his side. Josh had his hands folded across his chest, acting very nonchalant. The Hounds circled Wes.

"Let her go. I'm here now. She's no longer of any use to you."

"Well, now, that's not exactly true. See, I know how much she means to you. I can see into your soul, remember? She consumes three-fourths of it."

Wes's face turned red. Katie couldn't tell if it was from anger or embarrassment. A small part of her softened. Did he really feel that way about her? Did he really keep her in his soul? No! Stop that! You're dealing with a demon. They lie. Josh just said that to get a rise out of Wes. Still, if Wes didn't care in some way, he wouldn't be there for her.

Josh smiled. "I also know what you've done to her. How you've turned her feelings of love into hate. I know how you crushed her dreams and broke her heart. I've seen the resentment in her soul."

Wes's fists relaxed. Sadness shrouded his face. His gaze drifted down to Katie for a brief second, then drifted back to Josh. "I've seen it too," he spoke softly.

The look of pain on Wes's face was almost too much to bear. If she had been in a different situation and wasn't afraid for her life, she might have cried for him. How could she have put him through that? She never meant to hurt him. She just wanted him to know how bad he made her feel. But those sorrows didn't last for long. She had more pressing concerns, mainly if someone was going to die and if there was anything she could do to stop it.

"Oh, he already knew how much it hurt you," Josh said, seemingly reading Katie's mind. "He felt it in his heart and soul every time he left you hanging. His heart ached, his soul cried out."

Wes turned his gaze back on Katie. He held his hands out to her. "I never meant to hurt you. Never. I had no choice." Tears filled his eyes.

Anger surged through Katie's body. Using all her might, she struggled to stand. With some effort, she got to her feet.

"How dare you," she hissed. Her voice was low, barely over a whisper. "After all these years, after all I've told you, you could have said something to me."

It irritated her it took a situation like this for Wes to open up. He'd had ample opportunities to prepare her for a moment like this. Instead, he kept his mouth shut, made her vulnerable.

A tear fell onto Wes's cheek, and he shook his head. "What would I have said? Would you have believed me?"

"I loved you, Wes. I would've believed anything you told me. I would've tried to help you through your problems. Instead, you kept me in the dark, treated me like an idiot. Made me feel hated."

Wes choked. "I'm sorry. I did it to protect you."

Katie narrowed her eyes to slits. "I don't need you to protect me."

Josh laughed. "Ooooh! She's a feisty one."

His voice broke Wes's gaze from Katie's face. He glared at Josh, then looked back at Katie. "You can't believe anything he says. He's evil. He lies to get what he wants."

Katie huffed. "That may be, but he's still kept more promises than you have."

Wes's gaze dropped to the floor.

Josh laughed again. "She has you there, buddy. What are you going to do now?"

The Hell Hounds drew in closer to Wes, their lips curled up, exposing their teeth. With a sniff, Wes wiped his face with both hands. He looked up. Anger and hatred once again covered his face.

"You still won't win. Even if Katie doesn't love me anymore, I'm not going to let you have her."

Josh shrugged his right shoulder. "She's the one who makes that decision, not you."

Wes yelled and ran forward. A Hound lunged and grabbed the back of his shirt, but it wasn't fast enough. The material tore and Wes continued toward Josh. He tackled him to the hard ground, then sat on his chest and proceeded to punch him in the head.

Blood spattered from Wes's fist and Josh's face. Josh's head bounced off the concrete floor with every punch, but Wes only got three of four hits in before the dogs dragged him off their master.

"I will kill you!" Wes screamed. "Kill you!"

The dogs' teeth dug into his flesh, and he yelped in pain. Katie watched blood ooze from his arms as the dogs continued to drag him across the floor. Josh picked himself up and brushed the dust from the shirt. Blood dripped from his face.

"That may be. But you'll have to wait until I get back to Hell to do it."

Katie's eyes scanned the area, looking for something she could use as a weapon. Her heart thudded in her chest, fear tingled her extremities. Her gaze fell on the pile of trash. She ran toward it. Her heart sank as she examined it. Decayed boards with rusted, broken nails were stacked to her waist, along with some rusted wire, broken plastic, and layers upon layers of dirt. She toed the pile, hoping to find something buried underneath. It paid off. She bent down and picked up a pipe. It wasn't any thicker than her two fingers, but it was twice as long as her arm and weighty. It would do the trick.

A yell echoed through the large space, and Katie turned back toward Josh and Wes. The dogs had gotten Wes prostrate on the floor, and they held him in place with their jaws around his ankles and wrists. Blood drained from the puncture wounds. Josh stood over him, smiling. Why wasn't he concerned with what Katie was doing? Was she really that little of a threat he didn't need to keep an eye on her? Part of her couldn't help feeling rejected. Wes was right; Josh didn't want anything to do with her. Josh was only using her to get to him, and now that Josh had Wes, Katie didn't matter. That really pissed her off. She wasn't going to be anyone's pawn, and she wasn't going to be the reason for anyone's death. Her grip tightened around the pipe.

Josh lowered himself onto Wes's chest, and the nail on his index finger grew to ridiculous lengths. It caught and reflected the light like a sword blade. Wes struggled underneath Josh's weight, causing the teeth at his wrists and ankles to rip his flesh open further. Blood pooled under his extremities.

"I've waited a long time to kill a Praesul. I'm going to enjoy this." He dragged his nail across Wes's midsection, slicing open his shirt and drawing a line of blood from his abdomen. Wes yipped, then bit his bottom lip to keep the scream from erupting from his mouth.

Katie didn't waste any more time. With the pipe raised over her right shoulder, she ran toward Josh. When she was close, she swung as hard as she could. The metal connected with his skull with a crunch, and Josh fell backward. One of the dogs released its grip on Wes's ankle and lunged at her. The teeth sunk into her left forearm.

"Aaaaah!" She raised the pipe again and smashed it into the creature's head. The only thing that accomplished was causing the thing to dig its teeth deeper into her arm.

Wes kicked his free leg at the other hound. Successfully, he got it to release him, then focused on the ones at his wrist. Confusion followed, and the dogs were unsure where they needed to be. The one from his ankle shook his head and attempted to get a grip back on his leg, but Wes moved too much. The one on his left hand let go to help his companion subdue Katie. It leapt on her chest and knocked her to the ground. The pipe skittered across the floor. Jaws moved toward her neck.

"NO!" Josh's voice boomed through the room. "Don't hurt her!"

The dog growled but obeyed its master. It remained on her chest, and the other let her arm go. Katie pushed the creature to the side and clambered to her feet. Blood dripped down her fingers. It felt numb and useless. She scanned the floor for her pipe.

Wes had made it to his feet and stared at Josh, who seemed to be having trouble keeping his balance. Through the mess of blood on his face, Katie noticed a small dent in his forehead where she hit him. Did she really strike him that hard? She didn't think she had the strength. The boys faced off, ready to attack each other again, if they could find the strength. The dogs circled Wes, waiting for the chance to grab his limbs once again.

Katie found her pipe and picked it up. She wasn't going to wait. With one hand, she raised it over her shoulder and smashed it into the closest Hell Hound's head. It whined and its legs gave out underneath him. She smashed it again to silence it. The others didn't like that. They turned their attention to her and bared their teeth. She whacked the other one nearest her with the pipe, knocking its legs out from underneath it. Before it could recover, she kicked it in the head with all of her might. She felt the impact through her maroon Chuck Taylor. For a second, she wished she'd had a chance to put on her tennis shoes. The other two stopped and glared at her.

"Come on!" she yelled. "I'll take care of you, too!"

The dogs snarled at her but didn't come any closer. Josh's laugh resounded through the warehouse.

"You've got spunk. I like that."

"I don't care what you like," Katie spat.

"Yeah, if you're not careful," Wes wheezed, "she'll use that spunk on you."

Katie pointed the end of the pipe at him. "I didn't do this for you," she hissed.

Wes snapped his mouth shut and averted his gaze to the floor.

"I don't really care what kind of tiff the two of you have going on, but I'm not going to be a part of it anymore. I'm done."

Josh held his hands out to his sides. "Fair enough. I wouldn't want you to have to witness your friend's death." He pointed at her. "But you and I aren't done. I'll find you when I'm done here. We really need to talk."

His comment disconcerted her, but she didn't want to stick around any longer to figure out what he meant. This wasn't her battle. She wasn't going to fight anymore. Katie was about to turn and head for the door when Wes threw something through the air. She had no idea where it had come from, but he apparently used the distraction to grab it. From where Katie stood, it looked like water. It splashed against Josh's face, and instantly his skin steamed. He screamed and covered his face with his hands. Wes wasted no time. He lunged forward again, pulling something out of the back of his waist band. He kicked Josh in the chest and knocked him over. Then, while sitting on him, plunged a gold knife through his eye. Josh's screams instantly stopped, his body went limp. The dogs turned and ran toward Wes, but he was ready. More water arched through the air, and when the droplets touched them, they exploded. Black ooze and bone scattered about the room. Katie covered her eyes to protect them. The adrenaline drained from her body, and she sunk to the floor.

Her head spun, her stomach cramped. She thought for sure she was going to puke. Pain throbbed through her arm. Her vision blurred. She was going to pass out. But before she could, she felt Wes's hands on her shoulders.

"You're fine. Take deep breaths."

Her first inclination was to shove him away. She didn't want him anywhere near her, but she didn't have the strength. That anger was enough to revive her, and the wave of dizziness subsided. It also cleared her vision, and she glanced over Wes's shoulder. Josh stood behind them, the knife sticking out of his eye, pointing at them. She sucked in a sharp breath and tightened her grip on the pipe. It probably wouldn't do her any good, but it was better than nothing.

"This isn't over," he growled. "I will come back for her. She will be mine." He pulled the knife out of his eye, and his body disintegrated into dust.

Wes took a deep breath and wiped his forehead with the back of his hand. "Glad that's over." His face pinched with pain. "Katie, you got your phone on you?"

The pipe clanked onto the floor as she frantically patted her pockets and found it in her right front one. "Yeah."

"Good. Call me an ambulance." With that, he fell over backward, unconscious.

*   *   *

Katie sat next to Wes's hospital bed with her arm wrapped in a bandage after receiving thirty stitches. She had been cleared to go home, and her mom was ready to take her, but she asked if she could stay for a little while longer, just to keep an eye on Wes. His wounds had been cleaned and stitched up, and aside from needing a transfusion, he was going to be just fine. Katie wasn't exactly sure how she felt about that. On one hand, she was extremely happy he was still alive. Even though he'd broken her heart a bazillion times, she didn't want to see anything bad happen to him. On the other, it would have made things much simpler if he wouldn't have made it. It would have depressed her, yes, but she would have moved on. Did that make her heartless? Or a bad person? What was going to happen to them now?

She reached forward and gently traced her fingertip across his forehead. His skin was pale and wrinkled with concern. As she pulled her hand away, he opened his eyes and stared at her.

"Hey." He smiled. His voice was soft and croaked.

"Hey."

"Where am I?"

"The hospital. You lost a lot of blood, but you're going to be just fine."

He stared at her intently. "What did you tell them?"

Katie sighed and leaned back in her chair. "Well, I couldn't exactly tell them you were in a fight with a demon from Hell who sicced his Hell Hounds on us, could I?" She returned his intense gaze. "I told them we skipped school to talk. We went to the warehouse for privacy and were attacked by a rabid dog." She shrugged. "I don't really know if they believed me, but they didn't ask any more questions."

Wes attempted to push himself up. Katie placed a hand on his shoulder.

"No, just relax. It's fine."

Wes ignored her and got himself into a sitting position. He turned toward her and grabbed her face gently in both hands. "Josh wasn't joking. He will continue to come after you. He will not stop until you are his."

A lump formed in Katie's throat. "Why?"

"To hurt me. But also because he likes you."

"How can that be? He's a demon. Can he have those feelings?"

Wes sighed. "He saw something in you, Katie. Something dark, something evil. He wants you for his own."

Fear grew in the pit of Katie's stomach. "What do you mean?" Her voice was barely over a whisper. "I'm not evil."

Wes pulled her closer and gently kissed her lips. Katie wanted to protest, to pull away, to scream at him and make him answer her question, but she couldn't. His lips were warm and soft, radiating security through her entire being. It felt natural, right, like she was exactly where she was supposed to be. After a few moments, he pulled away.

"I'm sorry I never told you about my, ah, other life. I couldn't. I needed to keep you safe."

Katie nodded. "I know. Just tell me one thing. The other night, when you came into my room, whose blood were you covered in?" It was pointless to try to get the answers she wanted out of him, so she figured she'd try to get answers to the multitude of other questions she had.

Wes's gaze dropped. "My dad's."

Her eyes grew wide. "Is he all right?"

Wes nodded. "He'll survive. Just like I will." He met her gaze. "But as long as Josh is still out there, I'm not letting you out of my sight."

Katie rolled her eyes and pulled away from Wes. "I'll find a way to take care of him."

Wes wrapped his arm around the back of her neck to keep her from going too far. Katie didn't fight against his grip and rested her forehead against his.

"Josh was nothing compared to the other creatures out there. He's a low-level demon. A baby."

Katie closed her eyes and reveled in the warmth of Wes's touch. "Well, then I guess you'll have to teach me how to fight them."

Wes kissed her lips again. "Gladly."

The squeak of shoes on linoleum caused the pair to look up at a nurse, who smiled.

"Glad to see you're awake. I'll need to check your vitals."

He released his grip on Katie, and she stood to leave. "I need to get home anyway. Although I'm not looking forward to facing my mom. She wasn't very happy that we skipped school. I'll come back tomorrow. If I can." She headed toward the door, but was stopped by his voice.

"You used to have a crush on me, ya know."

Katie turned and smiled at him. "You're right. I did."

CHAPTER 5

KATIE LAY ON HER BED, her left arm folded across her chest. Her right arm lightly touched the wrap, as if to protect it, and stared at the ceiling. Her lips still tingled from when Wes kissed her. Again, it wasn't the first time their lips had connected, but it was definitely different. She swore she felt his love that time. It was no longer a secret that he deeply and honestly cared for her. So why was she struggling to feel the same way? Why didn't she feel elated and happy that she had finally gotten him to admit he had feelings for her? Was it because there was the underlying tension that he was going to abandon her again? It was still a possibility, despite the fact he had let her into his life. Or had he?

There was that doubt again. At the hospital, she pretended everything was all right. She acted like they were okay, like things had gone back to normal, but they hadn't. Things would never be the same again. And she wasn't sure she could continue to act like she liked him, especially since she wasn't exactly sure how she felt.

She shook her head and took a deep breath. A Praesul. Was that even possible? She looked up the word on the internet when she got home from the hospital, but it wasn't much help. It was defined, but the definition barely seemed to fit with what Wes did. What exactly did he do? Josh said he protected the world from demons, but what did that entail? And were there that many demons coming into the world to constitute an entire secret society? There must have been. After all, Katie couldn't deny what she had seen with her own eyes. Or could she? Logically, she could think of several different reasons for what happened, first and foremost in her mind being drugs. She wasn't one to experiment with drugs, but that didn't mean Wes or Josh hadn't slipped her something when she wasn't looking. After all, Wes had shown up in her room in the middle of the night covered in blood. What if he did something to her then? Did she believe he would? No, but then again she didn't think he'd be a demon slayer, either. The former sounded much more logical than the latter. She needed something tangible to cling to, and being slipped a hallucinogen explained everything.

But it didn't ease her tension completely. It raised more questions than answers. The most important of all being why would they, either Wes or Josh, give her a hallucinogen? What could they have possibly gained out of the situation by doing that? It didn't make any sense. Katie's head ached, so she rolled onto her side. It was close to 11:00. She'd gone to bed around 9:00, telling her mom she was tired and needed to rest. That hadn't been a lie. She was tired. She'd spent the day running on very little sleep. But her brain wouldn't stop with the questions long enough for her to close her eyes. She needed answers.

Her mom had actually handled the situation fairly well. After all, Katie had the marks on her arm that proved a dog bit her, and the doctor confirmed it, so why would her mom think she was lying? She got into a little bit of trouble for skipping school, but not as much as she expected to. Maybe Mom was just happy she was all right and hadn't been totally mangled. Not like Wes and his dad. She hadn't seen Wes's dad, but she could assume it was pretty bad considering the amount of blood that was on Wes.

The thought made her shiver. Would she see Wes's dad now? Now that she knew the secret, did that mean she was part of their club and had to hang out with the entire family? Somewhere in the back of her mind, she knew his dad wasn't the monster she made him out to be, but the other part told her it was hard to let go of preconceived notions and prejudices. So much was happening in such a short amount of time, she didn't know how to handle it. She needed to talk to someone, preferably Wes, but it was much too late to call. Besides, she didn't think he had his phone on him in the hospital. She sighed and closed her eyes, attempting to fall asleep.

Her phone vibrated on the nightstand, causing her eyes to fly open. She reached for it and held it in front of her face. A chill ran through her. A text from Josh. Did she dare read it? Why would he send it? What could he possibly still want with her? Oh, that's right. She was still the link to Wes. Josh's way in to hurt him. Jerk. Curiosity got the best of her and she opened the message.

I miss you.

She pushed her eyebrows together. What an odd thing to say. First of all, they hadn't known each other that long; secondly, Josh was using her; thirdly, and probably most importantly, he was a demon. How could he possibly miss her?

Leave me alone, she texted back. Katie knew it was probably best if she didn't respond to the text at all. She should just delete it and ignore him, but at the same time, she was curious. Was Josh really what Wes said he was? It didn't seem possible. He seemed so nice, so human. Well, all except for surviving a knife in the eye and fading into dust. If it turned out she had been given drugs, she didn't want to lose contact completely. Staying in contact with Josh could prove to be potentially dangerous, maybe even deadly, but she'd never know unless she tried. Besides, he might be the answer to some of her questions. Texting wasn't going to hurt her, but she'd have to be cautious if he wanted to meet in person.

Her phone buzzed.

There is so much you haven't seen, so many questions that need answering.

Katie read the text before turning off her phone and setting it back on the nightstand. Josh was right, but she wasn't going to worry about it that night. She needed rest and time to figure out what was really going on. With a sigh, she walked to the bathroom and took two sleeping pills. She was tired of thinking, and she knew she'd never get to bed without them.

*   *   *

The alarm pulled her out of a dreamless sleep too soon. With a heavy arm, she hit the snooze and rolled onto her side. A few more minutes was all she needed to be ready for the day. She closed her eyes and drifted back into oblivion. When the alarm went off again, she flopped onto her back and stared at the ceiling. She still didn't want to get up, but she knew she didn't have a choice. Katie turned off the alarm and headed into the bathroom. Maybe a shower would help perk her up.

After wrapping a plastic bag around her arm, she stepped into the warm stream of water. Anger and frustration seared through her body. Stupid Josh and his Hell Hounds! If they hadn't attacked her she wouldn't have to spend extra time in the morning getting ready to take a simple shower. Damn Wes and his secret life! It was his fault she was targeted in the first place. If she could go back and do it again, she'd tell both boys to go to Hell. She didn't want to be anyone's pawn.

She finished her shower and got dressed. Mom was in the kitchen when she got downstairs to eat her breakfast.

"Feeling all right today, Katie?" She kissed the top of Katie's head.

Katie's mood hadn't improved, so she grunted as she poured herself a bowl of cereal.

Mom patted her shoulder. "I'm sure things will get better as the day goes on. Try to stay in school today, okay?" She raised her eyebrows at Katie.

Katie rolled her eyes. "I will." She turned to her bowl and shoveled the food in her mouth. Mom disappeared upstairs to finish getting ready.

When Katie was done eating, she brushed her teeth and grabbed her backpack from her room. She unplugged her phone from the charger and turned it back on, placing it in her pocket as she headed out the door. After pulling the door closed, she turned and stopped on the porch. Her heart leapt into her throat. Was she still dreaming? What was Josh's car doing parked in front of her house? The phone buzzed in her pocket, and she pulled it out. Apparently, Josh had sent another text after she turned it off.

Let me answer them for you.

Katie suppressed the shudder that ran down her spine. She glanced back toward the street, thinking maybe it had been a figment of her imagination that his vehicle was there. It wasn't. Josh climbed out of the car. Placing his hands on the roof, he smiled at her. Katie's resolve faltered with the dazzle of his looks.

Maybe Josh's presence meant that yesterday didn't really happen. After that smile, she really hoped that was the case. Josh was amazingly hot and could be so nice when he wanted to be. Katie wrapped her arms across her chest and her fingers brushed against her bandage. Reality crashed in on her. Desperately, she glanced up and down the street, expecting—hoping, someone was going to save her. Except for her and Josh, the street was empty. The one person who could save her was in the hospital. As usual, Wes was leaving her alone in her time of need. She could go back in the house and wait for Josh to leave. She probably should. Instead, she squared her shoulders and lifted her chin. She didn't need Wes to save her. She could take care of herself.

Katie stepped off the porch and walked to the sidewalk. Josh's smile grew wider, revealing his perfect white teeth, and he walked around the car and opened the passenger door. Katie smirked, then turned on her heel and walked down the sidewalk.

"Oh, come on!" Josh called after her. "I promise I won't hurt you."

Katie stopped in her tracks. Her arm throbbed. Anger coursed through her and she set her jaw. So many different phrases ran through her head, mainly where he could shove his promises, but she didn't say a word. Mustering every ounce of strength in her body, she continued to school.

Suddenly, Josh appeared before her. Katie jumped at the unexpectedness of his presence. She glanced back over her shoulder to make sure it was actually him. He wasn't by his car. She turned back around to face him. He held his hands out to his sides to show he wasn't a threat.

"Katie, c'mon, seriously. I know you have a lot of questions. I have the answers. Hear me out."

"Hear you out? You've got to be kidding! You say you don't want to hurt me, but what about this?" She held up her arm. "Your dog, your Hell Hound, did this to me. After you kidnapped me and used me to get to Wes."

Josh shrugged. A sheepish look crossed his face. "I admit, we got off to a bad start, but—"

"A bad start? You threatened to torture me almost to death, to hurt Wes!"

Josh's hands dropped to his sides. "I did do that. I'm sorry. If it's any consolation, I wouldn't have killed you. And I told you that. Plus, you killed two of my Hounds."

Katie was taken aback. She hadn't expected an apology. She didn't know what she'd expected Josh to do, but it wasn't that. Shouldn't a demon be more evil? Would it show remorse? And she did feel bad about killing the dogs. As vicious and hideous as they were, they were still living creatures—at least she thought they were—and she'd never hurt an animal before. It had been self-defense, but that didn't alleviate the guilt.

"I had no choice." Her anger softened. "They attacked me."

"I know. But they shouldn't have." He took a step forward. "Please, let me make it up to you. I can answer your questions."

Katie stared at him, searching his face for any sign of deception. They only thing she saw were his striking blue eyes and wonderfully charming smile. There was no hint of evil or treachery about him, only the illusion of adolescent innocence. Katie desperately wanted to believe him. In the short time she'd know him, he'd never lied to her. He probably wasn't lying now. She took a deep breath.

"I'm going to be late for school."

She moved to step around him, within arm's length, but he reached out and lightly grabbed her arm. There was nothing menacing in the action, only a desire to get her to stop. His touch was surprisingly warm.

"At least think about it."

Katie nodded, and Josh released her. She continued to school, her mind racing.

Katie made it through the day on autopilot. She went to class and pretended to take notes, but she had no idea what was going on. She couldn't get Josh and Wes and demons out of her mind. Was Josh really as bad as Wes made him seem? Or was it just jealousy that fueled his actions? It would be nice if that were true, but Katie knew better. Josh had tried to kill Wes. She had seen it with her own eyes. The stitches on her arm reinforced Josh's evil intentions. Sort of. After all, he did call the Hound off and seemed genuinely sorry she had gotten hurt. But he was a demon. It could have been an act.

At some point in the day, Katie's best friend, Deb, attached herself to Katie's side. She vaguely recalled Deb saying she was concerned and asking how she was doing. Katie couldn't remember what she said, but she knew she didn't say a word about demons. Who would have believed her? Part of her was still convinced she had been drugged.

Somewhere in the back of her mind, she knew she would have to tell Deb the truth about what was going on. She was the only person besides Wes who knew everything about Katie's life. Maybe she would have some good insight into the situation. Maybe she would tell Katie she was crazy. Katie wouldn't mind. In fact, it was the one thing she wanted—she needed—to hear. But it wasn't the time yet to say anything. There were things Katie needed to figure out first.

Katie expected to see Josh at school, but he wasn't there. Was that a relief or distressing? She wasn't sure. She wished she didn't have to think about it. Why couldn't she forget both of them and go on with her life? Why was she thinking and stressing about both of them? It was bad enough when she worried about Wes and what he was going to do. Adding Josh into the mix nauseated her. Couldn't they both just leave her alone? She expected to see Josh in the hallway after each class or by her locker. He didn't show up either place. He wasn't in gym class, either. But that didn't bother Katie. After the last two times, she didn't want to go near the locker room. Thankfully, because of her arm, she didn't have to participate in class.

By the time the day was over, Katie was exhausted. Her only desire was to crawl into bed and take a long nap. Maybe she'd wake up to discover the whole thing was a horrible nightmare. She barely had the energy to raise her feet to get upstairs, but she made it and flopped into bed, her eyes closed before she hit the pillow.

A buzzing woke her later. She sat up and stared around the room. Where was that coming from? Her phone! She climbed out of bed and searched for her backpack. It lay in the middle of the floor. It took her a while to find the phone, and when she did, it had stopped ringing. She looked at the caller ID and frowned. She didn't recognize the number. Oh, well. If it was important, they'd leave a message.

Yawning, she stretched her arms over her head. Her muscles pulled and popped, and when she was done, she brought her arm down. A glimmer of hope that the bandage was gone tingled through her. It dissipated quickly when she noticed the wrap. Her stomach growled. She glanced at her phone to check the time: 4:30. Mom would be home soon to make dinner, but a small snack wouldn't hurt. She made her way downstairs into the kitchen. The phone buzzed in her hand. The caller left a message. She dialed the number for her voicemail and typed in the code.

"Hey, Katie. It's Wes. Just calling to see how you're doing. I thought you were going to visit, but I guess you're busy. Call when you get the chance."

Crap! She forgot she told Wes she'd be at the hospital. She hung up and leaned against the counter. Should she still go? Did she want to? If she didn't show up, it would be payback for all the times he made her promises and never fulfilled them. Part of her thought that was poetic justice; it was what he deserved. The other part of her was too tired and confused to have an opinion.

"He misses you."

The voice was sudden and unexpected, causing Katie's heart to leap into her throat. Her breath caught. No one was supposed to be in the house. She spun toward the table, her hand feeling the counter for a weapon. She expected to see Josh. Instead, a middle-aged man sat at the kitchen table. Katie's fingers brushed against the cool, hard handle of a knife. She scooped it up and held it in front of her. It became evident she held a butter knife, but it was better than nothing. Her breathing came in rasps; her palms started to sweat. She cautiously glanced toward the kitchen door with her eyes. With a little luck, she could make it before the man had a chance to grab her. She took a slow step closer to the opening. She didn't want to alert the man to her plan. Her phone was still in her hand. Could she dial 9-1-1 without him attacking her?

The man held up his hands. "I'm not going to hurt you. I'm sorry to scare you. I'm Wes's dad. Randy."

CHAPTER 6

THE MAN TRIED TO BE NONTHREATENING by keeping his voice low, soft. It didn't comfort Katie. How was she supposed to know if the man was telling the truth? She'd only seen Wes's dad once. And that was a long time ago. Visions of her childhood fears ran through her mind, and she pictured the person in front of her killing someone. Maybe this guy was another demon in disguise. She didn't know. She had no idea what they were capable of doing. She hadn't even known they existed until the day before. And she still wasn't convinced what happened was real. Even the fact that his face was covered in purple bruises and stitches lined his forehead and right cheek didn't help. She tightened her grip on the knife and took another step closer to the door.

"My mom is going to be home any minute," Katie squeaked. She tried to sound brave, tough, but it didn't work. She took another step.

The man nodded. "I know. I told her I would be here. To check on you." He placed his hands in his lap and took a deep breath. "I don't blame you for not relaxing. I can only imagine what's going through your mind. But, please, trust me. I don't want to harm you."

Despite everything, Katie couldn't help but feel comforted by the man's last words. There was something about him, something familiar and safe feeling. It reminded her of Wes. No matter how upset she was with him, no matter how much he hurt her, she always felt safe with him. Randy—if that was really his name—made her feel the same. That unnerved her.

"What do you want?"

He shook his head. "Just to talk. Maybe answer any questions you might have about what happened yesterday."

She huffed. "Yeah. Like you would have those. You weren't even there. You don't know what happened."

"That's true. But Wes told me what happened. And I've been in similar situations. I've been around demons for a long time, Katie."

His words rang through Katie and instantly made her mad. If he knew so much about demons, why hadn't he done something to protect her and Wes? Why did he let them get hurt? He could have at least warned them. He could have saved them!

She snarled. "Why didn't you stop him?"

A questioning look wrinkled his forehead. "What?"

"Why didn't you stop him before he took me and lured Wes into a trap? If you know demons so well, why didn't you save us?"

Randy's eyes flicked to the ground for a moment. When they came back up and met her gaze, tears glazed his eyes. "Fair enough question. You might not like the answer, though. I stayed out of it because Wes said he had it handled. He told me he could take care of it. Plus, I was busy with my own situation." He gestured toward his face and body. "But that's no excuse. It's blatantly obvious I should have been there. Wes's feelings clouded his judgment. Caused him to make stupid decisions."

So was it stupid for Wes to want to make sure Katie was safe? What exactly was Randy inferring? Was it stupid to get her involved? Or was the way he handled it stupid? Randy kind of left his words open to interpretation. Katie was already sensitive, so she took his statement as a personal attack. Katie opened her mouth to tell him what an awful father he was for putting Wes into such horrible situations, but the words never came out of her mouth. A door opened and closed, and her mom entered through the garage. She stared from Katie to Randy, then stepped in and gave Katie a kiss on the forehead.

"You doing all right?"

Katie nodded curtly.

Her mom turned to Randy. "Thanks for coming by. I appreciate you worrying about my daughter. How's Wes doing?"

He smiled. "Much better. He should be getting out tomorrow."

"Oh, that's wonderful," Mom responded. "And you're looking stronger today. Is there anything we can do to help out?"

Randy pushed himself up from the table with effort. He grimaced as his straightened up. "If you wouldn't mind, I could use Katie's help later tonight moving some stuff into Wes's room. I got some presents for his welcome home."

Katie's mom smiled and glanced at her daughter. "She'd be glad to help. I'll have her over there at seven."

Katie wanted to protest, to say she had other plans, but she knew it would fall on deaf ears. Even if she had plans, Mom would make her change them. It was best not to argue. She shuddered at the thought of being alone with Randy in his house. God only knew what she'd find in there.

Mom stepped forward to help Randy, but he waved her off. She followed him to the door and showed him out. Katie watched them from the kitchen, her eyes narrowed to slits. She attempted to project her thoughts into the air, to get Randy to change his mind and tell her she didn't have to help, but it didn't work. He waved from the door before stepping out. Her mom told him goodbye, then turned back into the house and headed upstairs to change out of her work clothes. Katie followed her.

"You know, Mom, I have a lot of homework to do tonight. Maybe I should help Mr. Akers another time."

Mom turned, a smirk on her face. "I'm sure you can spend an hour to help Randy get Wes's room ready. If you start your homework now, then you'll have plenty of time." She raised her eyebrows.

Nuts! Katie thought. It was just as she suspected. Mom would have a rebuttal for any argument she threw at her.

"What happened to him? How did he get hurt?"

Mom changed into a pair of sweats. "Car accident. Pretty nasty one from what I hear. He's lucky to be alive."

Katie raised an eyebrow. "And you believe that?"

Mom stared at her, confusion covering her face. "Of course I do. Why wouldn't I?"

Katie shrugged and sat down on the bed. "I don't know."

"It was in the paper. Third page. The car was all mangled. Looked horrible."

"How well do you know Mr. Akers?"

Mom's confusion deepened. "What do you mean?"

Katie huffed. "What I mean is, we've lived her for eleven years, and this is the first instance I remember him entering our house. How often do you talk to the man?"

Mom pressed her lips into a thin line and headed out of her bedroom. Katie followed her down to the kitchen. Mom pulled meat and vegetables out of the fridge and started preparing them for dinner.

"Randy, your father, and I used to be really good friends. When his wife was still around, we had dinner all the time. You wouldn't remember, you were pretty little. We've known the family since we've lived here. Since you were eighteen months old. You and Wes have grown up together."

"What happened to his wife?" The question came out softly. Katie wasn't sure she wanted to know the answer. Visions of demons ripping a woman apart drifted through her mind, causing her to shudder.

Mom stopped chopping carrots and faced her daughter. Sadness covered her face. "She died in childbirth. The baby didn't make it either. It was a girl. Wes would have had a little sister. It all happened right before you guys started kindergarten. Randy took it real hard. Stopped coming over for dinner, despite our constant invitations. We respected his desire for privacy, though it broke both of our hearts. I still talk to him occasionally when I see him in the neighborhood, but those moments are few and far between." She took a deep breath and wiped at her eyes. "This is the first time in a very long time that he's been in the house. I think Wes's accident with that dog really shook him up." She turned back to the vegetables and the cutting board.

"What does he do for a living?"

Mom set the knife down and faced Katie. "What's with all the questions? Why are you interrogating me about Randy?"

Katie threw her hands into the air and became indignant. "Uh, maybe because you told him I would help him out in his house. I don't know the guy. How do I know he's not a creep or pervert? I would like to have some idea of what you got me into before being alone with a guy in his house."

Mom gave her a sideways look. "You have nothing to worry about from Randy. I wouldn't have volunteered your services if he was a creep. What kind of mother do you think I am?"

One who has no idea what their neighbors really do, she thought.

"You'd better get upstairs and get your homework done. You're helping Randy no matter what."

Katie rolled her eyes and headed up to her room.

In reality, she had no idea if she had homework or not. She had no recollection of what happened at school. Maybe she should call Deb and ask. They didn't have any classes together, but Deb always knew what was going on. She plopped down at her desk and pulled out her phone. She sighed. Was she really in the mood to talk to anyone? No doubt, Deb would ask how she was doing and ask a bunch of questions about what had happened. Katie wasn't sure how to answer. More than likely Deb would also give her a lecture about hanging out with Wes. Deb wasn't a fan of the guy, especially since she had to hear all about it after he broke Katie's heart. Katie wasn't in the mood to hear about what an awful person Wes was and how she was an idiot to keep falling for his tricks. She could send a text. It was easier to lie that way. She nodded. That's what she would do. Just as she was about to send the message, her phone buzzed. Another text from Josh.

How was your day?

Katie shook her head in disgust. He was relentless and infuriating. Why couldn't he just leave her alone? What did he want from her? She knew she shouldn't respond, but the question seemed so harmless, so mundane. Almost normal. It seemed as natural as if Deb had sent the text. Again she wondered if Josh was as bad as he was made out to be. She replied.

Horrible. But you would know that. You're the reason.

I'm not trying to make life difficult for you. Meet with me. Let's talk.

Can't. I have prior engagements I have to take care of tonight. Thanks to my mom.

Sorry to hear that. I want to see you.

Try going to school.

Maybe tomorrow. I hope to talk to you soon.

Katie sighed and set the phone on the desk. Rubbing her hands over her face, she wondered what was going on. She couldn't keep doing this to herself. She needed to cut herself off completely from Josh. But it wasn't that simple. She knew so little about him, and she wanted to find out more. He was dangerous, there was no denying that, but he swore that violence wasn't directed at her. Still, she didn't like being used. But was he still using her? After all, Wes was laid up in the hospital. If Josh really wanted to finish the job, he could walk in there and Wes wouldn't be able to fight back. Maybe that was too easy. Maybe Josh wanted to toy with Wes for a while. Make him squirm. Hadn't he mentioned in the warehouse that he wanted to hurt Wes deeply? Wouldn't he do that if he tortured Katie? She shuddered at the thought. She really needed to cut off all communications with Josh.

As much as she wanted to believe he wasn't as evil as he probably was, there was no sense taking unnecessary risks. With effort, she picked up her phone and went to delete and block Josh's number. Right before hitting the button, it vibrated, causing her to drop the phone onto the desk. She glanced at the number. The same one that had called earlier. The one Wes called from when he left the message. Must have been his hospital phone. She picked up the phone and stared at the screen. She should answer it. Let Wes know she was all right. But she couldn't bring herself to push the button. Eventually, the phone stopped ringing. Would he leave another message? She placed it down and stared at it, waiting for the indicator that he left a voicemail. It never came.

Sighing, she stood and went back downstairs to watch TV before dinner. At that point, she really didn't care if she had homework. There was no way she was going to be able to focus to finish it anyway.

Mom sat next to her on the couch and placed a hand on her knee. "You doing all right, Katie? After you went upstairs, I realized we haven't really had a chance to talk about what happened yesterday."

Katie shrugged and focused her attention on a string on her pants. She appreciated that her mom wanted to know how she was feeling, but what was Katie going to tell her? She couldn't exactly tell the truth. Mom wouldn't believe it. The story Katie told her mom about the warehouse and the stray dog explained her injuries and some of Wes's, but not all of them. Mom didn't question the other injuries, but maybe she didn't know the extent of them. Katie needed an ally, but would she find one in Mom?

"Must have been pretty scary, huh?"

Katie nodded but didn't raise her head. "It was."

Mom nudged her with her arm. "Sounds like you're lucky to only have gotten bit on the arm. And you saved Wes's life by attacking the dog with a pipe. What made you think to do that?"

Katie shrugged. "I don't know. Just acted on impulse, I suppose."

Mom wrapped her arm around Katie's shoulders. "It's a good thing you did. Wes is lucky you were around."

"Mom, how well do you know Wes?"

She stroked Katie's hair. "Not as well as I used to. When Randy fell into his depression and locked himself in the house, he took Wes with him. I tried to reach out to him, to make him feel loved, but he seemed afraid of getting too close. I don't know. Maybe he thought I was trying to replace his mom. Deep down inside, maybe I was. It killed me to see him so sad. He had been such a happy, carefree boy. A smile always came easily to his face, and he joked often. That went away after his mom died. It broke my heart." She laid her cheek on Katie's head and pulled her closer. "Sometimes, when he's around you, I see glimpses of the boy he used to be. The carefree and happy child. You bring out the best in him."

"Do I?" Katie sat up and stared at her mom. "If he's so happy around me, why can't he stand to be around me? You don't see what happens at school. How he pretends to be my friend, comfort me when I'm in pain, making promises he never keeps. He's broken my heart more times than I can count."

Sympathy crossed Mom's face and she brushed her fingers across Katie's cheek. "I know. I've seen the pain on your face. The way you longingly stare out the window. That broke my heart more than anything. It's hard to love someone who's so damaged."

Katie set her jaw. "I don't love him."

"Maybe not anymore, but you did at one time." She pulled Katie into a hug. "I know how hard it is to care so deeply for someone and not have them care back. Given enough time, your heart becomes hard; your sympathy disappears. I don't blame you for how you feel toward Wes. And I'm sure you don't want to hear this, but I don't think he was trying to hurt you. I don't think he knows how to show his love."

Katie snuggled closer to her mom. It felt good to be in her arms. Even though she couldn't tell her exactly what was going on, it was still nice to be comforted. "Or maybe he's harboring deep, dark secrets."

Mom stroked her hair once again. "That could very well be, honey. No one knows what went on at the Akers house but Randy and Wes. Neither one of them dealt with Maureen's death in a healthy way."

"So what should I do?"

Mom clicked her tongue on the roof of her mouth. "I don't know. That's a decision you'll have to make on your own."

Katie grimaced. That wasn't what she wanted to hear. Mom was supposed to tell her to stay away from them. That they were nothing but bad news. Mom was supposed to tell her that if she remained friends with them, she'd only wind up getting hurt. That would have made things so much easier.

"What would you do?" Katie wondered.

Mom sighed. "The same thing I've been doing for years. I wouldn't give up. I would continue to let them know they were loved and I was there to help. I would keep hope and faith that one day they would break out of their depression and let their friends back in."

"What if they don't?"

"I'm sure they have their reasons for doing it. But it's not my place to judge, and I will continue to pray that they find their way back to happiness."

Katie scowled. Leave it to Mom to see the good side of everything. Would she feel the same way if she knew the truth about what was going on?

"No matter what you decide," Mom stated, "I'll support your decision."

The timer in the kitchen went off, and Mom stood from the couch to check on dinner. Before she left the room, Katie stopped her with a question.

"What if I decide I don't want to help Mr. Akers tonight. Would you support that?"

Mom smiled. "Unfortunately, no. Randy never asks for favors. It's not going to kill you to help him for one night." She turned and headed into the kitchen.

Katie's shoulders slouched. Mom didn't know what she was talking about. It could possibly kill her to have contact with that family. It almost already had.

CHAPTER 7

KATIE STOOD ON WES'S PORCH, wondering why she was there. Various images of what lay beyond the door ran through her mind. She imagined a living room with no furniture and the carpet covered in plastic sheets. As soon as the door closed behind her, Randy would overpower her and lay her on the plastic sheet and cut her apart a piece at a time. Either that or the house would look completely normal, with a couch and a TV and pictures of him and Wes hanging on the wall, and then he'd take her down to the basement, where she would be taken to a room with padded walls that had thick chains waiting to be clamped around her wrists and ankles. He would secure her before subjecting her to torture and eventually killing her. Katie shuddered.

Why hadn't she told her mom her arm was sore? Surely, she would have let Katie stay home if she were in pain. At the moment, her arm was aching. She glanced across the street at her house. Multiple lights were on, making the place look warm and inviting. Unlike the house she stood in front of. The porch light wasn't even on. Katie was bathed in shadows. Who doesn't turn on the porch light when they are expecting someone? It added to the chill that already crept across her skin. She turned back to the door and sighed. Might as well get it over with. She knocked on the door, a soft tap that she hoped no one would hear. If Randy wasn't home, how could she help it? At least she tried.

Almost immediately the door swung open. Katie's heart skipped a beat. Orange light from the foyer spilled onto the porch. Randy leaned against the door frame, smiling. A garbage bag hung from his hand.

"I wondered how long it would take you to knock. I've been waiting for five minutes to take this out." He lifted the bag.

A million different excuses of why she hesitated ran through Katie's head, but she didn't say one out loud. Instead, she pointed to the trash.

"Can I take that for you?"

He cocked his head to the side and stared at her through narrowed eyes. You plan on running away afterward?"

She huffed. "No. I'm trying to be nice. I saw how much effort it took you to walk from my kitchen to the front door." She stepped to the side and held her arm out. "But if you want to take it yourself…"

In response, Randy handed her the bag. Katie walked to the side of the house, where the can was, and placed the bag inside. As she turned to go back to the house, she glanced longingly across the street. The thought had crossed her mind to leave and go home, but she didn't want Randy to tell her mom. She could only imagine how much trouble she'd get in.

Randy gestured for her to enter and she stepped across the threshold, bracing for the worst. The door clicked shut behind her. Oh, God. What am I doing? She fought back the urge to run. Glancing over her shoulder, she once again took in Wes's dad. This close, the extent of his injuries became more apparent. She noticed the swelling and how raw and painful the wounds looked. He stepped past her and farther into the house. His limp was noticeable, and he held his left arm at a ninety-degree angle close to his body. He wasn't a threat. Katie could take him if she needed to. The thought didn't make her feel better.

She followed him cautiously into the house. It comforted her slightly to know he walked in front of her. At least that way she knew he wasn't going to knock her out from behind. From the door was a short hallway. Pictures of sunsets and mountains lined the walls, along with a cross on each side. A table sat in the middle on the left; mail was piled on top of it. The hall opened into a living room, the kitchen was off to the right. On the very back wall was the sliding glass door that led to the back yard. The stairs were on the left wall. It looked exactly like Katie's house but reversed. She hadn't expected that. Randy gestured toward the tan couch that sat in front of the entertainment center.

"Please, have a seat. Would you like something to drink?"

Katie shook her head and moved around the couch to sit. Randy lowered himself into the recliner on her right. He grimaced as he adjusted in his seat.

"Did you really get into a car accident?" Katie placed her elbows on her knees and clasped her hands. She tried to portray an air of confidence, even if she didn't feel it.

Randy waggled his head from side to side. "A car was involved, but it wasn't your typical accident."

"So what happened?"

He leaned back in his chair. "Wes and I were out on patrol."

Holy crap! He was actually going to tell her the story! She thought for sure he would tell her a pile of lies or that she wouldn't understand, but he just launched into the narrative. She leaned forward.

*   *   *

Wes was still agitated from the events that had transpired earlier that day. He couldn't sit still in the car. His leg bounced up and down, and his gaze darted everywhere but on the house in front of them. They were parked under some trees, camouflaged by darkness. The house was off the main road, private but not really hidden. It lay in a community of other cabins, all close enough so no one felt isolated, but far enough apart that the owners could be alone.

The rumor was that the house was being used as a portal for demons to cross into the human world. As Praesuls, it was Randy and Wes's job to check it out and shut it down if necessary. The job was dangerous and required concentration. If a portal was involved, there was no telling how many demons were there—or how many could be summoned in a short amount of time.

Wes slammed his fist into the car door. "I should have taken him out. Right then and there."

"And told Katie what?" Randy's voice was even and calm.

Wes threw his hands in the air. "I don't know! I would have figured something out. You didn't see how he glommed onto her. How receptive she was to his advances."

Randy turned his head to look at his son. "You can't blame Katie. For all she knows, he's human."

Wes punched the door again. "I don't blame Katie. I blame that parasite. And myself." His mood softened, and he lowered his gaze to his lap. "I'm losing her, Dad. You should have seen the hate and anger in her eyes, in her soul." He looked at his dad. "I really hurt her."

Randy placed a hand on Wes's shoulder. "No one said this life would be easy. We all have to make sacrifices for the greater good. You know that."

Wes nodded and dropped his gaze back to his lap. "I do. But I'm not going to let Josh have her. She can hate me all she wants, but I won't let him turn her."

Randy squeezed his son's shoulder. He wanted to tell Wes that the battle wasn't his to fight, but he didn't get the chance. The door to the house slammed shut, drawing their attention forward. Randy squinted into the darkness. The only light came from the moon, and the porch was covered, shrouding whoever in shadows. From the silhouette, Randy could tell the outline was human, but the black tint on the soul let him know it was actually a demon in disguise.

Wes leaned forward in his seat. "What do you want to do?" he whispered.

The car was far enough away that the man—or whatever it was—couldn't hear them, but neither wanted to take the chance.

Randy shook his head. "Nothing yet. We need to find out for sure if there's a portal in there."

The man stepped off the porch and walked to the truck parked on the side of the house, twirling his keys on his fingers. The engine started with an obscene roar in the quiet night, while the headlights harshly cut through the darkness before the truck disappeared down the road. Father and son stared into the darkness for several long moments before reaching for the handles. Stepping out, they stood by the car and stared at the house.

"In and out," Randy whispered. "No telling how long he'll be gone or if others are in there. After a quick reconnaissance, we'll get the tools out of the trunk and take care of this." Wes nodded.

Randy was sure he'd find a portal inside the house. In his line of work, rumors were never wrong. Besides, it wasn't hard to mistake a portal as anything but a portal. Still, they needed to find out exactly what they were dealing with. There was no sign or schedule for when demons came through the opening. And there was nothing more dangerous than being in the room when they decided to come through. Plus, they didn't know if anyone else was in the house. Just because they saw a guy leave didn't mean he was the only one who was there. A quick walk around would give them all the answers they needed.

Closing the car doors softly, they made their way down the hill. Randy took the lead, and Wes hung back to keep watch. Randy tiptoed to the side of the house, and Wes took position in the trees a few feet away. Randy signaled to his son to make sure he was ready. Wes nodded back, and Randy drew a gun from his belt. He sidestepped to the nearest window and peered in. A pulsating blue glow met his eyes. As he suspected—or already knew—the portal was active. That meant one of two things: a demon had just gone through to the other side or one was getting ready to enter the human world. He could only see a sliver of light, which meant the portal was just out of his line of sight. He'd have to find a window with a better view to get a better idea of which way the demons were moving. He wasn't going to waste his time doing that, though. He knew the portal was there. Whether or not a demon was coming or going didn't matter. What mattered was closing the portal quickly. If demons were coming, closing the portal would keep them out of the human world. He pushed himself away from the wall and hurried back to the car. Wes took up position behind him and followed.

"It in there?" Wes whispered as they slowly opened the trunk to pull out their weapons.

"Yep. And it's active."

"We'd better hurry then." Wes reached frantically into the trunk for his crossbow and holy water bombs.

Randy shared his desire to get the job done quickly; while he focused on grabbing his own weapons, he neglected to hear the soft footsteps coming up behind them. After arming himself, he turned to walk back to the house and was backhanded, sending him flying across the forest floor.

"Dad!"

He barely heard Wes calling him as he landed hard on the ground, the air knocked out of him. He rolled to get to his feet, sensing a presence extremely close. Rough hands wrapped around his collar, and he was jerked upward. Black dots danced in front of his eyes. Between the dots, he caught a glimpse of his attacker. The demon stood close to seven feet tall, its black leathery wings folded behind it. Red eyes burned into Randy's soul. Yellowed teeth dripping with spit snapped at him It must have been the demon coming through the portal. He and Wes weren't fast enough. It hissed and threw Randy backward. Pain radiated up Randy's spine. His head flew backward. For a moment, he was suspended against the car, thinking his back had been broken and he was going to die. As he slid to the ground, the pain renewed through his body, making him aware of every bone, muscle, and joint. He would have preferred not to be in agony, but that meant one thing, and he said a quick prayer of thanks that he was still alive.

Gun shots echoed all around him. He turned to his left and saw Wes's legs coming around from the back of the car. The muzzle flashed at the corner of his eyes. Guns were an effective tool against demons, especially when the bullets were blessed, but they weren't the best. Believe it or not, demons were fast enough to dodge most bullets, and they could see them coming. A few from Wes's gun hit the mark, but more often they sailed into nature beyond. The demon advanced toward them.

Randy had to get to his feet. He had to take the demon down. He knew Wes was more than capable of doing it, but he didn't want him to do it alone. Mustering all the strength he could find, and using the car for support, he pulled himself up and grabbed a holy water bomb from his belt. He threw it at the demon, but his aim was off; his eyes wouldn't focus. The bomb hit at the creature's feet. Some droplets splashed onto its taloned toes, causing wisps of smoke to curl in the air. The demon screamed. Randy's vision cleared, just in time for him to see the demon lock him in its gaze. It charged forward, spreading its wings and taking flight. Randy grabbed another bomb from his belt. The creature was within ten feet. He cocked back his arm and threw. The water hit it square in the face at the same time a crossbow bolt skewered through its head. A gasping scream escaped its lips before it fell out of the sky onto the car. Randy jumped out of the way to keep from being hit. The weight of the demon crushed the roof in. Randy slowly got to his feet and stared at his son. Wes panted, the crossbow still raised. He circled the car toward Randy, making sure the demon was dead.

"You all right?" Wes asked.

Randy nodded. "Just need to catch my breath."

The sound of crunching metal echoed through the woods. The demon on top of the car slid to the ground. Randy instantly jumped to his feet, grabbing at the crossbow on his back. He wasn't fast enough. The car flew at them. Wes and Randy jumped sideways in opposite directions. Randy didn't make it far enough. The hood clipped his leg. Burning pain traveled from his knee up to his thigh. For the second time that night, he landed hard on the ground. He rolled over, frantically searching for Wes. All he saw was another large demon looming over him. He tried to back away, to grab any weapon from his belt, but there wasn't time. The creature slashed his clawed hand downward, catching Randy across the face. Blood splashed from the gash onto the forest floor, into his eyes, blinding him.

"The honor is mine, Praesul." The demon's voice crackled around him. Its hand reached out and grabbed his neck.

Randy fought to stay conscious. Pain radiated through his entire body. It was the only thing that made him realize he was still alive. Thinking of Wes, he once again fumbled for anything on his belt. The demon's hot breath tickled his neck. He felt the points of its teeth ready to penetrate his flesh. With the little strength he had left, he smashed the holy water bomb into the side of the demon's head.

Squeals of agony penetrated the night. Randy flopped onto the ground. The last thing he was aware of before passing out was the stench of burnt flesh.

*   *   *

"I awoke in the hospital. Wes was seated by my bed." Randy shook his head. "He looked awful. Thankfully, though, the demons hadn't hurt him. I suffered the brunt of their wrath. He saved my life."

Katie nodded. "He showed up in my room later that night covered in blood. Stained everything he touched. I thought he had killed someone."

"He was pretty distressed that night. I wanted to comfort him, assure him that everything was going to be all right, but they had me doped up on so many painkillers. I was in and out of consciousness."

"You weren't in the hospital for very long."

"Why would they keep me? Nothing was broken, no internal damage. They patched me up and sent me home with a bottle of feel-good pills." He shifted awkwardly in his seat. "I hate that I have to go back to see Wes in there."

"Do you worry about him in there? I mean, what if Josh wants to finish what he started. Wes is defenseless."

Randy shook his head. "Josh can't hurt Wes."

"What's to stop him? Do you have someone guarding him? The hospital is a public place. Anyone can walk in there."

"Any human can walk in there. Demons in disguise can't."

"Are they like vampires and have to be invited in?"

Randy chuckled. "No. They are free to go wherever they please, as long as it's not holy ground."

Katie pushed her eyebrows together. "Is the hospital holy ground?"

"What hospital is he in?"

Katie had to think for a moment. She hadn't paid that much attention to where they had been taken. If finally came to her.

"Saint Mary's."

Randy nodded slowly. "It is tied to and blessed by the Church. Josh can't set foot in it. But even if Wes weren't at Saint Mary's, there are things that could be done to ensure his safety." He pointed at her. "Things you might consider doing to protect yourself."

Katie refrained from rolling her eyes. Randy was trying to be nice and protective, but why had it taken him so long to act that way? Why wasn't he concerned about her well being years ago? If he wanted to make sure she was safe, why didn't he make his son stop hurting her? The only thought that ran through her mind when he talked about protection was hanging a garlic wreath around her window and a cross on her wall. Would that really do any good? It might keep Josh out of her house, but it wouldn't stop him from contacting her on the street or at school.

Randy narrowed his eyes and cocked his head to the side. "You don't know much about demons, do you?"

Katie shrugged her right shoulder and picked at an invisible string on the couch. "Just what I've seen in the movies."

Randy leaned his head back in an "Ah" gesture. "Well, unfortunately, the movies aren't always right. I assume you're referring to possession films?"

Katie didn't look up but nodded. She felt foolish, unprepared. Should she know more about demons? Should she have paid closer attention in Sunday School? Did they even talk about demons in Sunday School? It seemed like a topic that might cause some distress in the kids.

"Possessions do occur," Randy continued. "But they aren't as rampant as those movies would lead you to believe. And only certain types of demons possess." He leaned forward in the chair and placed his elbows on the arms. "What do you think the ultimate goal of a demon is?"

Katie stopped picking at the couch and looked up. "I don't know. To torture and kill humans?"

"That's a good guess, but not exactly true. Demons do torture and kill, but usually only individuals who have a close connection to God."

"Like you."

Randy smiled. "Yes, like me. Otherwise, a demon wants your soul. It's a lot easier to tempt you into sin if a demon appears as your friend. Most people can be talked into doing anything by someone they trust. Demons will do and say whatever it takes to make you trust them."

Katie thought back to the texts Josh had sent and the things he told her on the street. He seemed so sincere, so genuine. He almost did seem trustworthy. He made her question his motive and nature. That was incredibly cunning on his part. Not that Katie was all that good at picking up when people lied to her. Wes had done it for years and on several different occasions and she never figured it out. Did that make Wes better than Josh or just the same? How was she supposed to tell the good guys from the bad if they acted exactly the same?

"I don't want to keep you for too much longer. I'm sure you would rather do anything but hang out with me." Randy smiled.

Katie cleared her throat. If Randy only knew how right he was.

"Wes is coming home tomorrow, and I think he'd really appreciate it if you were here."

Katie shifted uncomfortably in her seat. "Well, um, you see..."

What was she going to say? Did she want to see Wes tomorrow? She was still trying to figure some things out—things on her own.

"I can get you out of school."

That made Katie pause. She might not be sure she wanted to see Wes, but she was sure she didn't want to go to school. She couldn't stand floating through another day pretending to pay attention. She could stomach a few hours of Wes to get a whole day away from school.

She sighed, trying to play it cool. "I suppose if it will make him happy."

"It will. I'll pick you up at nine." He pushed himself out of his chair. It took several moments and a grimace of pain on his face to get to his feet.

For a moment, Katie wondered if she should help him. Her thoughts drifted to earlier in the night when her mom tried to help him and he waved her away. She didn't want to emasculate him though, so she stayed where she was. If he asked for assistance, she'd help him.

When he was on his feet, Katie got to hers and headed for the door. She was several steps in front of him and intended on leaving without saying much more. She stepped into the darkness and focused her gaze on her house.

"See you tomorrow," Randy called from the door.

Katie turned and waved to acknowledge him, but never slowed her pace until her front door was closed behind her.

CHAPTER 8

MOM GLANCED AT KATIE from the couch, craning her neck around.

"You get everything taken care of for Wes's return home?" Mom wondered.

Katie nodded. "Yeah."

Mom turned back around. "Good."

Mom's phone rang, and Katie assumed it was Randy calling to ask if Katie could get out of school tomorrow. Katie was confident Mom would say it was fine, especially if Randy was the one asking. She smiled slightly. At least there was one thing to look forward to in this whole mess.

She headed up to her room. Exhaustion surged through her body; her arm still ached. She needed to take some ibuprofen and climb into bed. Even if she wasn't going to school tomorrow, she wanted to get as much sleep as she could. The weekend was coming up, and even though she didn't have any plans, she wanted to be ready for anything. Well, at one point, she'd had plans to go to a movie with Josh, but after the warehouse debacle, Katie was sure those plans were cancelled. Maybe she would call Deb and they could go somewhere. Shopping sounded like a good plan. Or maybe just a hike in the woods. Anything to get away from the craziness and people. Some alone time was really what she needed. But not too alone. If she was a target for demons, she didn't want to make it easy for them to get her.

After closing the door to her room, she pulled on her pajamas. Her phone buzzed on the desk. She stared at it. She had forgotten to take it with her. That wasn't very smart. What if she had needed it to call for help? She shrugged. It didn't matter. She hadn't needed it. Scooping it up, she glanced at the display. Wes had called again. Twice. But he didn't leave any messages. She rolled her eyes. That guy was persistent. He'd contacted her more in the last few days than he had the entire time she'd known him. She strained her mind to remember the last time he had called her. Had he ever? Maybe once or twice, but never that many times in a day. She flopped onto her bed. She'd see him tomorrow. No sense wasting time talking to him now.

Katie opened her browser. She typed in "demons" and waited for the pages to appear. She frowned. More than she had expected, and more varied. She didn't need to read the definition–she knew what a demon was–but there were multiple encyclopedias and disciplines that dealt with the evil creatures. Were they really that big of a blight on society? Where had she been that she hadn't noticed the problem? She clicked on a link of demon names. Maybe that would give her some answers.

She read the opening paragraph. It explained how different cultures from around the world had different demons that functioned in different ways. Some were tricksters, some were here to torment the living. There was list after list of names and descriptions of demons from around the world. Katie shook her head and closed the browser. That wasn't helping. It was making things worse. She didn't know what Josh was, so how was she going to find him in the list of names? If the list were shorter, that would be a different story. But it wasn't, and she wasn't any closer to understanding demons than she had been before being attacked by one. As much as she hated to admit it, she was going to have to learn about them from Wes and Randy.

That thought made her shudder slightly. She knew she was being unfair to both of them. In their own twisted way, they were only trying to protect those around them. At least Randy was open to share the story of his accident with her. He didn't have to, and he wasn't nearly as scary as she'd imagined him to be. Maybe she needed to rethink her attitude toward him. After all, she really couldn't blame him for not interfering in Wes's business. She would've hated it if her mom butted in to her life. Randy was just trying to let his son do what he needed to do. It was unfair for her to be upset with him. She sighed. It wasn't worth worrying about at the moment.

Leaning to her right, she plugged her phone into the charger before getting up to brush her teeth. It was quarter to nine—early—but she was tired. She contemplated watching TV with her mom, but pushed the thought out of her head. She'd fall asleep on the couch. Might as well just head straight to bed. She thought about reading a book, but her eyes probably wouldn't stay open long enough. No. It was best to give in and close her eyes. When she finished brushing her teeth and washing her face, she headed back to her room. Mom was coming upstairs at the same time.

"I was wondering where you were. You wanna watch TV with me?"

Katie shook her head. "No. I want to go to bed."

Mom wrapped Katie in a hug and kissed the top of her head. "Of course. You've been through a lot. You need to get some rest." She released Katie so she could head into her room. "Randy tells me you've offered to go with him to pick up Wes tomorrow."

Katie leaned against her door and nodded. "Yeah." She yawned. "Is that all right with you?"

Mom brushed her fingers across Katie's cheek. "That's absolutely fine. I'll call the school in the morning and let them know you won't be there. But you're responsible for making up any work you miss."

Katie sighed. "I know. I will."

Mom kissed her on the forehead. "All right. Good night. I'll see you in the morning. Love you."

"Night. Love you too."

Katie closed her door and headed for her bed. She slid under the covers, the coolness inviting on her bare feet. She settled onto her pillow, the softness cradling her head, and instantly fell into a deep sleep.

A throbbing pain pulsed through Katie's arm, pulling her out of her slumber. She raised her head wearily, trying to figure out what was going on. Why did her arm hurt? She blinked a few times to wake up further. At some point, she had rolled onto her injury. She pulled it out from under her and flopped onto her back. That wasn't how she wanted to get woken up. She fidgeted for a while, trying to find a comfortable position, but the pain in her limb wouldn't stop. She glanced at the clock: 3:33. Maybe she should get up and take some more ibuprofen. The thought of getting out of bed made her groan. Her arm may have been throbbing, but her bed was so warm, so comfortable, she didn't really want to leave. Maybe if she closed her eyes and thought about something else, the pain would go away. She squeezed her eyelids shut and attempted to let her mind drift into unconsciousness.

"You never answered my text."

The whisper sounded in Katie's ear, causing her heart to stop beating for a moment and her breath to catch in her throat. She shot up, ready to leap out of bed to the door, her eyes wide with fear. She clutched her covers, ready to pull them over her head, like they would form a barrier between her and whoever was in her room. A dark figure sat next to her on the bed. Her eyes drifted toward the door. She wouldn't make it before the person grabbed her, but if she screamed, her mom could be at her aid in a few seconds.

"I'm not going to hurt you." The voice was louder and familiar.

Katie leaned over and grabbed her phone. She would have turned on the light, but she knew it would be too bright, temporarily blinding her. At that moment, the last thing she wanted to do was lose sight of who was in her room. Using the light from her screen, she illuminated the figure. The blue hue cast weird shadows across Josh's face, making his features seem pointy and prominent. Shadows extended from the corner of his eyes onto his forehead, looking almost like eyebrows set at an angry angle. He smiled, but the gesture did nothing to hide the demonic look the light cast onto his face. Or was it from the light? Katie shuddered.

"What text?" It was all she could manage to squeak out. She wanted to ask how he had gotten in her room and why he was there, but her mouth wouldn't obey her will.

Delicately, Josh reached for the phone, his fingers brushing against hers. Katie shied away from his touch, yet found it strangely alluring. His fingers were warm, soft. She remembered how they felt on her face days earlier, right before his lips connected with hers. When she believed he was human. Oh, how she wished he was still human. He unlocked her phone and pulled up the texts. He turned the display so she could read it.

Have you decided if you want to talk to me yet?

He'd sent it during the time she had been at Randy's. Must have been around the same time Wes called her again. How did she miss that? Probably because she was so distressed Wes called again she didn't even think about looking at her texts. Plus, she was tired. That explained everything. Her mind wasn't working the way it was supposed to. She glanced from the phone to Josh's face.

"So you thought you'd just make your way into my bedroom in the middle of the night to see what I was up to?" The fear she felt initially drained from her body, replaced with irritation. This was the second time a boy had climbed into her room unannounced, and look how that had turned out. What was going to happen now with Josh?

He shrugged one shoulder. "Something like that." He leaned forward, resting on his elbow. His head was level with her chest.

The citrusy scent of his soap drifted into her nostrils. She closed her eyes and inhaled a deep breath. She opened them quickly and mentally chastised herself for the small indulgence. Josh was the enemy. No matter how wonderful he smelled or how warm his touch was, he had tried to kill her. He couldn't be trusted. She cleared her throat and clicked on the reading light next to her bed. It wasn't overly bright, but better than her phone. She squinted against the brightness. Josh held up his hand to shield his eyes.

"I'm trying to figure out how to convince you that you can trust me. That the other day in the warehouse was a misunderstanding."

"A misunderstanding?" Katie fought to keep her voice quiet.

Josh held up his hand to silence her. "If I could do it over again, I would do it differently. I can't, so now I'll have to make it up to you in other ways. What can I do? Tell me. I'll do anything."

Katie folded her arms across her chest. "The first thing you can do is get the hell out of my room and let me get back to sleep."

Josh smiled, and Katie's resolve faltered slightly. "I can definitely do that. I'm sorry for bothering you at such a late hour, but I wanted to see you. Make sure you were all right." He stood from the bed. "We'll continue our discussion at a more regular hour." He stared down at her for a moment, then headed for the window.

As soon as he was gone, Katie got up and flipped the lock. She didn't even check to see if he was in the yard. She didn't care. Throwing herself back into bed, she pulled the covers up to her chin.

Thankfully, her arm had stopped throbbing, but now her mind was racing. Maybe she should have gotten those precautions from Randy to keep Josh out of her room.

Katie punched and squished her pillow, trying to make it as comfortable as it was before. Why weren't boys climbing through her window when she wanted them to? And why couldn't they be normal boys? Did she do something in a past life to deserve this torment? She threw her head onto the pillow with a huff.

The only bright side was she didn't have school tomorrow. She could be tired around Wes. It might give her a good excuse to leave. She frowned. She was still unsure how she felt about seeing Wes. She should have been excited to be with him, thrilled that he was alive. Instead, she felt an emptiness, an indifference. Where had that come from? Would it ever go away? She sighed and stared into the darkness toward the ceiling. What she really needed was someone to talk to. An impartial observer who knew what was going on but had no stakes in either side. Where would she find someone like that?

Her eyes felt heavy and she let them drift closed. Somewhere in the back of her brain, she was surprised she could sleep after all the excitement, but she wasn't going to fight it.

*   *   *

"You should probably get up and shower."

Her mom's voice broke through her dreams, the remnants of which vanished the further she drifted into consciousness. She tried to grasp the fading image of a woman with brown hair surround by an ethereal glow. She faded into piercingly bright lights as her mom threw open the shades. Squinting, Katie turned to look at the clock. 7:50. Mom would be leaving soon for work. Katie lay on her back and rubbed her eyes.

"You call me if you need anything today."

"I will, Mom."

"And let me know how Wes is doing."

"Okay." Was there anything else she needed Katie to do?

"I hope you have a wonderful day." Mom kissed her on the forehead.

Katie forced a smile. "You too. Love you."

"Love you too." Her voice faded as she headed down the hall.

Katie stretched her arms over her head and stared out the window. The day looked so normal—like the world wasn't full of demons and boys who couldn't keep promises. Might as well get the day over with. She threw off the covers and headed for the shower.

At quarter to nine, she sat on her couch, waiting for Randy to show up while texting Deb to pass the time. Her friend sent a text wondering where she was, and Katie told her she was taking a mental health day. Deb was jealous. Katie wanted to make plans for the weekend, and Deb was happy to comply. She was in homeroom with nothing to do.

Katie was a little surprised Josh hadn't texted her again. After the late night visit and the need for her to answer his texts, she thought for sure he would have sent her a message. An apology at least. Hopefully, that didn't mean he was going to show up in her room again that night.

A knock sounded at the door, and Katie stood from the couch, texting Deb about how she wanted to do a little shopping on Saturday and then maybe go for a hike. Anything to get her out of the house and away from people. She barely looked up as she opened the front door.

"I really appreciate you coming with me to get Wes," Randy said quietly. "I know he'll be very happy to see you."

Katie responded with a grunt, finished her text, then placed her phone in her pocket. She stepped off the porch and glanced toward the street. "Where's your car?"

Randy pointed across the street. "In the garage. I'm not really in any shape to drive. I hope you don't mind." He smiled.

Katie was confused. "If you wanted me to drive, why didn't you tell me to meet you at your house? It would have saved you a walk across the street."

"I don't mind walking. I need to do it more often. Helps loosen me up." He proceeded down the walk and toward the street. His hand plunged into his pocket. Pulling out the keys, he handed them to Katie.

She took them and followed behind him. He barely walked faster than a snail; why would he want to make the trip twice? Maybe it was some kind of chivalrous act. She didn't know. She really didn't care, either. She wasn't in school. She had all day.

The pair slowly hobbled across the street. Randy seemed to be moving a little easier than he had the day before, but it definitely wasn't faster. Should Katie get the car and pick him up in the middle of the street? It might alleviate some of his discomfort. She shifted from one foot to the other as she tried to slow her pace to keep up with Randy. Her hands drummed on her thighs. She wasn't trying to be impatient or pushy, she was just trying to pass the time while she waited for Randy to catch up. Again, she wasn't in school. And with Randy, there was no chance Josh would stop her on the street. Or would he? Randy was injured. He couldn't fight back. He'd be easy pickings for Josh, should he decide to attack. They weren't protected out in the open, were they? A knot developed in her stomach and she glanced up and down the street, expecting to see Josh's car come flying toward them at a high rate of speed. The neighborhood was quiet. Like it had always been.

Suddenly, Randy stopped in the middle of the street and turned his head to the left. Katie's stomach twisted, her heart leapt into her throat. Did he sense something she couldn't see? Did he hear something she didn't? She stopped next to him, within a few inches, as if he could protect her from whatever was coming, her gaze directed the same way as his. A few hundred yards away from them was a dog standing right in the middle of the street. Katie let out the breath she held. It looked like a German shepherd, the ears alert and turned toward them. It lowered its head, studying them, then turned and trotted away. Randy waited until it disappeared before starting his painfully slow walk back toward the garage.

"Have to be wary of the stray population. Don't want an epidemic on our hands."

Katie stared at him for a moment, one eyebrow raised. There was one dog. One. And there was nothing to indicate that it was a stray. How did he know it didn't belong to someone? It was too far away to see a collar. And just because she'd never seen it around the neighborhood before didn't mean it hadn't been there before. She figured the comment was made in passing, sounds to break the silence between the pair. She shrugged it off.

CHAPTER 9

THE SMILE ON RANDY'S FACE as they pulled up to the hospital was so wide, Katie thought for sure it was going to pop the stitches in the side of his face. Luckily, they were able to pull right up to the hospital, as opposed to parking in the lot and making the excruciatingly long walk to the door. Wes sat in a wheelchair with a nurse behind him, waiting for them to stop. He also had an overly large grin on his face. Katie didn't think he looked too worse for the wear. He was a little pale, with dark circles under his eyes, but that was about it. She saw the bandages on his wrists and knew he had some on his ankles and around his stomach, but otherwise he looked like Wes. He definitely didn't get beat up as bad as his dad had.

As soon as Katie put the car in park, Randy clambered out of the car. Katie attempted to get around and help him, but by the time she got there, he was on his feet. The nurse helped Wes out of the chair, and father and son embraced. They wanted to squeeze each other tight, hold one another like they'd never let go, but they couldn't. Their bodies wouldn't allow it. Katie hung back by the car, not wanting to get in the way of the family reunion. When they finally pulled away, Katie saw the moisture in both of their eyes. Randy clapped his son's shoulder.

"I'm glad you're finally coming home."

Wes smiled. "Me too. We have a lot of work to do."

Randy squeezed Wes's shoulder. "That we do, son. That we do."

Wes's gaze drifted from his father and fell on her. Katie didn't think it was possible, but his smile grew wider. He stepped toward her, his arm held outward to wrap her in a hug. All of the frustration and anger she felt subsided slightly. She stepped into his arms and hugged him back. His lips were right next to her ear, his breath tickled her lobe. His blanket of safety wrapped around her.

"I'm glad you came."

Katie smiled and pulled away. She wasn't sure how to respond, so she said nothing. Inwardly, she hoped that Wes would be able to answer her multitude of questions. He had never been forthcoming with information before, but maybe that would change now that she knew what he was.

Wes turned to his dad. "Shall we head home? I'm tired of this hospital. I want to sit on my own couch and watch my own TV."

Randy chuckled. "Yeah. Let's get out of here."

Wes helped his dad into the back seat, then climbed into the front. Katie sat behind the steering wheel and headed for home.

Katie was thankful the ride was done in silence. It gave her the chance to stay inside her mind, think about what had just happened, sort out her feelings. It didn't make her angry to see Wes in front of the hospital. There wasn't an overwhelming urge to attack him, but she didn't feel much else. There was no tingling in her stomach, no relief that he was all right. There wasn't much of anything. When he wrapped her in a hug, the familiar safety surrounded her. It was comfortable, but also slightly irritating because of the most recent events. He should have told her long ago what he really was. She glanced at him from the corner of her eye. He stared out the window, the smile permanently etched on his face. He seemed happy to be out, like he'd been imprisoned and was experiencing fresh air for the first time in years. Katie was convinced he would stick his head out the window if it was rolled down. She pictured it in her head, and the thought brought a smile to her lips.

She pulled into the driveway and shut off the engine. Knowing what to expect, she quickly got out and helped Wes get his father out of the car. Randy didn't seem to mind, and thanked them both when he got to his feet. They headed into the house and into the living room. Katie wondered how long she was expected to stay. She wanted to head home and take a nap, maybe watch a little TV, but more importantly, she just wanted to be alone. She took a seat on the couch, and Wes sat next to her. Randy lowered himself into the recliner.

"So what did the doctor say?" Katie was tired of the silence. She didn't know if the father and son had some kind of mental telepathy going on, but they didn't talk much at all. It was driving her crazy. If she was going to be there, the least they could do was talk to one another.

Wes shrugged. "That I was lucky I didn't lose more blood than I had. He said I'll heal just fine, but it will take some time."

"How many stitches did you end up getting?"

Wes thought for a moment. "I think all total it was one hundred sixty some, plus some staples." He lifted his shirt, but the only thing visible was a white bandage. "Most of them are holding me together here."

Katie's stomach tingled with nausea. Her thoughts drifted back to the day Josh attacked them; the image of the blood dominated her mind's eye. She shuddered. Wes reached out and grabbed her hand.

"I definitely wouldn't have survived without you."

Katie glanced away. "You also wouldn't have been there if it weren't for me." She said the words under her breath, almost inaudibly. If Wes heard them, he didn't say a word, but squeezed her hand.

"What about you, Dad?" Wes turned his attention across the room. "How are you doing?"

Randy smiled. "You don't need to worry about me. I've been hurt a lot worse. I'll heal."

"So what do we know?"

Randy sighed. "Not a lot. Josh has been laying pretty low. I assume he's biding his time, waiting."

"For what?" Katie asked.

Randy shrugged. "It's hard to say. Demons are predictable in what they want, but how they go about getting it varies greatly. The only thing we know for sure is that he'll strike when he knows he can hurt Wes really bad."

"What do you think he'll do?" Worry and concern coursed through Katie's body.

The thought occurred to her that she should tell them about the texts and the late night visit, but it would probably upset them. Neither one of them was in any shape to run out and fight, which Katie was sure they would want to do. Besides, Josh hadn't done anything threatening; he was only trying to apologize. The fact that he had something to apologize for distressed her, but he also had some answers. Katie was willing to hear both sides until her curiosity was satiated, no matter how upsetting or how unsavory the company was.

"Well, for sure, he'll try to kill him again," Randy stated matter of factly. "But he'll toy with him before that. Put him in pain."

Katie's eyes drifted up and down Wes's body. "He's already in pain."

"Physical pain is only one part of it," Wes said softly. "People train themselves to overcome that. Since he was unsuccessful in killing me the first time, now he'll go after my emotions, my soul."

"How?" The question barely came out of her mouth. She wasn't sure she wanted to ask it. She was pretty sure she already knew the answer.

"He'll come after the people I love." Wes squeezed her hand again. "But you don't need to worry about that. My dad and I can protect you."

Katie nodded mechanically. Again, her gaze drifted from Wes to Randy, taking in their current states of abuse. She doubted incredibly highly that they'd be able to do much of anything. Randy could barely lower himself into a chair.

Was that why Josh continued to stay in contact with her? Was he still using her to get to Wes? In the back of her brain, she knew that had always been the case. She knew Josh didn't care about her, that she was just a means to an end, but there was a flicker of hope that it wasn't true. After all, he said he wanted to tell Katie what was really going on, explain to her the situation. He wouldn't need to do that if she was just a pawn. And last night, he could have taken her again, and no one would have known what happened. But maybe that was the point. Maybe he was biding his time, waiting for Wes to get out of the hospital. She didn't really believe that, though. No matter where Wes was, if Josh had killed Katie, it would have crushed him. It would have crushed him even more if it had happened while he was recovering. She glanced at the side of Wes's face. She imagined the pain and heartache would be unbearable for him if Katie died and he could do nothing to protect her. No, there was something more at play here. Josh was more complicated than she imagined.

Her thoughts drifted back to the warehouse when Josh commented about a blackness in her soul. Wes said he saw it too. What did that mean? Did that mean she was capable of evil like Josh was? It might explain her feelings of indifference toward Wes. A chill ran down her spine. What was she capable of doing? Did she even want to think about it?

"Why don't you two head into your room, Wes." Randy's voice broke her out of her thoughts. "Talk some things out. I'm going to lay down for a little while. We can figure out a plan later."

"Sounds good." Wes stood from the couch. "Come on. I'm sure you have a lot of questions."

Katie allowed herself to be led upstairs and into his room. As they stepped in, she was surprised at how bright and cheery his room was. Sunlight spilled in through the window reflecting off his light blue comforter. Bookshelves lined the wall, and on the right was a desk stacked neatly with piles of papers. Crosses hung on the parts of the walls that weren't covered by shelves. Katie blinked, as if she were in a dream. She expected Wes's room to be painted black, matching his secretive nature and tendency to be introverted. This was just the opposite. Wes sat on the bed and patted the space next to him. Katie pulled out his desk chair and sat down, her eyes wandering around the room.

Wes moved so he sat directly across from her. "I thought you were going to come visit me last night." His mouth turned downward. "I called several times looking for you."

Katie's gaze dropped to her lap. "I know. I had some other things to do. Plus, I didn't recognize the number."

Wes reached forward and gently rubbed the bandage on her arm. "How are you doing?"

She pulled her arm away and folded it across her chest. "I don't know. I don't know if what is happening is real. I'm confused and lost." It was easy for Katie to drift back into old patterns. Wes had always been the one person she could confide in and talk to. She completely forgot that she was trying to avoid him.

Sympathy crossed Wes's face. "I know. I'm sorry. I never wanted you to be brought into this world."

Katie clicked her tongue and slumped her shoulders forward. "I don't mind being in your world, Wes. I've always wanted to be there. But I would have liked to have had a little bit of warning, maybe some information about what I was getting into." She reached forward and touched his knee. "I told you all of my secrets. You know everything about me. Never once did you let me in. Ever."

Wes folded his hands into his lap, his eyes focused on his fingers. "I know. I'm sorry. There are rules. Things we can and can't do. I thought I was protecting you."

Katie had no idea why she was being so calm. She had every right to scream and yell at him for what he had done, and part of her wanted to, but what would it accomplish? She shrugged. "Things don't always work out the way you want them to." And boy, did she know that well.

Wes looked up and placed his hands on her knees. "Look, things are different now. You've been brought into the world, so I don't have to keep it a secret. Let's start over."

She sighed. "I'll try. But there is still a lot of hurt I can't let go of."

"You don't have to, but at least give me a second chance."

"It might take some time."

Wes sighed and turned away. "And that's fine. I don't deserve it, that's for sure." He turned back to her. "But I do love you."

Katie had waited so long for him to say those words, and now that he had, she didn't know how she felt about it. She should have been elated. Instead, part of her didn't believe it. Part of her knew he was going to leave her. Like he always did.

"Come on, Katie. You felt the same way about me once. Given time, don't you think you could feel it again? I promise, no more secrets, no more lies. Ask me anything. I'll tell you what you want to know."

"Why didn't you ever let me in? Why didn't you tell me what was going on when we were kids?"

"You wouldn't have believed me."

Katie cocked her head to the side and stared at him. "Don't give me that. You could have made me believe you. You could have shown me your world. You said no more lies, so stop lying."

Wes bit his lower lip. "I couldn't. My dad wouldn't let me." He said the words quietly, as if he were afraid his dad would hear. "He didn't want to see me go through the same heartache he went through."

"You mean when your mom...left?" She couldn't bring herself to say the word died.

Wes nodded.

"Did a demon kill her?"

Wes shook his head. It was obvious he really didn't want to talk about it, and that caused anger to flare inside of Katie. How were things supposed to change between them if he wouldn't change them? She leaned back in her chair and averted her gaze out the window. She pushed the feelings away and reminded herself that at least he was trying. She couldn't expect him to change overnight.

Wes must have sensed her irritation. He scooted closer and moved his hands onto her thighs. "Look, Katie, what we do is dangerous. By having close relationships, we put the people around us at risk. Demons don't play by any rules. They play to win. They want power, they want souls, and they will do anything to get them. We have to make sacrifices for the good of others. It's the burden Praesuls have to bear." He touched her cheek with his fingertips. "It's not easy, but we do what we have to do."

Katie pulled away from him. "Then why have friendships at all? Why not live in the mountains, away from people and only come down when you're needed?"

Hurt crossed Wes's face. "I'm still human."

"Are you?"

"Katie, that's not fair."

She took a deep breath. "I know. I'm sorry." She closed her eyes and swallowed hard.

"Katie, you're angry, you're hurt, and you're confused. I get that. But let me—"

Katie opened her eyes. "Do you really get it? What are you going to do to change it?"

Wes shook his head. "I don't know. I've done nothing to be trustworthy. I've hurt you...deeply. If you want to walk away and never look back, then do. But know that Josh won't stop. He'll continue to come after you. Only because he knows it will hurt me."

Katie stood and headed for the window. His words sounded so nice. They were everything she had wanted to hear from him. He was finally letting her in.

"All humans are unwilling pawns in the battle of good and evil, Katie. Most of them are just blissfully unaware of it. I'm sorry you got dragged into this, but I can't help you unless you allow me to. I will always protect you, but it's up to you if it's done from a distance."

Katie glanced at him over her shoulder. Anger, sadness, and confusion swirled through her. Part of her really wanted to believe him. She wanted to get to know Wes, the real him, and see what would happen if he let her in. She saw sincerity in his eyes, felt it in his touch. She believed it when he said he loved her, and part of her wished she could say the same thing back to him. At one point, she would have been able to. The other part of her held onto the hurt, the lies, the betrayal. It wanted to protect her from further damage. She was conflicted. She really needed someone to talk to, someone to give her advice. But who could she turn to? Wes had always been her confidant.

"Katie, just take some time. Think about it. I'll be here."

The desire to turn to him and embrace him overwhelmed her. His words melted something inside her, cast a net of safety over her. Her shoulders slumped, her resolve faltered. So what if he'd abandoned her a couple hundred times; he was willing to make up for it. They were given a second chance, things could be different. Part of her knew she would always regret it if she didn't give it a try. Josh had almost killed her and she was willing to hear him out, and she barely knew him. Couldn't she give Wes the same chance? She was just about to turn around to face him when her gaze fell on a picture on his bookshelf. It was of a smiling woman with blonde hair and a young girl, maybe around ten. The background was white, so Katie couldn't tell where the picture had been taken. Something about the woman's eyes seemed familiar. She picked up the frame and stared at it. She turned to Wes and glanced at him. That's where she had seen the eyes before. They were Wes's.

"Is this your mom?"

Wes stepped forward and looked at the picture. He placed his hand over Katie's. A sad smile crossed his lips. "Yeah."

"Who is this with her?"

"My sister."

"Your older sister? My mom told me your mom and sister died in childbirth."

Wes took the picture and placed it back on the shelf. He kept his back toward Katie for a long time, his head hung low. "My mom and sister aren't dead. They're someplace safe. Where demons can't find them. Where they can't be used to hurt us."

Katie's mouth dropped open. "They're still alive? Well, that's great! My mom told me you and your dad were so distressed when you...faked their deaths. What are they like? How often do you see them?"

Wes lowered his head and sighed. "Katie, I can't."

"Can't what?"

"I can't talk about my family. I can't reveal anything that could potentially put them in danger."

Katie felt a cold spot settle in her chest. "Don't you trust me?"

Wes turned slowly, sorrow filled his eyes. "I do trust you, Katie, but..."

That one word caused her breath to catch and the cold to spread to her extremities.

"If Josh captures you again, or any demon, I don't want them to torture the information out of you."

Katie lowered her gaze to the floor. Nothing was going to change in their relationship. It was blatantly obvious. He would always be afraid she was going to betray him. He would never allow himself to let her in. Without saying a word, she turned and ran out of his house.

CHAPTER 10

KATIE DIDN'T GO HOME. Wes would find her there. When she hit the street, she ran. She had no idea where she was going, but she just needed to be alone. Disillusionment and anger surged through her body, pumping her legs faster and faster. Her breathing rasped, giving her something to focus on besides what had just happened. She didn't want to think about it. How could he not trust her after all these years? What had she ever done to make him think she would betray him? She'd saved his life! She shook her head. Wes needed to be cleared from her system.

Her body finally gave out. Her legs wouldn't move anymore, her lungs burned for oxygen, and black dots danced in front of her eyes. She collapsed into the sitting position. With her head in her hands, she sucked in ragged breaths until her vision cleared and her breathing slowed. When some energy returned, she took in her surroundings. It took a moment, but she recognized where she was. She sat on the thin patch of grass in the parking lot next to her mom's work. Her subconscious must have taken her there. She needed someone to talk to, and if she could make anyone understand, it was Mom. Slowly, with shaky legs, she got to her feet and headed into the building.

Mom's office was on the third floor, and Katie leaned against the wall in the elevator to stay upright. Her body shook with exhaustion. Her mouth had gone dry. Thankfully, she could get a drink from the water cooler at the end of the hall. She downed three cups before heading to her mom's office. As usual, Mom was at her computer. She turned as Katie entered the room. Her eyes grew wide, she pushed her chair away from the desk and met her half way across the floor, scooping Katie into her arms.

"What happened? What's wrong?"

Katie wondered how awful she looked for her mom to express so much concern. Without a doubt, her face was red from running, her hair was probably a little disheveled, but she hadn't been crying, so her eyes wouldn't have been puffy. Maybe her mom saw the emotional torment under the surface. She didn't know. She didn't really care. Katie wrapped her arms around her mom's waist. It was just nice to be held.

"How well do you really know Wes and Randy?"

Mom pulled away and stared at Katie, concern and fear shrouded her face. "Why? Did they do something to you? Hurt you in some way? Do I need to call the police?"

Katie shook her head. "No, Mom. Nothing like that. I'm just wondering."

Mom placed her hands on Katie's cheeks and pulled her close. "Please tell me what's going on."

Katie grabbed her wrists and removed her hands. Maybe Mom wasn't the best person to talk to. She was really starting to frustrate Katie. "Wes and I had a fight. I will tell you about it in a minute. I ran here because I was so upset. Now, please, answer my question and I'll tell you what's going on."

Mom moved toward the chairs in front of her desk, pulling Katie behind her, and sat down. She motioned for Katie to sit next to her, which she happily did. Her knees were just about ready to give out.

"I'm not exactly sure I understand what you're asking me. How well do I know them?"

Katie nodded. "It's a pretty straight forward question."

Mom looked confused. "And one I thought we talked about the other night. I told you, after Randy's wife died, they shut themselves off from everyone. I don't know either of them at all anymore."

"What about before? Did you know them well before?"

Mom shrugged. "I guess. We had dinner with them a few times, but it's not like we shared secrets."

"Did you know Randy's wife really well?"

"Katie, I don't understand your line of questioning. Will you just tell me what's going on?"

"After she died," the word came out of Katie's mouth strained, "did they have a funeral? Do you know for sure that she was dead?"

The look of confusion on Mom's face turned into concern. "Of course they had a funeral. For both of them. And I didn't see the bodies, but I didn't need to. The look on Randy's face was enough to convince me."

Katie leaned forward in her seat. She wanted to tell her mom that they weren't really dead, that it was all a lie, but she couldn't get the words out. She couldn't betray Wes, even if he believed she could.

"Katie, what in the world is going on?"

"Wes and Randy aren't who you think they are."

"Katie, you're making no sense."

"They're Praesuls, Mom. They fight demons." She didn't feel bad about telling her mom that, it wasn't like the demons didn't already know what they were. Besides, she had to tell someone. She needed help figuring out what to do. "Randy wasn't actually injured in a car accident. He was attacked by a demon."

Mom pressed her lips into a thin line and stared at Katie.

"I can prove it!" Katie jumped from her seat. "Come with me. Wes and Randy will tell you everything."

Mom calmly stood from her seat and walked around her desk. Grabbing her purse, she pulled out her keys. Hope surged through Katie. Finally! Someone was actually listening to her. Maybe now she'd finally get some answers instead of more lies.

On the way out, Mom stopped at her boss's office and told her she had some family business to attend to. Mom told her she would call later with more details. She leaned forward on the desk and lowered her voice. Katie assumed Mom was giving her boss a few details about what was happening and glanced down the hall, anxious to leave. Her boss nodded and told her to take all the time she needed. As Mom walked out of the office, Katie noticed her boss pick up her phone, but thought nothing else of it.

Mom held Katie's hand in the elevator. Katie shifted from one foot to the other. Couldn't the dang thing move any faster? She practically ran to the car, pulling her mom behind her. She was half tempted to drive so she could get there quickly, but Mom wouldn't give her the keys. Katie stared out the window as they headed down the street.

It didn't take long for Katie to realize they weren't heading to Wes and Randy's house. They were going in the opposite direction. Confused, she turned to her mom.

"Where are we going? I thought you wanted to hear the truth."

Mom's voice was low, calm. "Katie, I think you might be having some kind of reaction to the dog bite. The doctor said it was possible. Rabies are quite common."

"Rabies?" Katie's voice was just below a screech. "I don't have rabies! I'm not making this up." She searched frantically for a way out of the car, but Mom was driving too fast. Maybe at the next red light. She leaned forward in her seat, waiting for her chance to get out. Mom reached across the seat and took a hold of her arm.

"It's going to be fine. The doctors will check you out and give you some medicine."

Katie tried to get her mom's hand off her, but she had too tight of a grip. As luck would have it, all the lights stayed green. Katie's breathing became rapid as they pulled in front of the hospital. This was not how she envisioned this happening. She really needed to get away. As soon as Mom let go to get out of her door, she'd be gone. But Mom didn't let go. Instead, the nurses were already waiting for her when they pulled up! How did they know she was coming? Katie screamed in frustration. This couldn't be happening! How could her mom do this to her? The men opened the car door and pulled her out.

"Let me go!" She kicked and wiggled in the man's grasp. "Let me go!"

Another grabbed her ankles and ushered her into the hospital. They plopped her onto a gurney and held her down. A female nurse approached from her right with a needle in her hand. Katie felt the cool wetness of the alcohol pad on her arm. She increased her efforts to get away, but the men were too strong. Her heart thudded in her chest, panic surged through her veins. She felt a small prick in her arm and liquid burn under her flesh. Within a few seconds, her body went limp, and her voice went silent. She had no fight left. The men released their grips and backed away from her.

"She should be fine now," the female nurse said. "That tranquilizer will keep her calm for a few hours. Let me grab some paperwork and we'll get her checked in."

Mom sat next to Katie on the bed and grabbed her hand. Katie would have jerked it out of her grasp, but she had no control over her muscles. She stroked Katie's hair. Tears rolled down her cheeks.

"I'm sorry, baby. I really am. But I want you to be well."

Katie would have rolled away from Mom, but she had no energy. Instead, she closed her eyes and tried to pretend she wasn't there. Katie barely heard her mom talking to the nurse, giving her the vital information to admit her to the hospital. The thought sickened her; the disappointment made Katie's chest ache. Mom's voice hitched often as she fought back the tears. Eventually, the nurse left with a squeak of shoes on linoleum.

A while later, Katie had no idea how long, the doctor entered the room. She opened her eyes for that, hoping he would see that she wasn't really sick, that this was all a misunderstanding. He smiled and held out his hand.

"Mrs. Barrett, it's nice to see you again." He nodded toward Katie. "And you too, Katie." He turned back to her mom. "I appreciate the phone call that you were on your way in. Made it easy to get that sedative ordered, just in case. From what I hear, she needed it."

Katie's mind barely comprehended what the doctor was saying. What phone call? Mom never made any call. Slowly, as if emerging from a fog, the vision of her mom's boss picking up the phone as they left materialized in her mind. Anger flared in her chest. That would explain why the nurses were waiting for her.

The doctor flipped through the pages of the chart, then set them on the bed and unwrapped the bandage on her arm. "Well, I don't see any signs of infection in the punctures. They look like they're healing rather nicely." He picked the chart up again. "You have concerns about rabies?"

Mom nodded. "Yes." Her voice croaked. "When you stitched her up the other day, you said it was a possibility and to keep my eyes on her. You said if she started acting abnormally I should bring her back right away."

He folded his hands over the chart and held it to his body. "It is still a distinct possibility. We'll have to do some blood work and keep her overnight for observation. If that's all right with you?"

"Yes. Please. I want her to be well."

The doctor plastered a sympathetic smile onto his face. "Of course. Let me get the paperwork filled out and we'll set her up in a room." He turned and left.

Katie wanted to protest, to yell and scream that she was all right, that her mom should call Wes and he would clear everything up, but what was the point? No one would believe her. Why did she think she could say anything to her mom? The one person who should have listened to her didn't. Where did that leave Katie? Alone. With no one to talk to. She squeezed her eyes shut once again.

The nurse returned later and wheeled Katie from the emergency room. Katie didn't open her eyes for the trip. She didn't care where she was going. What difference did it make? It wasn't like she was going to be able to escape anyway. The drugs kept her perfectly immobile. When they reached their destination, the nurse opened and closed some cupboard doors and placed something on Katie's feet. She opened her eyes and glanced down. It looked like a gown.

"You'll need to wear these while you're here," the nurse explained. "I'm sure your mom can help you into them."

"Of course," her mom answered.

The nurse stepped out of the room, and her mom placed her hands under Katie's shoulders, helping her into a sitting position.

"C'mon, Katie. Help me out here."

"Why?" The word croaked out of her mouth. Katie barely recognized the voice as her own.

Mom stopped fussing and sat down. Her face was red, puffy, and tear streaked. Mom looked horrible. If Katie wasn't so angry, she would have almost felt sorry for her.

"You need to get well, honey. I think you have some major issues. Please. Do it for me. Help me out. You know how I worry about you."

"And if I'm not sick?" Her tongue felt thick in her mouth, it was hard to move her jaw muscles.

"We'll worry about that when we need to worry about that."

Katie snorted and lifted her hands above her head as best as she could. No sense fighting against her mom. It wouldn't get her anywhere. In fact, it might bring the nurse back in with another shot. She didn't need that. She needed to bide her time, wait for things to wear off, then make her move.

"Call Wes." Katie hated that the words came out of her mouth, but he would tell her mom what was going on. He'd clear this whole mess up. He had to. He said he wanted things to change between them.

Mom pulled the shirt over Katie's head and slipped on the gown. "I will, honey. I will."

Katie lay back on the pillow and stared at the ceiling. Her mom took out the phone and dialed. The nurse came back into the room, so Mom left to talk in private. Good, Katie thought. This should be cleared up in the next few minutes. The nurse pulled a tray and IV pole behind her. Katie hoped Mom hurried. Otherwise, she was in for a long stay. She glanced at the door, expecting her mom to come back in at any second and tell the nurse to never mind.

The nurse wiped Katie's hand with another alcohol pad and readied the IV needle. Katie tried to move her hand out of the way, but the nurse tightened her grip on Katie's wrist and stared at her through slitted eyes. Not a good plan. Angering the nurse would surely get her another tranquilizer. She relaxed her hand and let the nurse do her job. As soon as the needle was in, her mom came back into the room.

"Is this really necessary?" she asked.

Yes, thank you! Tell her to take it out!

The nurse nodded. "It's protocol. If anything happens, we need direct access to administer meds. Plus, it makes it easier for us to draw blood." She held up two vials filled with crimson liquid. "I'll take these to the lab and we should have some answers soon." She pushed her tray out of the room.

Mom took a seat back on the bed. "Wes and Randy will be here soon."

Katie's head spun. That's not what she wanted. She wanted her mom to ask about it on the phone. But maybe this would work out better. Maybe talking in person would allow Mom to believe what they actually said. Maybe they were afraid of saying something over the phone and having it intercepted by an outside source. She wasn't excited about seeing Wes again, but if it got her out of the hospital, she'd endure it.

"Are you comfortable?" Mom asked.

"No."

"What can I get you? A blanket? Some water?"

"How about out of the hospital?"

Mom clicked her tongue. "You know I can't do that, sweetie. We need to find out what's going on."

"I told you what's going on."

"No, Katie, you didn't. You spoke a lot of nonsense. You told me Randy and Wes fight demons for a living. That's not you. You don't make up wild stories."

Katie stared at her mother. "Who said it was a story?"

"Honey, I know you believe it's true, but your mind is playing tricks on you. You're hallucinating, and I'm sure it's because of that dog that attacked you. It poisoned your blood and your mind."

Katie turned away. Wes would be there soon, and he'd clear everything up. Until then, she didn't want to say another word.

An eternity later, Wes and Randy stepped into her room. Their faces were somber, concern shrouded their eyes. Mom stood to greet them.

"I'm glad you're here," she spoke softly. "Katie wanted me to call you."

Wes stepped forward and leaned on her bed. "How are you feeling?"

"You have to tell her," Katie said. "You have to tell her everything. She thinks I'm crazy."

Wes turned to Katie's Mom. "What is she talking about?"

Mom shrugged. "I don't know. She came to my office ranting about how you two fight demons for a living." She turned to Randy. "She said you didn't get into a car accident but were attacked by a creature from Hell. What is she talking about?"

Katie waited anxiously. It was out. All they had to do was verify the facts. Tell her what really happened. Instead, they remained silent.

CHAPTER 11

KATIE WANTED TO LEAP FROM HER BED and scream. Were Randy and Wes really just standing there not saying a word? Why were they allowing her mom to think she was insane? Anger sizzled just below the surface, but the tranquilizer kept it from boiling over.

Wes leaned down and whispered in her ear. "I can't sacrifice the safety of my family. Your mom's safety. I can't tell her the truth."

Mustering all the strength she could, Katie raised her arm and slammed her palm into Wes's head. She meant to smack him on the cheek, but her aim was off and she hit him in the ear. Wes recoiled backward.

"Katie!" her mom gasped.

"Get out," Katie growled.

"Katie, look—"

"I said get out!" Katie punched the nurse's button repeatedly. The last thing she wanted was the witch to come back in, but if it got everyone else out, it was worth it.

Both the nurse and the doctor rushed into the room. They stared wide-eyed, trying to figure out what was going on.

"Get them out!" Katie yelled. "They are trying to hurt me!"

The doctor glanced from Katie to the others in the room. He pressed his lips together. "Out. Everyone out."

Mom's mouth fell open. "You can't ask me to leave. I'm her mother."

The doctor stepped in front of her. "Your daughter may be suffering from hallucinations and paranoia. The best thing we can do for her is to keep her calm. If she perceives you as a threat, you staying in here is only going to make things worse."

Katie liked the doctor. He seemed to be the only one on her side.

Her mom opened her mouth to speak, but the doctor raised his hand to silence her.

"Please. You want her to get better."

Mom nodded and headed for the door.

Wes stayed by the bed, shaking his head. "Don't do this."

"You had your chance," Katie snarled.

The nurse grabbed his arm. "You heard the doctor. Out."

Reluctantly, Wes rose and headed out of the room. He lingered in the doorway, his gaze pleading with her. The nurse pushed him out and closed the door. The doctor approached the bed and smiled at her.

"Try to get some rest. No one is going to hurt you."

Katie turned away. If he only knew.

*   *   *

A few hours later, Katie woke, unaware she had fallen asleep. Her head felt light, airy, like a balloon on a string drifting several feet above her body. Someone gently stroked her hair, but she felt disconnected from it, like it was happening to someone else. She wasn't in the mood for comfort, especially from her mom. Who let her back in the room anyway? Katie jerked backward to push the hand away. It worked for a few seconds, then the stroking started again. She rolled over to grab her mom's hand and tell her to get out. The words caught in her throat as her gaze fell on the person behind her. Josh smiled and folded his hands in his lap.

"Good morning, sleepy head."

Katie pushed herself into the sitting position and glanced around the room. Was she dreaming? She squeezed her eyes shut and reopened them. Josh was still there.

"I can assure you you're not dreaming." He pushed some hair behind her ear. "And it's not really morning. It's about ten o'clock at night. Although I'm sure the drugs they gave you have left you disoriented."

"How did you get in here?" Her tongue was still swollen and felt too big for her mouth.

Josh jerked his head to the right. "The door."

It took Katie a moment to understand what he said. It wasn't right. He shouldn't be there. But why? What had Randy told her?

"No, I mean the hospital." She remembered what he had said about holy ground. "How did you get into the hospital?"

Josh seemed pleased with himself. "You're not at Saint Mary's. You're at County."

County? What? That didn't make sense. The doctor knew her. He put the stitches in.

"They are short on emergency room staff, so doctors and nurses rotate between the two hospitals." Josh must have read her mind. "Wes tried to convince your mom to take you to Saint Mary's, but she wouldn't listen. She was much too distraught about your condition. Luckily for her, she had some tranquilizers in her purse. Keeps them there for emergencies. She's sleeping peacefully in the waiting room."

"What about Wes?"

Josh's face crunched in disgust. "Pfft. With your mom. Protecting her."

Katie's chest tightened. She shied as far away from Josh as she could, which wasn't very far. "What does she need protecting from?"

Josh smiled. "Me." He waved his hand through the air. "But you don't need to worry about that. Doing something to her would hurt you." He ran his hand over her hair. "And I'm not going to hurt you anymore."

She shrank from his touch.

Josh folded his hands back into his lap. "I understand your hesitation. I don't blame you for your mistrust. The only way to fix that is to give you some answers. Will you allow me to do that?"

Katie raised an eyebrow and stared at him for a moment before her gaze drifted around the room. "I can't leave."

"Why not?"

Katie opened her mouth to respond, then closed it again. Why couldn't she leave? What was keeping her there? The tranquilizers had inhibited her earlier, but they were wearing off. Even though she wasn't at one hundred percent and her head felt foggy, the feeling wouldn't last forever. Mom would be mad at her, but she'd get over it eventually, especially when she found out Katie didn't have rabies. Mom deserved to get upset. Maybe then she'd understand what she needlessly put Katie through. It would be justice. There was just one person Katie was sure they wouldn't get past.

"The nurse will never let us leave. How did you get past her anyway?"

Josh laughed. "Please. She wasn't standing guard at the door. Sneaking past people is my specialty. Besides, the shifts changed ten minutes ago and the new nurse already did her rounds. She won't be back for hours. But that doesn't really matter because we aren't going out the front door."

Katie pushed herself up. "Then how are we getting out?"

"A portal."

"A portal?"

Josh nodded.

"Are you taking me back to the warehouse?"

He chuckled. "No. We'll go someplace a little more...educational." He stood and walked to the chair on the other side of the room and grabbed Katie's folded clothes. "You'll want to change." He tossed them to her.

Katie went to grab them and was stopped by the IV. She looked at it in distaste.

Josh stepped forward and grabbed the tube. With a quick tug, he pulled the catheter free, then pressed on the hole with his index finger. Searing heat burned her skin, cauterizing the flesh and staunching the bleeding.

"Time is slipping by, and I have a lot to show you."

Katie pursed her lips and grabbed her clothes. "You gonna watch me change?"

Josh lifted his eyebrows suggestively and licked his lips. Katie cocked her head to the side. Josh turned his back to her and took a few steps away. Katie shrugged out of the gown and pulled on her clothes. What she was doing was crazy; she knew that, but what was the alternative? Staying in the hospital was out of the question. She didn't belong there; she wasn't sick. Wes obviously couldn't trust her with any answers, so Josh was her only choice. The decision didn't make her comfortable.

"Ready."

Josh turned. His smile spread ear to ear. He raised his right hand and whispered words under his breath. A pinpoint of light appeared before him, slowly growing until it touched the ground and was as tall as he was. He held out his hand for Katie. With the slightest hesitation and a deep breath, she took his hand. His grip was warm, his fingers wrapped gently around hers. Katie inwardly wished things were different between them—mainly that he wasn't a demon—because his touch sent sparks through her. They stepped into the light.

In the blink of an eye, they were out of the hospital and on the street in front of her house. Katie took in the surroundings, confused.

"Why did you bring me here? I thought you were going to give me answers."

"I am. But to take in the big picture, you have to start with the familiar. What do you see?"

"What do you mean what do I see? Nothing. It's my neighborhood at night. Everyone is doing their own thing. It's boring."

He turned around. "What do you see there?"

Katie looked where he indicated. "That's Wes's house."

"And what do you see?"

Katie shrugged and stared at the house, thinking she was supposed to see something she hadn't seen before. Maybe something mystical or magical, but there was nothing. Just a dark house.

"You're thinking about this too hard. I wasn't asking a trick question." Josh placed his hands on his hips.

Katie huffed. "I don't see anything. It's just a house."

Josh clicked his tongue. "And that's my point. All your life, this was just a house that Wes lived in. Unassuming. Average. And yet, just a few days ago, you learned Wes was more than he pretended to be."

Katie folded her arms across her chest. "What's your point, Josh? The world is never what it seems, it's what we perceive it to be. I learned that in English. You're not telling me anything new."

Josh held his hands out to his sides. "Fair enough. I guess we can skip that part of the lesson. Why don't you ask me something you want an answer to."

Katie stared at him for a moment and tapped her foot. Where to start? There were so many things she wanted to know.

Lights shone at the end of the street, illuminating the pair in harsh light. Katie squinted at the brightness, Josh stiffened. The car turned into a driveway several houses away. Josh grabbed Katie's arm and directed her to her yard.

"We'd better continue this conversation somewhere safe." He opened a portal and the pair stepped inside.

Katie's feet crunched on gravel, darkness surrounded her. A faint red light glowed off to her left, but it wasn't strong enough to illuminate the area. Humid heat surrounded her, stifling her breath and depositing a layer of moisture on her flesh.

"Where are we?"

"Someplace safe."

Katie shrugged. It didn't really matter where they were. As long as it wasn't the hospital, she was happy.

"Tell me about Praesuls," she said.

Josh took a seat on the ground and crossed his legs. Katie barely made out his outline, and seeing the expression on his face was impossible. It didn't matter, though. She heard him just fine, and that was all that mattered.

"Praesuls really got started and organized when the Roman Empire came into power. The leaders of the Empire were a paranoid lot, afraid of their own shadows." Josh chuckled. "I hear it was great fun to torment them. They were obsessed with power. Attaining and maintaining it. As they spread across the world, they came into contact with weird religions and a slew of demons. They had to do something to keep both at bay." Josh adjusted and leaned back on his elbows. "As you can imagine, the decadence and debauchery of the Romans was paradise for demons. So many sins, so many souls." He sighed. "To hear the stories from the Old Ones, taking a soul was like picking a flower. I wish I had been there for that. It sounds divine." His voice took on a dreamlike quality.

Katie waited silently for him to finish. He was quiet for several moments, and she imagined stories told by the Old Ones drifted through his head and he pretended he was with them harvesting souls. Eventually, he cleared his throat.

"A few of the more devout and pious took it upon themselves to save the masses. They believed humans were being led astray, that it was an innate desire to do good, but us demons were hindering that. They believed if they got rid of us, they would get rid of sin and evil. They created a sect of assassins to hunt us down."

"Is it true? Are humans naturally wired to be good?"

"Not exactly. When you're born, your soul is pretty much a blank slate. There's a fifty-fifty chance you could go either way. Most people are drawn to the good side because when they do a good deed, chemicals are released in the brain that make them feel even better. But the same thing happens to people who do evil. And your station in life doesn't dictate what side you're more prone to. It all boils down to choices. Does that make sense?"

Katie nodded, but she wasn't sure Josh saw it. A million more questions raced through her mind. She wished her mom had taken her to church more often or she would have studied the Bible on her own. If she had more knowledge of religion and God, the whole thing might make a little more sense. She had general ideas about good and evil, Heaven and Hell, God and Satan, but she was a little less clear about Free Will and the soul. Would Josh think she was a complete moron if she asked about that kind of stuff? Was there time to discuss it? At least he was answering her questions. It was more than Wes was willing to do.

Katie stepped forward and took a seat next to Josh. She folded her legs Indian-style; her knee touched his. If they were going to be talking about this for a while, she might as well get comfortable.

CHAPTER 12

JOSH LEANED FORWARD, his face inches from hers. She felt his breath on her cheek, smelled the mintiness of his toothpaste. That surprised her. From movies she'd watched and from the way Wes and Randy referred to demons, it seemed that demon's breath was always putrid and rotten. Of course, from what Randy had said, those movies weren't exactly accurate. Boy, he wasn't kidding. Katie knew very little about demon stereotypes, but she was sure Josh didn't fit any of them. He seemed so human. Aside from the episode in the warehouse, she hadn't seen him hurt a fly. Maybe he wasn't as evil as Wes said he was. Maybe he could be saved.

"How does one become a Praesul?" Katie knew she should move away, but she couldn't. The heat from Josh's body was comforting, especially with the darkness that surrounded her and not knowing what could be in it, waiting to attack.

"You would think there would be some special sign, like a calling or birthmark, wouldn't you?" Josh lowered his voice; his tone was seductive.

Katie found herself lost in his words, unable to speak. She nodded absently.

He chuckled. "Well, there's not. The only requirement is a desire to kill demons. You have to apply to the Church, and they bless you, but, otherwise, anyone can become a Praesul. If you asked a Praesul, they would probably tell you they heard a calling. That some higher being wanted them to do something good for the world."

Katie pushed her eyebrows together in confusion. That didn't seem right. It seemed like there should be more to it. Knowledge about Heaven and Hell, good and evil, maybe an undying devotion to God. Anyone could do it? Really?

"Back in the day, the religious leaders needed all the help they could get. Sin ran rampant; people didn't want to give up the luxuries and debauchery. If good wanted to win, they had to get help from wherever they could." Josh placed a hand on her knee. "But don't think that makes Praesuls weak or any less of a threat. They go through training, they get graced by a divine power. They are dangerous. They are powerful."

Katie's eyes drifted to his hand. She couldn't see it in the dark, but she felt the heat drifting through her jeans. Her stomach tingled.

She cleared her throat. "How many are there?"

"It's hard to say, Katie. They are very secretive, they keep their numbers hidden. Part of their defense is keeping their army hidden from demons."

"So how do you know when you've run into a Praesul?"

"There's a mark on their soul. A tiny hint of gold. Most of the time, demons don't look for it. It's a waste of time. Most of us are way too focused on harvesting sinners' souls and then going home. But if a Praesul happens across our path, we'll take every advantage to take them down."

"You mentioned in the warehouse that you weren't after Wes until you discovered he was a Praesul, but you also said you were harvesting souls at my high school. Who were you after?"

He raised his hand and placed his fingertips gently on her cheek. "You."

Katie recoiled backward, away from his touch. If he was offended by the action, she couldn't tell. On one hand, she wasn't surprised to hear Josh say that. She figured it was another of his lines to suck her into his plan to get to Wes.

"I know what you're thinking," Josh stated softly. "But it's not true. There were a few other students there that would be easy to lure to the dark side, some kids you consider Emos and some jocks that drink too much on the weekends. But when I saw you, I knew I had to have you. But not just your soul, all of you. I kept an eye on you, followed you in the shadows. It wasn't until I saw you and Wes near the locker rooms and had a good look at his soul that I figured out what he was. I lost my mind at that point. Got greedy. I knew if I could take Wes out, it would give me stature among the ranks of demons. I didn't care what I had to do to destroy him. When I realized how much it was affecting you, I had to back down. I couldn't stomach the look on your face. I couldn't stand to see you hurt."

Katie's mouth went dry, a knot developed in her stomach. "Why?" The word barely came out of her mouth.

"The dark spot on your soul. The propensity you have for evil."

Katie swallowed thickly. "What does it mean?"

"It means you have the ability to do devastating and awful things."

"What if I don't want to?"

Josh laughed. "That has yet to be decided. You are always free to choose what you will, what side you want to be on."

"And you're here to make sure I choose your side."

"Of course. You would be a valuable asset for Hell."

Katie felt queasy. That didn't sound like a very promising position. She'd always tried to do what was right, treat people with respect, and listen to her mom. She couldn't stomach violence. Wars and killing made her sad, mistreatment of any living creature made her nauseous. Josh had to be wrong. He had to be mistaken. There was no way she could ever be evil.

Josh abruptly got to his feet and held his hand out for Katie. "Come. Let me show you something."

Katie hesitated and stared at the shadow of his limb. She should leave, head back to the hospital room and wait for them to release her. They had to let her go in the morning. She wasn't sick. After that, she would go home and pretend like none of this happened. She would cut off communications with Wes and pray that Josh stopped coming around. She just had to get through the rest of the school year, then she'd be off to college. Somewhere far away where no one could find her.

And yet, part of her was curious to know what Josh had to show her. Was that the dark spot on her soul? The part that had a proclivity toward evil? Fear squeezed Katie's chest. If she went with him, did that mean she was giving in to her dark side? Would that make her one of them? Katie didn't want to do that.

On the other hand, if she went with him, she would have more answers, she would see exactly what Josh was. Maybe it would give her an answer of how to fight him, how to defeat him. No. It wouldn't make her one of them. If she went with them, she would see what her future might hold, and she would fight against it.

With a deep breath, she reached up and took Josh's hand. He pulled her to her feet, then directed her toward the red light. The rotten egg scent of sulphur tickled her nostrils, growing more intense the closer they got. The room grew hotter. Katie tensed and tightened her grip on Josh's hand. She was pretty sure she knew what they were heading toward. She was in a dark place with a demon, so she doubted they were close to a city park. Her body pressed closer to Josh's. It occurred to her that he might not afford that much protection, especially since he was the one leading her toward danger, but he was better than nothing. Katie couldn't rely on herself; she was far out of her element. She could only hope Josh wasn't lying when he said he wanted to keep her safe.

The light grew brighter, bathing the pair in an eerie redness. Katie's hands were sweating. Her heart rate increased. Part of her brain screamed for her to turn around and run, to get as far away as possible, but the other part was curious. It kept her emotions stilled just enough to keep her feet moving forward and her curiosity piqued.

The smell of sulphur became overwhelming. Katie gagged. Sweat dripped down her forehead and back from the heat. Low moans and whimpers reached her ears, along with the sounds of cracking whips and growls. Katie tensed even more. Josh leaned close.

"You have nothing to worry about," he whispered in her ear. "I'm not going to let anything happen to you."

For some strange reason, Katie found the words comforting. While her fear didn't dissipate completely, she relaxed and loosened her grip on his hand. She remained close to his body, finding comfort in the proximity.

They were completely encased in heat and red light. The ground gave way before them into a pit. A pool of red liquid dominated the middle. It looked like lava, but it didn't. From what Katie had seen from films at school, lava was thick and slow moving, with an orangish tint to it. This was a deep red and fluid, almost like water. Maybe the films she'd watched were wrong. Either that or that wasn't lava. Steam rose from the lake, curling upward with jerky movements, as if it were alive. The cave extended far beyond Katie's vision and was filled with shapes that looked distinctly human, as well as winged creatures that walked on two legs and animals that looked like dogs. The red light messed with her vision, making it hard for her to tell exactly what she looked at. Shadows moved across the landscape, not really connected to bodies or things, but seemingly with a mind of their own. More moans rose from the depths below, sending a shudder through Katie's body. They sounded sad, in pain.

Katie wasn't sure what was going on, but from her vantage point, it looked like the human-shaped creatures were hauling the red liquid from the lake in buckets. The line started on the left and extended to the right, appearing from and disappearing into darkness. The burdens looked heavy, the place unbearably hot. If one of them stepped out of line or slowed, a winged creature pushed them back. Katie watched one collapse, and a winged creature lifted it up roughly by the hair. A moan escaped from the human's mouth. She pressed even closer to Josh.

"Is this Hell?"

He nodded. "A section of it. The depths and dimensions of eternal damnation vary greatly. There are various levels and punishments."

"What are they doing?"

"Meaningless work. Torture in Hell doesn't have to have a rhyme or reason, as long as it punishes the offender."

Katie turned to him, confused. She didn't know much about Hell, but she figured if a soul went there, the punishment it received would be equivalent to the sin. One more thing she was going to have to find the answer to.

Josh placed his hand around her shoulder, drawing her into his body. White eyes glowed from the dog-like creatures below. They growled and snapped at the human figures to keep them moving and in line. Hell Hounds. Renewed fear surged through her. Her arm throbbed. She wrapped her arms around Josh's waist, hoping the proximity to him would guarantee her safety. Even though Josh was the one who brought her there, and part of her hated him for that, he was also the only one who could get her out. She wasn't going to let him get away from her. If she were honest with herself, she would admit there was something comforting about standing with him overlooking the lake. The way Josh's body felt next to her was familiar. The thought made her breath catch in her throat. He tightened his grip around her shoulders.

"The scene before you isn't as horrific as you think it is."

She pulled slightly away and stared at him with eyebrows pushed together.

He laughed. "Okay, it's bad, but it's not without its purpose." He pointed to the line below them. "All of those humans you see are sinners. They did something bad in life to make them wind up here. They are paying the penance for their bad deeds."

"What did they do?"

Josh shrugged. "I'm not exactly sure. Probably nothing too major. Perhaps they didn't repent their sins. For each one, it will be something different. But for each one it was something minor. Trust me, the bigger the sin, the greater the torment. This is nothing compared to what some souls go through for eternity."

For some reason, her mind drifted to the Greek stories she read in English class about Sisyphus and having to roll the boulder up the hill for eternity and Tantalus with his burning thirst and inability to drink. Those punishments seemed almost as pointless as the souls beneath her gathering liquid for an unknown reason. While she didn't want to do any of them for eternity, they didn't seem that bad. Granted, the repetition and pointlessness would drive her crazy, but it wouldn't be as bad as having birds eat her insides while she watched or having her skin removed in sections until the end of time. She shuddered as she thought some people had to go through that...and worse. Her mind couldn't even fathom what worse was.

"My point is that whatever they have to endure, they deserved. They didn't lead good lives, Katie. They led awful, evil lives. They did things to hurt other people. They sinned. Us demons, we make sure that they pay for their crimes."

Katie scoffed. "From the sounds of it, you also help lead them down the road of bad deeds."

Josh stared at her for a moment. "We don't make them do anything they weren't contemplating doing in the first place. We just give them a little nudge in the direction they really wanted to go."

Katie rolled her eyes. Was that how they justified it? She knew humans weren't perfect. They killed and maimed and did awful things to each other. Those people totally deserved to rot in Hell. But how many souls down there could have possibly been redeemed? How many of them were just a little bad, but then a demon came along and made them really bad? What if they were caught in the wrong place at the wrong time? It seemed hardly fair they would have to pay for it for the rest of time.

And yet, a voice at the back of Katie's brain told her that everyone had a choice. It was up to them to give into a demon's temptation or to turn away. What did that say about her? She had every opportunity to tell Josh to get out and turn her back on him, and she was right next to him, her arms around his waist, in Hell. She always considered herself good, but how would this be perceived? Would it damn her soul for eternity?

Something buzzed by her ear as she contemplated her soul's fate. Instinctively, she swatted her hand through the air. Whatever it was grabbed onto her middle finger, and pinpoints of pain radiated through her flesh. She brought her hand around in front of her face. Latched onto her digit was a small demon, about the size of a wasp, with its teeth buried in her flesh. The creature was roughly human shaped with black, membranous wings. Its eyes glowed white, its black skin was pulled tight over its bones. Katie flicked her hand through the air trying to dislodge the beast. She only succeeded in getting it to bite harder. A squeak of pain escaped her lips.

"Here, let me see." Josh held out his hand for Katie.

She moved her hand toward his, and he gently grabbed her wrist. The demon looked up at him and pulled its fangs from her flesh.

"Yeah, you gotta watch for those Tormentors. They'll get you anyway they can." He held out his hand, and the demon crawled into his palm, hissing at Katie as he did.

Katie wrapped her hand in her other hand and pulled it to her chest. "Tormentor? What do they do?"

Josh brought the demon close to his face and nuzzled it. Katie was shocked at the sheer pleasure that danced across his features. The demon was hideous, especially with her blood dripping from its mouth, and Josh coddled it like a kitten. He turned back to Katie, a smile spread wide on his lips.

"They land on you, right about here." He brought his finger behind Katie's ear and traced it gently across her skin. Her flesh prickled. "And they whisper things in your ear."

"What kinds of things?" Subconsciously, she moved closer to his body, licking her lips.

Josh leaned into her, bringing his face closer to hers. "Whatever it takes to get you to sin."

Katie pulled away from Josh and stared at him wide eyed. Her face crunched in anger. "So that was your plan all along? Bring me down here, answer my questions, all the while waiting for the opportune moment to attach a Tormentor to my head?"

Katie found it hard to keep her emotions in check. How could she have been so foolish? She should have known Josh would do something so devious and underhanded. He was a demon, he couldn't care for her. How could she have been so stupid to believe that he did? She backed even further away from him, wrapping her arms around her chest. She wanted to get away from him, but not too far. She was still in Hell. She needed his protection. He was her only way out. She glanced nervously around, making sure none of the other demons had seen her and wanted to come after her.

Josh's face dropped. He glanced from the Tormentor back to her. "No, Katie. It wasn't like that. I swear. I brought you here to give you answers. I would never betray your trust like that." He glanced back at the tiny demon, who glanced from him to Katie.

The demon shook its head curtly, then hissed at her and flew from Josh's hand toward the lake below. Katie watched it leave, disgust coursing through her body. Josh's foot crunched on the gravel as he stepped closer to her, drawing her attention away from the winged beast. She glared at him as he took another step closer.

"Katie, please. I'm sorry."

She tightened her grip around her chest. "Just take me back. I'm done."

CHAPTER 13

KATIE STEPPED OUT OF THE PORTAL into the bathroom of her hospital room. Josh didn't think anyone would be in her room, but he wanted to be on the safe side. Katie didn't care. She just wanted to get away from him. Why didn't she expect him to be so sneaky? Why did she let her guard down and trust him? Was there a guy anywhere in the world that wasn't underhanded or a liar?

The part that bothered her the most was the fact that she couldn't get the look he gave her out of her mind. He held the Tormentor in his hand and looked truly surprised she had accused him of siccing the thing on her. And that thing was so vicious. If it wanted to attack her to whisper things in her ear, wouldn't it have been nicer? It bothered Katie to think Josh was telling the truth when he said he didn't plan anything. It made her head spin. Things weren't supposed to be like this. There were certain ways "good" was supposed to act and very specific traits that made someone "evil." None of those applied in this situation. What was Katie supposed to think? What was she supposed to do?

Josh stepped out of the portal behind her, but the light didn't disappear like it had before. Katie kept her back turned toward him, avoiding eye contact. If she looked into his eyes, saw the sorrow and desire to apologize—whether it was sincere or not—she would find herself letting him back in. She couldn't do that. Not right now. She needed time to sort things out in her mind. Josh placed a hand gently on her arm.

"I'll give you some time and space." His voice was soft, apologetic. "Text me when you're ready to talk."

Katie didn't respond. The light vanished. Josh was gone. She sat down on the toilet and placed her head in her hands. What was she going to do? A few days ago, she had no notions of good and evil, Heaven and Hell, except for the few memories she had from Sunday School. Now, she was faced with picking a side. And the thing that made her skin prickle and her chest tighten was that she was seriously considering joining the side of evil. It shouldn't be a consideration. It shouldn't even be in the realm of possibility, and yet she found Josh's words ringing true. She found his explanations viable. Wes had burned bridges with her. He didn't trust her, so he refused to let her in. And he was supposed to be the good one. He was supposed to keep her safe, but he had dragged her into the middle of his holy war.

Part of her knew it was unfair to accuse him of that. After all, he'd tried to keep her out of it by keeping her at a distance. But when Katie tried to make it easy on him by stepping out of his life, he dragged her back in. In a way, it was his actions that had doomed them both. Would things have turned out differently if Josh didn't know Wes was a Praesul? Josh said that he was there for Katie and a few others, so what would he have done differently to tempt her to his side? Surely she would have never gone to the warehouse. Maybe she would have never witnessed Josh try to kill Wes.

Katie lifted her head and ran her hands down her cheeks. She could drive herself crazy thinking about all the what-ifs. Things had already happened, so she had to deal with the facts. She couldn't change anything, and the first thing she needed to deal with was getting out of the hospital. After that, she needed to find someone to talk to. She stood and opened the door. Her room was still dark, and the clock on the stand next to the bed said it was 11:30. Katie could have sworn she'd been gone longer than that. It certainly felt longer. Her mind drifted back to the day in the gym and how time had slowed down. Maybe that had happened again. It would allow her to have been gone for a lot longer than the clock showed. No doubt that was what had happened.

She took a step into the room and stopped. Someone was sitting on her bed. It was impossible to tell who, but Katie's heart thumped a little harder when she thought it was the nurse. How mad was she that Katie wasn't in bed? How long had she been there? Then it occurred to Katie that she was coming out of the bathroom. No one could be upset with her for answering the call of nature. Removing the IV and changing into her clothes was a different matter though. Katie squared her shoulders and stepped farther into the room. She had nowhere to go. Might as well face whatever repercussions she had to face.

"Taking matters into your own hands?"

Katie instantly recognized the voice. Randy. Her worry and concern turned into anger. "You're not supposed to be in here." She walked to the chair where her clothes had been and took off her shoes.

"And you are, so I guess we're both breaking the rules."

Katie was thankful the room was dark and her back was to him. Her cheeks burned, her stomach tingled. How long had he been in the room? Did he know where she'd gone? That she had been with Josh? What would he say? Would he make her stay in the hospital longer to "keep her safe"? Maybe she should make a run for it now. She glanced at the door and gauged her chances of getting away. Randy was still injured, so outrunning him wasn't an issue, but he was right next to the nurse call button. More than likely she wouldn't get past them.

"Well, either way, I'm glad I caught you before you left. I wanted to apologize for earlier."

Thank goodness he thought she was leaving instead of just getting back. Outwardly, she huffed and turned around, her arms folded across her chest. "A lot of good that does me now."

With difficulty, Randy stood from the bed. "The life of a Praesul is lonely and full of sacrifice. Sometimes we have to put the needs of many ahead of an individual."

Sadness replaced the anger. Was that all she was to them? A means to an end? She pushed the hurt away and allowed anger to replace it. "The needs of many? You mean your needs."

"Katie, I have to protect my family. If the demons discover where they are, they will use them to destroy Wes and I. What we do protects the world. If you have to stay the night in the hospital to ensure Wes and I stay alive to fight demons, it's a small sacrifice for the greater good."

Katie's mouth fell open. Did Randy admit he had used her? She snapped it shut and set her jaw. "And where does it end?" There was an edge to her voice. The fact that she was remaining so calm scared her. The desire to shout constricted her throat, but it never came out. "What if my death would save millions? Would you lead me to the slaughter? And who are you to decide?"

"Katie, I know it's difficult for you to understand. There's still so much you don't know. I work for the greater good, to do what is best for the majority. I don't enjoy making the decisions, but I do what I have to do. What is ordained of me."

How could they be so callous when picking who to save? She knew both Wes and Randy loved their family but he just said he worked for the greater good. Katie was the one being tempted by a demon. Randy's family was safe. If anyone needed help, it was her. Did she mean so little to them they didn't care what happened? The coldness in her chest extended into her stomach. What had she ever done to them to make her not worth saving?

"Get out." Katie jerked her head toward the door.

"Katie, please, I—"

Katie grabbed his arm and pulled him toward the door. "I don't care. Out."

Randy almost lost his balance from the tug, but regained it and hobbled to the door. Katie didn't watch him leave; she had turned her back on him again. The soft click of the door as it shut was the only indicator he had left.

Most of the anger drained out of Katie and her knees shook. She sat on the bed to keep from falling over. It wasn't her intention to be that mean to Randy. She had no desire to hurt him, but she didn't really appreciate being the sacrifice in their war. No one should have to be. It distressed her that for them it was so easy to throw her life away. Why were they making her choices for her? Where was her Free Will? The only one who wasn't forcing her to do anything was Josh. The only thing he was doing was giving her answers. Maybe in the future he would expect her to do something, but Katie was confident he would ask her to do it, not force her to.

Katie took off her clothes and climbed back into the hospital gown. The thought had briefly crossed her mind that she should walk out, but she was more than confident Randy was outside her door. He would stop her. Besides, she was tired. The tranquilizer wasn't completely out of her system, and her adventure to Hell had worn her out. She was stuck, so she might as well take advantage and rest up. She pulled the blankets to her chin and rolled onto her side. She pushed the events from her mind. She was tired of thinking about them. They gave her a headache.

A few hours later, the nurse came in to check on her. Even being quiet, Katie sensed her presence and it jerked her awake. Thankfully, the nurse only stayed long enough to check her blood pressure and left. If she noticed the IV was no longer connected, she didn't say anything. Katie rolled over and fell back asleep.

The next time she opened her eyes, rays of muted sunlight tried to penetrate the closed curtain. Katie frowned. She didn't feel rested. Her hip hurt. She wanted to be in her own bed. The only bright spot on the day was that she'd be going home in a few hours. There was nothing wrong with her, so they couldn't force her to stay. She and Deb had plans, and she was going to fulfill them no matter what. Some time away was exactly what she needed.

She contemplated taking a shower, but then thought better of it. She didn't have any shampoo or soap or clean clothes, so it was pointless. She would wait until she got home. Still, she might as well get dressed and ready to go. No sense wasting time. After pulling on her clothes, she pressed the nurse call button.

"Yes?" the voice asked.

"When is my doctor supposed to be here?"

"He should be doing his rounds in the next half an hour."

"Good. Make sure I'm his first stop. Otherwise, I'm walking out." Katie wished there was a way to disconnect the conversation, but since there wasn't, she got up and went to the bathroom.

The doctor was in her room within fifteen minutes, along with her mom. Man, she looked awful. Her eyes were darkened by black circles, the lids were puffy from crying, her hair stuck out in various directions, and her clothes were wrinkled. Katie almost felt sorry for her. Almost. But her mom had brought it on herself by not listening to Katie in the first place. She had to pay the price. Katie sat on the edge of her bed, her hands folded neatly in her lap, and waited for the okay to get up and go. The doctor was the only one who had been on her side, she wanted to show a little bit of respect. He smiled at her.

"How are you feeling today?"

Katie shrugged. "Fine."

He flipped through a few pages of her chart before turning to Mom. "The tests came back clear. Katie has no signs of infection. She's free to go."

Her mom's forehead wrinkled with the effort. "How can that be? The things she was saying, she was acting crazy."

The doctor closed the folder. "I don't know what to tell you Mrs. Barrett. Perhaps it was a cry for help. All I know is that it wasn't an infection. We can't keep her here. I would suggest going home and getting some good rest. If Katie continues to act abnormally, I can recommend a psychiatrist for you to speak to."

Mom nodded. "Okay. That sounds good."

The doctor glanced back at Katie. "I'll see you in a few days to remove those stitches." He turned and headed out of the room.

Katie and her mom stared at each other for a moment. Katie fought back the urge to say, "I told you so." Sympathy crossed her mom's face. At least Katie thought it was sympathy. With fatigue lining her features, Katie couldn't be sure what her mom felt. She stepped across the room and sat down on the bed. Katie desperately wanted to get up and move. Being so close to her mom made her stomach turn. She turned her head away instead.

"It's all so weird. I thought for sure you had picked up rabies." Mom ran her hand through Katie's hair. "Especially after the stories you were telling me yesterday."

Katie rose from the bed and stepped across the room. Still, she didn't speak. What was the point? Her mom wouldn't believe anything she said anyway. Plus, Katie was sure she wouldn't be able to speak civilly. Since shouting at her mom would get her nowhere, she kept her mouth shut.

The nurse entered the room with paperwork and her mom signed. Katie didn't wait until the ink was dry. With long strides, she headed out of the room and into the hall. When she made it to the front door, she had to wait for her mom, since she wasn't sure where the car was. Inwardly, she wondered if Wes and Randy would be there for her release. When they didn't show up, she wasn't surprised. Why would they be there for anyone else? Everyone was supposed to cater to their needs, but Heaven forbid they think of others. She climbed into the car and stared out the window.

The ride home was done in silence. Mom pulled the car into the garage and turned it off. Katie opened the door and headed into the house. She made a beeline for her room and plugged her phone into the charger. It had died at the hospital. She sent a text to Deb.

We still on for today?

She headed for her dresser and grabbed some clean clothes. The phone dinged on the nightstand. Katie picked it up.

Are we? Heard you had to go to the hospital.

Yeah, out now. I'll tell you about it when you get here. Can you pick me up in an hour?

Your mom okay with that?

Not her choice.

Okay. See you in a bit.

Katie set the phone down and headed into the bathroom.

The hot water helped melt away some of Katie's stress. She let it run over the back of her head and shoulders. She tried to keep from thinking about the hospital, Wes, and Josh, instead focusing on what she and Deb were going to do. It worked, for the most part, until Katie heard the bathroom door open and close. She held back the groan of irritation.

"Katie, honey, can we talk?"

Her mom could be so annoying! Of course she waited until Katie was in the shower. She was cornered, had nowhere to go.

"I really need to finish getting ready."

"Where are you going?"

"Deb and I are going out," Katie snapped, unable to hold the anger back.

"Okay. When will you be home?"

Katie flung open the curtain and stared at her mom through slitted eyes. "Whenever I feel like it." She pulled the curtain back closed with force.

"Katie, baby, I'm sorry for what happened. I'm sorry I took you to the hospital. I was worried about you. I had to make sure you weren't sick."

Katie slammed off the shower and grabbed a towel. She glared at her mother before grabbing her clothes and heading for her room. Mom was right behind her, and Katie slammed the door in her face.

"You're entitled to be mad. I would be too if I were in your shoes. I'll give you some space, but I want to talk to you. I want you to tell me what you were trying to tell me about Randy earlier."

Katie rolled her eyes. Of course now she wanted to talk about it. Once she found out she was wrong. She couldn't believe Katie before. Well, maybe Katie didn't want to talk about it later. Maybe she was done trying to get people to listen to her. That was something she was going to have to decide later.

"I love you, Katie. Please don't forget that."

Katie's anger softened a little after Mom's words. Katie knew Mom loved her, but that didn't change the fact she wouldn't listen to her.

She finished getting dressed and sat down on the bed. Deb would be there in ten minutes, but she didn't want to wait for her downstairs. Mom would try to talk to her again. She thought about waiting outside, but what if Wes saw her out the window? She really didn't want to have to talk to him. No, it was best to stay in her room, where she was safe, until Deb showed up. She contemplated sending Josh a text, to see how he was doing, but didn't. Uncertainty lingered about whether or not the Tormentor was part of his plan. Until she sorted things out in her mind, it was best to leave him alone.

A horn honked, and Katie jumped from the bed. She grabbed her purse and headed downstairs. Her mom called after her as she ran out the front door, but Katie didn't acknowledge her. She jumped into Deb's car and faced her friend.

"Oh, my God. You're never going to believe what I've been through."

CHAPTER 14

REALIZATION HIT KATIE that she couldn't tell Deb exactly what had happened. That would mean telling her about the warehouse, about what Josh and Wes were. No doubt, Deb would never believe her. Her mom didn't believe her. Plus, even though Deb was her best friend, she was terrible at keeping secrets. It was one thing for Deb to think she was crazy, but for the whole school—possibly the whole town—to think that was too much. Deb's eyes widened and she smacked Katie on the arm.

"Well? Are you going to tell me or what?"

Katie playfully shoved her back. "My mom thought I had rabies."

Deb's face crunched in amusement and confusion. "What? Why would she think that?" She pointed at Katie's arm. "Because of the dog bites?"

Katie nodded. "Yeah. That and Wes and I got into this big fight and I guess I went a little crazy when I tried to explain it to her."

Worry crossed Deb's face. "Oh, no, Katie. Please tell me you aren't pining for him again."

Katie held up her hands defensively. "Absolutely not. I just had to drive his dad to the hospital to pick him up."

Deb knew most of the stories about how Wes had stood Katie up and broken her heart. They had been friends since the eighth grade. She always told Katie to forget about him and move on. She always said he was bad news. If Deb thought Wes was bad, what would she think about Josh if she knew the truth?

"You better not be falling for him again. I'll kick your ass. Seriously. I'm not listening to you whine about him anymore."

Katie pursed her lips and placed her hands in her lap. "I promise I'm not falling for Wes again. He's ancient history."

"Good. The rumor around school is you and Josh Evers are a thing. Is that true?"

Katie became sheepish and turned her gaze away. To the school and the vast majority of town, Josh was still a teenager. A good looking, athletic student. Katie was rarely ever the topic of gossip. Not that she minded—she was more than happy to stay out of the limelight and crosshairs of teenage drama. It embarrassed and flattered her at the same time to know that people were talking about her and Josh. After all, he was the most popular guy at school. It made her heart ache that he couldn't be normal. If her classmates only knew.

Deb smacked her arm again. "It is true! Why didn't you tell me? Why did I have to hear this from Brenda?"

Katie shrugged. "I'm still not sure what's going on between Josh and I. It's complicated."

"But he kissed you, right? Brenda said she saw him kiss you in the hall."

Heat warmed Katie's cheeks. "Yeah. He kissed me in the hall."

"Oh, my God!" Deb's voice screeched through the car, piercing Katie's ears. "You have to tell me all about it. I want every sordid detail."

"Deb, really, there's not much to tell. It was just a kiss."

Deb pounded her hands on the steering wheel. "You see what happens when you finally let go of childhood flames? The world comes knocking on your door!" She leaned her head back against her seat. "I am so freaking jealous of you right now! Josh Evers. Hottest guy in school." She sat up and pointed a finger at Katie. "Promise me you'll fill me in on anything that happens between you guys."

Katie nodded. "I will. Don't worry."

"You better."

An engine revved next to Deb's car, and Katie glanced over her friend's shoulder out the window. Wes's truck pulled into his driveway. Katie's chest tightened, her limbs tingled. The last person she wanted to see was him. He got out of the truck and stared at Deb's car.

"Deb, drive. Let's get out of here."

Deb wrinkled her nose, then glanced over her shoulder to see what Katie looked at. When her gaze fell on Wes, she put the car in gear and headed down the road. Katie looked out the back window. Wes watched them drive off.

"So, I was thinking, instead of going shopping today, some of the senior class is meeting at the reservoir. You know, just to hang out. A last fling before the weather gets cold. I thought that sounded fun. What do you think?"

Katie turned and stared at her friend. Normally, that wasn't the type of scene Katie liked to hang out at. It made her uncomfortable, out of place. But at that moment, she really didn't care where they went, as long as she didn't have to be around Wes, Randy, or her mom. Maybe it would be the perfect chance to not have to think about the events of the past few days, a chance to just be a teen.

"Sure. Why not. But I don't have a swim suit."

Deb smiled. "No worries. I brought you one of my bikinis. Your suits are so dowdy."

Katie feigned anger. "And how did you know I would agree to go to the reservoir?"

Deb glanced at her. "I didn't. To be honest, I planned on taking you no matter what. But if you really wanted to go shopping, we would do that first."

Katie chuckled. Once Deb had her mind set to do something, it took a lot to get her to change it.

Deb pushed Katie's leg. "C'mon. It will be fun. It's the perfect chance to get away."

"I didn't say it wouldn't be fun. I'm sure it will, but I can't exactly go in the water with this." She held up her arm with the bandage.

"It'll be fine. You can hang out on the beach. Get some sun."

Katie nodded. It would be fine. It was the perfect chance to relax. It was exactly what she needed. She was a little nervous about wearing Deb's bikini, though. Deb had a tendency to show off a little more skin than Katie was comfortable with. Not that Katie had anything to hide. She was in good shape, being on the volleyball team, and wasn't exactly lacking in the assets department. In fact, there had been many times during her games she wished she didn't have the curves she had; they seemed to get in the way. Still, just because she was endowed didn't mean she wanted to show it off. This one time she would let her inhibitions go, only because she needed to get her mind off demons.

"So, what did the doctor say?" Deb's tone took on a seriousness. "Do you have rabies?"

Katie stared at her through narrowed eyes.

"I'm not trying to be rude," Deb said quickly. "But you haven't been acting like yourself lately. I mean, two days ago you were like a walking zombie. If I was your mom and you came up to me acting hysterical after being out of it, I would probably think that same thing. No offense."

Katie shook her head. Deb was right. She hadn't been acting like herself lately. Her world had been turned upside down, she wasn't sure she knew who she was anymore. Maybe it was unfair of her to be so mad at her mom. After all, she was just reacting to how Katie was acting. It was completely plausible to believe she had picked up rabies and it altered her personality. Still, her mom should have listened to her, given her a chance to explain herself before dragging her to the hospital. And Katie's actions certainly were justified when it came to Wes.

"No," Katie answered. "I don't have rabies. And I'm sorry for the way I've been acting. Things have been kind of weird lately."

"Weird how?"

Katie took a breath. "It's hard to explain. And I don't have things straight in my head. Let me figure it out, then I'll talk to you about it."

Deb glanced at Katie out of the corner of her eye. "Okay. If that's what you want. But know I'm here for you no matter what."

Katie smiled. "I appreciate that."

"Now let's drop this bad mood and have some fun!" Deb plugged her iPod into the radio and cranked up the volume.

Both girls sang at the top of their lungs as they headed to the reservoir.

Deb found a parking spot at the top of the hill and shut off the car. Reaching into the back seat, she grabbed a duffel bag and smiled at Katie.

"You can change in the outhouse. Which one do you want to wear?" She dug through the bag. "The turquoise one with sequins or the stripy one." She held them up for Katie to see.

Katie chewed on her lower lip. She had seen Deb in them both, so she knew they were lower cut than she liked, but the one with stripes had more of a tank-top top, so she opted to go with that one. She had on a pair of jeans shorts, so she decided to put that over the tiny bottoms. Deb handed her the suit with a smile. She opened the car door and got out with the bag. Katie followed behind her.

After dressing and applying sunscreen, the pair headed down toward the water. Katie noticed the normal weekend boaters and families, but she didn't see any high school students. She followed Deb around the dam to the upper lake. Of course the teens would want to be away from the other people; no doubt they were engaging in activities society would frown upon. Katie was surprised at how many kids there were. If she had to guess, it was half of her graduating class—mainly the popular ones and those involved with sports. She glanced down at her cleavage and felt exposed. Was it too late to put a shirt on? Deb would probably tell her it was.

She followed her friend into the thick of the crowd. Deb knew practically everyone at school. She made it her business to know what was going on with everyone. With blonde hair and a quick smile, hardly anyone minded that Deb wanted to know everything. She was also Student Council President and had a great sense of humor. Sometimes, Katie wondered how they were best friends. They were complete opposites. Katie rarely craved being in the limelight, while Deb would steal it from her own mother. Deb ran into the group and instantly started hugging people. The boys were more than happy to comply. Katie hung back and waited for her friend to finish her hellos.

While Deb was talking to a group of basketball players, someone nudged Katie on the right arm. Katie turned. Zack Nelson. The quarterback.

"Katie, right?"

She had to physically keep her jaw from dropping open.

He offered her a red Solo cup. "You want a beer?"

Katie held up her hand. "No, thanks. I can't drink today. It will mess with the medication I'm taking."

The lie came easily. It had occurred to her in the car that alcohol would be at the beach, so she thought about plausible excuses. Katie really didn't feel like getting sloppy drunk in the middle of the day around a bunch of people she didn't know. She wasn't really a drinker. She'd had a few here and there, but she didn't want to get in trouble with her mom. Alcohol had caused a lot of problems in the family, so she tried to avoid it whenever possible. Of course, explaining that to the quarterback would make her look like a weirdo, so she opted for a simpler answer.

He shrugged. "Whatever. What happened to your arm anyway?"

"A dog attacked me."

He took a long drink out of his cup. "No kidding? I'm not surprised. Seen a ton of them around town lately."

Katie thought the comment was strange. An influx of dogs? Why would that happen? Didn't Randy say something the other day about dogs becoming a nuisance? She pushed the thought from her head. She didn't care. She was here to have fun, to get away from it all.

"So I assume you can't get into the water with that either, huh?"

Katie couldn't believe Zack was still talking to her. They had a class together, Sociology, but she didn't think he knew she existed.

"Nope. Unless I want to wrap a plastic bag around my arm."

Zack chuckled. "Too bad."

Katie smiled. A silence drifted over the pair. Zack took another drink of his beer.

"Well, I'll see you around. I assume you'll be here later in the day?"

Katie nodded. "Sure. Why not?"

He pointed his finger at her and clicked his tongue.

At that point, Deb ran up to her, a smile stretched from ear to ear. "Oh, you dog!"

Katie rolled her eyes. "I have no idea what that was all about."

A knowing look crossed Deb's face. "Oh, I do."

Katie stared at her. "Well, are you going to fill me in?"

"It's simple, really. Now that Josh has shown an interest in you, everyone else is curious to know why. They're feeling you out, checking out what you have to offer." Deb laughed. "You could probably let anyone of the guys 'feel you out' if you wanted."

Katie smacked her arm. "Very funny, Deb."

"It's true. Just now, Andrew Spence was asking about you. Wanted to know if you and Josh were serious."

Katie tried not to let her enthusiasm show. Andrew Spence was on the basketball team. Since both of their sports took place in the gym, she often saw him and his teammates during practice. He had extremely blond hair, almost white, and green eyes. He was already over six feet tall and muscular. Katie never really thought much about him, mainly because her eyes were only focused on Wes. But she heard the stories about him, about what a nice guy he was and how he would do almost anything for a friend. She wondered if those rumors were true. Given the chance, Katie would like to find out how kind he could be. Anything would be better than what Josh and Wes put her through.

"And what did you tell him?"

Katie hoped that Deb's answer would give her some clarity on how others viewed their relationship.

Deb stopped at an empty spot on the beach and pulled out a blanket. "I told him I didn't know and that he would have to ask you."

Katie took a seat. "Yeah, I'm sure that will happen."

Deb's response wasn't exactly helpful in giving her an idea of what was going on. But what did Katie really expect? Not many people saw her and Josh together. It all seemed so secretive. And Katie wasn't sure she wanted anything serious with him. He was evil, manipulative, yet so incredibly hot and nice when he wanted to be.

Deb sat next to her and nudged her with her body, pulling her back to reality. "Just go with the flow, Katie. How often do you have so many boys interested in you? Even if you and Josh are serious or get serious, this isn't hurting anything. Besides, if you and Josh don't become a thing, this keeps your options open."

Katie leaned back on her elbows and stared at the water. "What makes you think I'm looking for something serious?"

Deb shrugged and pulled out the bottle of sunscreen. "Serious, a fling, whatever. The point is, now that you're no longer aching for Wes, there is a world of guys out there. And you're a very attractive girl. Any of them would be lucky to have you." She rubbed some lotion on her shoulders. "And the ones you reject, you can send my way and I'll comfort them."

Katie laughed. "Maybe I'll keep them all for myself."

Deb snorted. "Like you would know what to do with one of them. You've spent your whole life up to now going after a boy who couldn't care less if you existed. You have no idea what real boys want."

Again, Deb was right. Katie didn't know what boys wanted or liked. She had an idea from movies, but she'd never experienced it in real life. So much time had been wasted trying to figure out Wes and doing things she thought would make him happy. Where did that get her? Nowhere. Heck, for all she knew, boys could have always been interested in her, but she was so focused on Wes, she never noticed. Well, all of that was going to change. No longer would she waste time on people who didn't give her the attention she deserved. She was going to live and experience what the world had to offer. What boys had to offer.

The sunscreen lid snapped shut and pulled Katie out of her thoughts. Deb smiled at her.

"Don't feel bad about it. I'm sure we can find plenty of boys who are willing to instruct you in the art of loooove."

As if on cue, footsteps sounded next to Katie. She turned and looked at Andrew and two of his friends—Paul and Stan. Andrew smiled at her.

"I heard you couldn't drink because of your medication, so I brought you a water." He held the bottle out for her.

"Thanks." She took it from him and he took a seat next to her. Katie's chest felt warm from the gesture. It was the nicest thing any boy had done for her recently.

Stan sat by Deb and Paul sat in front of them. A giddiness surged through Katie—or maybe it was nerves, she couldn't tell. She'd never been in this situation before. But she wasn't going to let her fears stop her. She was going to do her best not to embarrass herself.

"So what happened?" Andrew asked. "I heard you got attacked by a skunk or something."

"A skunk?" Deb scoffed. "Who told you that?"

"Brenda."

"Of course she told you that." Deb's tone was defensive. "It was a dog. Do you know of skunks that can jump high enough to grab a human by the arm?"

Andrew turned his gaze toward Katie. "Really? A dog did that?"
Katie nodded.

"What kind of pills did they give you?" Paul asked. "Anything good? You wanna share?"

Deb threw a small rock at him. "Knock it off, Paul. Like you need anything else."

Paul threw the rock back. "I was just asking."

Andrew leaned in close to Katie. "Just ignore him. He acts like a pill popping freak, but he's not. Just does it to be cool. Besides, I wouldn't let him take your meds."

The smell of pineapples and beer drifted into Katie's nose. His shoulder almost touched hers and she felt the heat rising from his skin. Her stomach tingled, and she found herself lost for words. She forced a smile and her gaze drifted around the beach. To cover the silence and make it less awkward, she opened the water and took a drink. Her sight fell on a group of teens several yards to her right and the water lodged in her throat. Coughing, she sat up and spit water all over her legs. What in the world was Josh doing there?

CHAPTER 15

DEB WIPED OFF THE BEADS OF MOISTURE that had inadvertently splashed her before rubbing Katie's back.

"Jeez, Andrew. Are you trying to poison her?"

He held his hands out to his sides and lifted his shoulders, as if asking why he would do something like that.

Katie gained control of her coughing and took another sip of water to alleviate the scratchiness in her throat. Her gaze was locked on Josh's. He smiled and raised his red plastic cup. The girl standing next to him followed his line of sight. When she saw Katie, her nose wrinkled in disgust and she placed a hand on her hip. Josh took a drink and then made his way toward her. Anticipation coursed through Katie. On one hand, it made her giddy to see Josh, especially since he wore long swim trunks with no shirt. Every one of his well-defined, well-tanned muscles glittered in the sun. On the other hand, it was hard to straighten things out in her mind if she didn't have a chance to be away from him.

Andrew cleared his throat and moved slightly away from Katie. He must have noticed Josh's approach and didn't want to get in trouble for hitting on her. Not that he was really doing much. Bringing someone water and telling them they were protected from rowdy friends would hardly be considered more than friendly, but Katie was aware of the intention behind it. More than likely, Josh was too, but what was he going to do about it? Why did he even care? It wasn't like they could have a real relationship.

Josh stopped in front of them and his smile grew wider. "Hey, guys. What's going on?"

Paul and Stan mumbled something under their breaths, Andrew glanced at him briefly, then played with a pebble near him.

"Nothin,'" Andrew said softly. "Just hangin' out."

Josh nodded toward Deb. "You just hangin' out too?"

Deb smiled and leaned back on her elbows. "You know it."

"You all look like you could use some more beer." He held his hand out. "C'mon, Katie. Let's get your friends some drinks."

Katie didn't want to take his hand. She wanted to tell him to go back to Hell and let her live her life. She wanted to scream at him to stop acting human and be what he really was. Or did she? She knew that was what she was supposed to do, but she didn't. She liked how all the eyes on the beach drifted toward her. She liked the evil stares from the other girls who were jealous Josh Evers wanted her and not them. She liked the attention. She reached out her hand and let Josh pull her to her feet.

"You all want one?" She pointed at each in turn and waited for their affirmative, then she and Josh headed down the beach toward the keg. He placed his hand around her waist.

"May I say you look absolutely stunning." His eyes drifted up and down her body. "You should show off your curves more often. Show these boys what they're missing."

Redness crept into Katie's cheeks and she tucked a piece of hair behind her ear. The embarrassment quickly turned to irritation as Josh pulled her into his body.

"What are you doing here?" She tried to keep her voice low so no one heard. "I thought you said you would wait for me to text you."

They reached the keg and Josh grabbed the tap. After pumping it a few times, he filled his glass. He nodded toward a sleeve of other cups and Katie grabbed four. Joshed started filling them.

"C'mon, Katie! You really think I'm going to miss this? The sin, the debauchery. With a little luck, I'll get me some souls." He handed her a full cup and took an empty one. "I am surprised to see you here. I wouldn't consider this your normal scene."

Katie took the second full cup and handed him another empty one. "And what exactly is 'my scene'?"

He shrugged one shoulder. "I don't know. Something safe, something low key." He handed her the third full cup.

"I'm branching out. Trying something new. I can't sit around by myself forever."

Josh finished filling the last cup and smiled. "No, you can't. And you shouldn't. Life is too short not to try new things."

She grimaced. "I'm not sure I'm overjoyed to see you. No offense, but I was hoping to get away from you for a while. Clear my head. Relax."

Josh folded his arms on the tap and leaned forward. "I can leave you alone. If that's what you really want. This place is big enough for the both of us." He pointed toward Andrew. "I know it would make him incredibly happy if I left."

Katie glanced at Andrew. He smiled. She forced one back. It would give her a chance at a real relationship if Josh was gone. Her and Andrew could spend some time to get to know each other and talk...about what? She didn't know the first thing about what regular boys wanted to talk about. She'd only talked to Wes, and that conversation focused solely on her. Surely someone else would find that topic boring. Besides, didn't the boys only find her attractive because they thought Josh had her? Would they feel the same if they thought she and Josh had broken up? She swallowed thickly, an uneasiness developed in her stomach. She wanted to go home.

"Tell you what." Josh placed a comforting hand on her arm. "I'll help you carry these drinks over, and if you want me to leave, rub your eyebrow like this." He ran his middle finger over his right brow. "Deal?"

She nodded.

"Cool. Now, are you sure you don't want one of these? Might help loosen you up."

Katie contemplated it for a moment. Beer would help her relax, put her at ease, but was that really a good idea with a demon running around? Not only that, but it was 11:00 in the morning. It was too early and it was best to keep her senses sharp.

"I'll be fine."

"Suit yourself." He grabbed three cups and the pair walked back to the group.

Katie handed one cup to Deb and the other to Andrew before taking a seat. It didn't escape her notice that Andrew had moved to the other side of the blanket closer to Deb. That was both a relief and a disappointment. Relief because she had no idea how to act around a real boy and a disappointment because Andrew was her chance at a real relationship. Well, maybe he was. Who really knew for sure? Still, she wanted the chance to find out.

Josh handed his cups to Stan and Paul, keeping one for himself, and sat next to Katie, close enough for his thigh and shoulder to touch hers. She couldn't have moved away if she wanted to, unless she wanted to sit on Deb's lap. He took a drink of his beer.

Really? That was how he was going to approach the situation? He was going to pretend the day before didn't happen? He was going to totally forget about the incident with the Tormentor and ignore that Katie was still upset with him? Of course he was. Maybe Katie's feelings didn't matter to him. Perhaps this was his way of torturing her. But it didn't feel like torture. It felt nice, right. What if Katie was overreacting? What if Josh was acting like there was nothing to be upset about because there was nothing to be upset about.

The memory of his face and how he looked when she accused him of being sneaky and underhanded came to her mind. Why would he need to sic a Tormentor on her? He already had her in Hell; if he'd wanted to prevent her from leaving, he could have. She was helpless in his realm, and yet he'd taken her back to the hospital when she wanted to go. Was it possible she'd misread the entire situation? She had been tired, drugged, fuming from the betrayal Wes, Randy, and her mom had put her through. Maybe she was looking for others to do the same thing when in reality, they had no intentions of hurting her. Josh was so unlike anything she had ever experienced, yet she was treating him like Wes. That was unfair. He was a demon, yes, but he'd had many opportunities to kill her and never taken them. Maybe it was time to stop being so defensive and let him give her some answers. She was going to need them if she wanted to avoid becoming like him.

"So what's the plan for today?" Josh licked his lips.

"The boys and I were just talking about going water skiing." Deb nodded toward Stan. "Apparently Stan's cousin has a boat and will take us out."

Katie frowned. "I can't go on the boat. I can't get my arm wet."

Deb looked her up and down, disappointment on her face. "You don't have to ski. You can just sit on the boat."

Katie pushed her eyebrows together. "I'm not sure that's a good idea. I could still get splashed."

Deb's shoulders slumped.

"You guys can go," Josh interjected. "I can hang out with Katie." He nudged her with his shoulder.

"Or I can stay with her," Andrew volunteered. "If you want to ski, Josh."

Deb brightened up. "We won't be gone for very long." She winked at Katie. "And it looks like you will have plenty of company."

Katie pursed her lips and lowered her voice. "I thought you and I were going to hang out today."

Deb stood. "And we will. Just as soon as I get back from skiing." She tipped her cup to her lips and chugged the beer. Streams ran down her chin and glistened on her chest. "Oops!" She wiped at them with her hands, licking the liquid off her fingertips.

The boys stared at her, their mouths hanging slightly open. Katie held back a laugh. Leave it to Deb to figure out how to become the center of attention and turn all the boys' heads. Not that Katie was surprised. That was part of the reason she and Deb got along so well. Katie was the shy, introverted girl, and Deb was the outgoing loud-spoken one. They complemented each other. Katie liked that Deb was everything she wasn't. It allowed her to experience things through her friend without taking too much of a risk. Katie straightened up. Plus, it gave her an opportunity to learn something. Deb had had several boyfriends since junior high. She knew how to act around boys, what they liked. Katie could pick up a few pointers and use them later.

Deb tossed the empty cup onto the blanket. "You guys ready?"

Stan jumped to his feet. "I am." He finished his beer and threw his cup next to Deb's.

Andrew glanced over at Katie and Josh, twirling the cup in his hand. "What do you want to do, Josh?"

Josh placed his arm around Katie. "I think I'm going to hang out here for a while. You go and have fun. If I want to ski later, I'll let you know."

Andrew nodded and placed his cup in the sand. He didn't bother finishing it. The three of them interlinked arms and headed toward the docks before stopping and turning toward Paul.

"You coming with us?" Deb asked.

He shook his head. "Nah. I'm gonna hang out on the beach and see what's going on here."

Deb shrugged, and the three of them continued on their way.

Paul turned toward Katie and Josh. "I'm off to see what other kinds of recreation I can find." He smiled and got to his feet.

Confusion rushed through Katie. "What is he talking about?"

"Pills." Josh released her shoulders and finished his beer. "You wanna see me work?"

Katie stared at him. "What?"

Josh finished his beer and burped. "Well, you never rubbed your eyebrow, so I figured you wanted to hang out with me longer. I figured I could show you how I harvest a soul."

Shock hit Katie. Was that something she wanted to see? Was it part of the answers she was looking for? She had inwardly decided hanging out with Josh would be all right, but now she second-guessed the decision. If she really wanted to, she could have gone out on the boat. She could have wrapped her arm in a plastic bag to keep it protected. It would have looked ridiculous and embarrassed her slightly, but then she would still be able to hang out with Deb. It annoyed her a little that Deb so easily ditched her to hang out with the boys. Katie was really hoping for some girl time so they could talk. Maybe they should have gone shopping. They would have been alone then. Not a lot she could do to change it now, and she kicked herself mentally for that. What was it about Josh that made her lose the ability to think rationally? Was it some kind of demon power he had over her? Was it the blackness in her soul that drew her to him?

She sighed. If she were honest with herself, she would admit she was curious to know exactly what Josh did. Again, she reminded herself that maybe if she saw firsthand what he was capable of, it would give her information of how to fight against him. Besides, what else was she going to do? Her friend had left her on the beach.

Josh nudged her again. "C'mon. You know you wanna. You know you can't resist my charms." He flashed her his most adorable smile.

It bothered her to no end that he was right. She couldn't resist him. No matter how hard she tried, no matter what he did or put her through, she found part of her didn't want to.

"Fine." Katie tried to sound exasperated. "What are you going to do?"

Josh stood. "First, I'm going to refill my drink, then I'm going to give Paul what he wants." He helped Katie to her feet and held her hand as they walked back to the keg.

"How many of those are you going to drink?"

He shrugged. "A few. It doesn't matter, though. I could down the whole keg and it wouldn't have an effect on me. Demons can't get drunk."

Katie nodded her head, then let her gaze drift around the beach. Deb waved to her from the docks, and Katie grudgingly returned the gesture. Josh filled his drink and scanned the area. He pointed to a group off to the left.

"Paul's over there. Shall we?" He grabbed Katie's hand again and led her to the group.

It could have been Katie's imagination, but she thought a look of desperation crossed Paul's face. He was laughing with a group of teens, but it seemed strained, forced almost. Her mind drifted back to the conversation about pills and what kind she was on. At first, she thought he was joking about wanting her pain pills. Not that she had any on her. She had left those at home. She hadn't needed them. The pain wasn't that bad. She knew kids her age took them to get high, but not anyone she knew. She figured it was mainly the Emos and Hoods that did that kind of stuff. Her belief was that maybe Paul was just saying that to look cool in front of everyone. That was what Andrew said he was doing. They were friends, so Andrew would know. Now, though, she wasn't so sure. Again, it could have been her imagination, but he seemed twitchy, stiff. His arms were straight at his side, his left hand clutching the pocket on his swim trunks. It was possible Andrew said what he said so Katie would relax and not be afraid. Or maybe Andrew really didn't know Paul. What she witnessed was not the actions of a guy who wanted to look cool; it was the desperation of an addict. She had seen the symptoms multiple times on documentaries they were forced to watch in health class and the many crime shows she watched with her mom.

When a moment presented itself, he grabbed one of the guys–Katie thought his name was Derrick, but she wasn't sure–and spoke to him quietly. Derrick pulled away, shaking his head, his hands out to his sides, and redness crept into Paul's features.

"Come on, man. Help me out."

Derrick turned his back and walked away.

"Here's our chance." Josh sounded almost giddy.

Paul's eyes scanned the beach, his forehead creased with concern. He chewed on his thumbnail.

"Hey, Paul!" Josh called. "I've got what you want."

Paul's eyes widened and lit up. Josh jerked his head to the left, indicating Paul should follow, and he eagerly did. The three of them headed for the bathrooms that serviced the area. They were nothing more than holes dug in the ground with walls constructed around them, but they did what they needed to do. On a hot day, the smell would be less than desirable, which meant a lot of people wouldn't want to hang out by them. It would give Josh and Paul the privacy they needed to conduct their business. Katie wasn't sure she wanted to be a part of it anymore, especially when the stench of human waste hit her nostrils. It was nice to be in the shade of the building, though. Katie hadn't realized how hot the day was getting.

Paul approached, looking pale and a little sweaty. "What is it you think I need?" He tried to keep his voice calm, but Katie was sure she heard the desperation in his tone.

Josh reached into his pocket and pulled something out. He held his hand open to Paul, and Paul's eyes lit up. To Katie, they just looked like two small white pills. Nothing worth getting excited over. Josh folded his hands back over the pills.

"You want them?"

Paul's eyes looked like they were going to bug out of his head, and he nodded enthusiastically. "I do. How much?"

"I'm not looking for money."

Paul raised an eyebrow. He glanced suspiciously at Josh and Katie. "I'm not doing anything kinky, so don't even go there."

Josh laughed. "That's good to know. No, that's not what I had in mind."

Paul licked his lips, his eyes kept darting to Josh's hand and back to his face. "What do you want then?"

"Your soul."

Confusion covered Paul's face. "My soul?"

Josh nodded.

Katie's gaze drifted from Josh to Paul and back, trying to take in the whole situation. What was Paul thinking? Would he go for such a deal? Did he think the whole thing sounded ridiculous? If Katie had heard the conversation days before, she would have thought Josh was insane. She probably would have made it, thinking she had nothing to lose. Was that what was going through Paul's mind?

A nervous, shallow chuckle escaped Paul's lips. "Sure, man, whatever. Take my soul." He held out his hand. "Just give me the pills."

Josh released Katie's hand and stepped forward. He placed his hand on Paul's chest. Paul stared down and tried to back up, but he couldn't move. His eyes widened in horror and his mouth opened to scream, but no sound came out. A golden light glowed from Paul's chest, outlining his ribs in shadow. Katie's stomach tingled. She wanted to rush forward and grab Josh's hand, pull it away from Paul, but she was also frozen in place. The light grew, entwining itself around Josh's hand. She glanced at him. A smile covered his lips, a smile she had never seen before. It was evil and self-satisfied. Katie sucked in a sharp breath. The body of Josh turned into a transparent shell, and inside of it was something with dark and mottled flesh, like it had been badly burned, and pulled tight over the bones. Like the Hell Hounds she had seen in the warehouse, the creature didn't seem to have any muscles. Its eyes were white, glowing. A red tongue ran over pointed teeth. She blinked, trying to clear the image from her head, and when her eyes opened, Josh stood before her, the gold glow collapsing in on itself until it was the size of a marble. He quickly popped it into his mouth and swallowed.

Katie turned to Paul. He was still frozen in the same spot, his eyes cast down like Josh's hand was still on his chest.

"Here ya go," Josh said.

Paul blinked and looked at the open hand in front of him. He snatched the pills from Josh's hand and downed them with the beer he carried. He pointed at Josh.

"Thanks a lot." He turned and headed back toward the party.

Katie stared after him, her mouth gaping. Josh grabbed her hand and led her away from the outhouses.

"He won't remember any of it," Josh whispered in her ear.

Katie couldn't find her words. Did she really just see what she thought she saw? What exactly had she just seen? She brought her hand to her head to stop it from spinning. Part of her told her she needed to get away from Josh, to run as far as she could, but where would she go? Deb brought her here, and she didn't have the keys to the car. Surely someone could give her a ride home. Then again, she wasn't sure she wanted to go. If anyone could answer the questions she had about what had just happened, it was the guy holding her hand, the guy who just performed an unholy act. She turned to look at him. He smiled. Movement caught her eye and she glanced over his shoulder. She opened her mouth to warn Josh, but it was too late. With the element of surprise and a log, Wes knocked Josh to the ground.

CHAPTER 16

JOSH WAS JERKED FROM KATIE'S GRASP. A scream built up in her throat, but it never had the chance to leave. With inhumanely fast speed, Josh was on his feet, spinning to meet his attacker. His eyes glowed white. His jaw was clenched, his hands balled into fists at his sides. A growl emitted from his lips. When his vision fell on Wes, all of that drained away and a laugh escaped his lips. Katie had a hard time understanding what was so funny. Her heart pounded in her chest, her palms were sweaty. The anticipation of what was going to happen next hung thick in the air.

"Oh, Wes. It's just you. I thought I was facing a real threat."

Wes raised the log and pointed it at Josh. Where had he gotten a log? Katie didn't remember seeing any lying around.

"I'm done warning you, Josh. Stay away from her." He said the last part slowly, emphasizing each word so Josh would know he was serious.

A crowd formed around them. The buzz of whispered questions reached Katie's ears. They wanted to know what was going on. Who was the guy with the log? Why had he attacked Josh? Was it because of her? Fingers pointed at her, gazes drifted in her direction.

Josh held his hands out to his sides. "What are you gonna do?"

Katie saw the indecision on Wes's face. He wanted to attack, to take Josh down and beat him into Hell, but could he do it in front of all these people without them interfering? Plus, he wasn't at one hundred percent. He still had his injuries from his and Josh's first meeting. That hadn't gone too well for him. The only reason he had gotten out of it alive was because of Katie. Was she going to help him again? His eyes briefly took her in, but she averted her gaze to the sand. Why was he putting her in this situation? How could he expect her to do anything for him after he refused to help her in the hospital? Wes held out his hand.

"Katie, come with me."

Katie's head shot up. Her eyes widened, and a grimace covered her face. Was he serious?

Josh stepped in front of her. "I'm pretty sure she's going to stay right here with me."

"Yeah, loser!" Someone called from the crowd. "She wants to stay with the cool people."

Wes's eyes drooped in sadness. "Katie, please. I need you to come with me."

Josh reached behind him and grabbed Katie's hand. She took it and pushed herself closer to Josh's body. The crowd around them drew in, moving closer to Josh to emphasize they had his back.

Wes was not in a good situation. Katie glanced around. He was easily outnumbered twenty to one. Surely he knew he couldn't win. He would turn around at any moment and leave. He had to. Katie was mad at him and didn't want to talk to him again, but she also didn't want to see him get hurt. She stared at him, her eyes pleading with him to leave.

Josh laughed again. "I'm fairly certain Katie has made her point. If anyone needs to leave, it's you."

"No one wants you here, geek!" A girl's shrill voice echoed across the beach. "Go home to your video games."

Wes never took his eyes off Katie. His hand shook slightly, then fell to his side. The log thumped into the sand. Relief washed over Katie. Wes was going to leave. He would be safe. Rage burned across Wes's eyes, and he charged forward. Josh dropped Katie's hand and lunged forward to meet him on the sand. His fist connected with Josh's face, and then the two of them fell to the ground in a flail of arms and legs as they tried to punch and kick each other. Shouts erupted from the crowd, encouraging the two to kill each other. If they only knew that would happen if everyone wasn't around.

Nausea settled in Katie's stomach. She wanted to scream at Josh and Wes to stop fighting. She wanted to tell the teens around her to quit encouraging them. She wanted to go home and crawl into her bed, pretend the day didn't happen. But she didn't do any of that. She couldn't. Frozen in place, she stared at the two fighting like she was caught in a trance. They continued to roll around on the ground, each trying to get the upper hand on the other. It surprised her how much fight Wes had in him. Where did he get the strength after being in the hospital and having so many stitches? He shouldn't have been able to put up that good of a fight. Perhaps it was determination. Maybe he wanted Katie so badly to go with him he could transcend pain and discomfort to accomplish his mission. Whatever it was, it was too late. He'd had ample opportunities to express his feelings to Katie. It shouldn't have taken such extreme measures to get his attention.

The crowd parted opposite of where Katie stood and three guys rushed toward Wes and Josh. Katie faintly recognized one of them as Zack. The other two must have been other members of the football team. Without blinking, they reached into the tangle of limbs that was Josh and Wes and pulled them apart. It took two of them to pull Josh away, but Zack was enough to handle Wes. Blood was smeared across Wes's face, and small pools formed on his shirt. Josh's face was red, his lip swollen. They glared at each other, each looking like they wanted the other to burst into flames.

"Enough!" Zack yelled.

Josh immediately went limp in the two guys' arms, and they let him go. He wiped at his mouth, never taking his eyes off Wes, who jerked himself out of Zack's grasp.

"What's going on here?" Zack asked. His tone softened slightly, but there was a hardness to it. "Is this about her?" He pointed at Katie.

All eyes turned toward her. She wrapped her arms around her chest and hunched her shoulders forward. If she could have folded in on herself and disappeared, she would have.

Zack slapped his hand against his leg. "Look, I'm not trying to get in anyone's business, but we all came out here to have a nice, relaxing day. You two want to fight over her, assuming she's worth it, by all means, but do it somewhere else. Don't ruin everyone else's good time." He folded his arms across his chest and stared at Wes and Josh, expecting an answer.

Katie turned and ran to the bathrooms. She didn't want to be back in the smell, but she had to get away from the looks of contempt, of blame. Being the center of attention was nice, but not like that. She wanted to be envied, not hated. Slamming the door behind her, she held it shut with her hands as she caught her breath. This wasn't exactly how she planned on spending the day. It was supposed to be her one chance to get away, to relax, to not think about Wes or Josh or Heaven or Hell. She and Deb should have gone shopping.

She went to lock the door, to make sure no one barged in on her, only to find the lock was broken. Of course it was. Nothing else had gone her way that day, why would the lock work? She sighed and took a seat on the "toilet." Really it was nothing more than a seat over a hole in the ground. She placed her head in her hands. With any luck, no one would come after her. Hopefully they were so disgusted with her they would shun and outcast her. But what if they didn't? What if Wes or Josh came in? What would she do? Panic settled in her chest and she raised her head, surveying the room for something to prop against the door until she could figure out how to get home. It wasn't her first choice to hang out in the bathroom, but where else was she going to go? She had to wait somewhere for Deb to come back. There was nothing she could use unless she could figure out a way to wedge a roll of toilet paper under the door.

She stood and reached for a roll. It was worth a shot. Before she could pick up the paper, a portal appeared before her and an arm pulled her into the light.

Katie blinked and found herself standing on a grassy hill surrounded by wildflowers. Tall, snow-covered mountains towered above her on all sides. A breeze blew, bringing with it a slight chill, causing goosebumps to form on her skin, but it wasn't unpleasant. The scent of lavender filled her nostrils. She inhaled a deep breath. The smell was more than welcome after being in the outhouse at the reservoir. She turned to her right, to figure out who had brought her here. It could have been either Josh or Wes, although she was fairly certain exactly who it was. She folded her arms across her chest as Wes came into view. His brow was wrinkled in anger, and he paced in front of her, his eyes glued to the ground, occasionally glancing up at her. He wanted to say something, that was obvious, but he was trying to figure out the best way to say it without sounding like a complete jerk. Katie didn't think that was possible.

"He took you to Hell." The words were quiet but laced with venom. His jaw muscles tightened after he said them, and the vein on his neck bulged.

"So?"

Wes stopped pacing and faced her. Rage burned through his eyes. "So? SO? Do you know how much danger you were in down there? Do you have any idea what could have happened to you?" He lost control of his temper and screamed the words at her.

If Katie could have turned and walked away from him, she would have. She would have flipped him the bird over her shoulder and headed into her house, intent on never speaking to him again. As it was, she had nowhere to go. Her only option was to suffer his verbal abuse until he decided to take her home. She dug her nails into her upper arms to keep from lashing out at Wes. The temptation to punch him in the face burned through her. Who did he think he was, talking to her like that?

"Josh was with me. He said he would keep me safe."

Wes placed both hands on the side of his head and tugged at his hair. "YOU CAN'T BELIEVE ANYTHING A DEMON TELLS YOU! They lie about everything."

"I'm here, aren't I? He must have not been lying if I made it out of Hell."

"He's trying to draw you in!"

Katie huffed and forced a chuckle. "Maybe if you weren't so worried about keeping Josh out, you could draw me in too."

Wes stopped pacing and looked toward the sky. The anger drained from his features, and his breath became ragged. His knees gave out and he collapsed onto the ground. For a second, Katie thought his injuries had gotten the better of him, that he had passed out from the pain. How was she supposed to call an ambulance? She didn't even know where she was. Concern coursed through her body and she was about to run to him, but he pounded his fist into the ground and placed his forehead in the grass. Katie took a step back and gave him his space. If he was upset, he deserved to be. He turned and looked at her, his face red, tears threatening to fall from his eyes.

"You don't think I hate myself for that?" His voice was low, filled with emotion. "My entire life has been spent trying to protect you, keep you away from the horrors I face on a daily basis, and all I succeeded in doing was putting you right in the middle of it."

Katie glared down at him. There were so many things she could say, both to validate his point and tell him it wasn't completely his fault. Secretly, it made her happy to see how upset he was, to see him beat himself up, especially after what he did to her in the hospital.

"How did you know Josh took me to Hell?"

Wes wiped at his eyes and turned so he sat in the grass. His gaze was focused on something to his right. "My dad figured it out after talking to you in the hospital room. At first, when he saw you coming out of the bathroom, he thought you were just getting ready to leave. He thought it was odd that you took your shoes off when you saw him, but he figured it was because you knew you were caught and wouldn't be able to get out. It took him a while to realize you were just getting back from somewhere. After you were released, we went into the bathroom and reversed the portal. We went to where Josh took you."

"So then if you can do that, can't Josh do the same thing to find us?" Katie felt hopeful that Josh would show up and rescue her. If anything, he could take her home and let the nightmare of a day end.

Wes shook his head. "He can't follow us here. We're on holy ground."

Katie's shoulders slumped. Of course. Leave it to Wes to take them somewhere safe where no one could find her. "What's the big deal that he took me to Hell? At least he was willing to give me answers, show me what was going on. You haven't done that."

Wes's head jerked upward and anger flashed across his face again. "You're lucky you came out of Hell. Once there, all the rules go out the window. The demons could have enslaved you, taken your soul without your consent. You might have never come home, and I wouldn't be able to save you."

"Like you're saving me now? Have you ever thought that maybe you're wrong about Josh? That he's not as bad as you think he is?"

Wes stood from the ground and approached her. He grabbed both her arms and looked her directly in the eye. Katie wanted to back away, to tell him not to touch her, but his grip was too tight, his look intent.

"He's even worse than you can imagine. That's how he got you. He made you believe he is something he isn't. He made you believe he has human feelings and can be saved. He can't. He doesn't want to be. He likes what he does. He enjoys causing suffering. Trust me, I've been dealing with them my entire life. I know about them, more than you do."

Katie raised her hands and forcefully removed Wes's from her arms. She shoved him backward. "Don't talk to me like that! How dare you chastise and belittle me. Just because you've known about demons for your entire life, that doesn't mean I have. You've had every opportunity, every chance to tell me what you knew, to arm me with information, and you didn't. Now that the world of Heaven and Hell, angels and demons, has crashed in around me, you can't get mad at me for not approaching it the way you would. You can't expect me to know what to do. I'm going into this blind. And that's because of you. I have to figure things out on my own because you've refused to be there for me since the beginning." Katie pointed at herself. "I'm going to deal with this in my own way." She jabbed her finger into Wes's chest. "If you had wanted to protect me, you should have done it way before now."

Surprisingly, Wes smacked her hand away. Katie's eyes grew wide. The anger crunched Wes's face.

"So I've made mistakes. Who hasn't? I'm human. I can't go back to the past and change things. The only thing I can do is fix things now. In the present. But you're not making it easy. Are you trying to prove a point? Are you trying to rebel? What's the point of taking Josh's side and listening to what he has to say? Is this your way of punishing everyone? Because I can tell you now, the only person you're going to hurt is yourself."

Katie had never seen Wes so angry before. All the self-loathing and sorrow drained from him completely. There was nothing she could say in her defense.

"I've tried to save you, Katie. Maybe I went about it in the wrong way, maybe I should have told you what was going on, but I didn't. I'm trying to fix that now."

"Trying to fix that now? How are you trying to fix it? At your house after I picked you up from the hospital, you told me you couldn't trust me with information about your mom and sister because I might tell a demon about them. How can you love me if you can't trust me? And why would you save me if I'm such an awful person?" Her voice cracked and she sucked in a ragged breath.

He waved his hand through the air, as if to push away the words Katie had just spoken.. "If you don't want my help, I'm not going to force it on you. Ultimately, you're the only one who can save yourself. I'm not going to make you do anything you don't want to do."

Katie's limbs tingled with irritation. Her throat felt tight, her hands balled into fists at her sides. She fought back every urge to punch him right in the face. "Typical, Wes. As soon as things get hard, you leave. I know you can't change the past, but you're not doing much to change the present either. Don't yell at me to stay away from Josh because YOU don't like him. Show me what you know. Let me experience what you go through. Maybe then I'd understand. Don't just abandon me." Katie huffed. "Oh, wait. That's what you're good at. Why would you change now?" Her body shook and she folded her arms across her chest to keep it under control. "Maybe your family really didn't go into hiding to be safe. Maybe they went there to get away from you."

Katie felt bad about saying those last words. They might have pushed things too far, and the look that crossed Wes's face emphasized that. It was a combination of sadness and pure hate. But the words were already out there. She couldn't take them back. Besides, part of her wanted Wes to feel just as bad as she did. She wanted him to know how much hurt, sorrow, and loathing flowed through her at the moment. She knew those words would cut deep.

Without saying a word, Wes opened a portal. Katie didn't care where it went. All she wanted was to get away from him. She turned her back on him and stepped through the light. When she blinked, she found herself in her bedroom. Glancing over her shoulder, she expected to see Wes step in behind her. Thankfully, he didn't. The portal vanished. With a deep breath, she collapsed onto her bed. Anger coursed through her veins, along with regret. She'd known Wes for a long time. Did their friendship really just end because of another guy? Well, not just a guy, but a demon. She hated to admit it, but there was an emptiness in her chest, close to the area she had seen Josh place his hand on Paul to extract his soul.

Even though she had resolved to cut Wes out of her life, she didn't think this was how it would end. It made her sad, but there was also a feeling a relief associated with it. That scared her more than anything. She really needed to talk to someone. She needed guidance. But who?

Her phone buzzed and she pulled it out of her pocket. There were thirteen messages on it, all from Deb. Katie sighed. She had a lot of explaining to do, but how much of the truth could she actually reveal?

CHAPTER 17

I'M FINE. Will talk to you later. Promise.

Katie wanted Deb to know she wasn't totally blowing her off, but she wasn't quite ready to talk to her yet. She needed to get her thoughts together; she needed to be alone. There was one place Katie could go where she was sure no one would bother her. She rose from the bed and headed downstairs.

"Katie?" her mom called. "Is that you? I didn't hear you come in."

Katie didn't respond. She grabbed the keys to her mom's car and headed out the door.

She stared at the headstone, reading her dad's name and birth and death dates over and over in her mind. Thirty years was too young. There was a time when she thought that was old, decrepit, but now she knew it wasn't. He never had time to realize his dreams, see his daughter grow up. There were so many things he could have done, accomplished.

Katie sat in the grass and faced the marble slab. When was the last time she had been there? It had been years, she knew that. A lot of it was because of anger, resentment, hate that he left her so early. She convinced herself that it was because she was busy, but she knew better. As she sat there, she wondered if things would have turned out differently if he were still there. Would she have pined after Wes for so long if her dad was there to give her advice? Would she have gotten sucked in by a smooth-talking and attractive demon? She didn't know. But she also knew worrying about and having the scenarios go through her mind weren't going to change anything. Her dad was gone, and he had been for eleven years. She couldn't change that; she could only deal. Maybe there were things she could have done differently, but what was the point in worrying about them? They couldn't be changed.

The real reason for coming to the cemetery was because she could be alone. It was quiet, peaceful and hardly anyone knew where her father's grave was. It was the perfect place to collect her thoughts and not be bothered. The location of his grave was perfect, too –under an ash tree, so she was shaded from the sun, and away from the main gate. She lay down in the grass and stared at the leaves. If someone passed by, they wouldn't be able to find her among the headstones. She was truly able to be alone with her thoughts.

Katie thought about her dad and sin and salvation. Where had he gone when he died? She wanted to believe it was Heaven, but as she lay there, she realized she really didn't know her dad. She was six when he died, hardly any time to get to know him. Mom rarely talked about him, only making comments here and there about how he would have liked something or it was a shame he wasn't there to see them. Her parents had met in college at a party. Mom didn't give too many details, such as if they were drinking or doing other bad things. Dad had asked her to the movies, and at first she wanted to decline, say she had studying to do, but she didn't. She went with him. They dated for two years before getting married, but Mom was vague on the details, believing Katie was too young and would find the love aspect gross. After a while, Katie quit asking. Wes was in the picture and Katie was sure she could figure out on her own what it meant to be boyfriend and girlfriend. Instead, Katie was misinformed about how relationships worked. Wes was constantly abandoning her, and her father was gone, so Katie was convinced that was how loved worked. The guys left when they were needed most.

That was normal. All those shows on TV were wrong. No one got a happy ending in real life. It took Katie a long time, practically until her senior year in high school, to realize relationships weren't full of heartache. Once she'd made the decision to look for that happy ending, she tangled herself in more despair and treachery. The only hope she could cling to was that she could force a happy ending. Josh wasn't Prince Charming—well, he looked like Prince Charming, but didn't have the right background—but he wasn't Captain Abandonment, either. He at least gave her something to work with.

Katie still wasn't sure how a real relationship worked, but she didn't blame her father for that. She couldn't. He had been killed by a drunk driver. She blamed the other driver. It was his fault she had a screwed up outlook on love. If he hadn't taken everything away from her...but that was a waste of energy too. Even if she had the chance to yell and scream at the guy, what difference would it make? Her dad wasn't going to magically rise from the ground and they would be a happy family. No, what was done was done. Nothing could change it.

Still, she was curious to know what kind of person her father was. She assumed he was nice and kind, only because the fleeting comments her mom gave made him seem that way. But Josh also seemed nice and kind, too, and yet something dark and evil lurked just below the surface. The same thing could be said about her. She tried to live right and treat people with respect, but did it always turn out that way? There was a dark spot in her soul, the potential for evil. Who did she inherit that from? It was easy to say her dad because he wasn't there. Her mom tried, she really did, but she wasn't perfect and Katie didn't always make things easy. Maybe her dad would have turned out to do awful things, but his life had been cut short and he never had the chance. Maybe that was why he died so young. Perhaps his crimes would have been so heinous they would have changed the course of history. The thought didn't exactly cheer Katie, but it helped her make sense of the situation.

Katie also had to consider that the whole thing was a lie. Not the demons or Hell–those she had seen for herself–but the things Wes and Josh had told her. How could she possibly believe anything that came out of their mouths? Wes had been lying to her since kindergarten, maybe before. Josh was a demon. Supposedly everything he said was a lie. Katie hadn't seen him act like that, but she had to be on her guard. After all, Wes and Josh were locked in a battle with one another and using Katie as the bait. They were going to say whatever they needed to say to get what they wanted. And Katie had to stop falling for it.

Yet, part of her found it hard to believe Josh didn't have some feelings for her. He'd had a chance to kill her—multiple times—and didn't. He took her to Hell and, according to Wes, he could have taken her soul, but he didn't. Katie was willing to give Josh the benefit of the doubt because in the short time she'd known him, he'd never given her a reason to doubt. He laid everything out in front of her—no matter how ugly or undesirable—so she could make her own decisions. At least he was willing to share his life with her. That meant something, no matter how dark and twisted it was. He trusted her and let her in. He took a chance doing that. If Katie had been repulsed by him, she could have found a priest or another Praesul to banish him. He didn't know what would happen, but he was willing to put himself at risk...for her. What other guy in Katie's life was willing to put himself in danger for her?

"I knew I would find you here."

The voice startled Katie and she bolted upright. Deb stood next to the headstone directly in front of Katie, her hand on her hip, a genuine look of concern on her face. Katie wasn't sure if she was relieved or irritated to see Deb, but she was thankful it wasn't Josh or Wes.

"I went by your house after you sent the text." Deb explained. "Your mom said you took the car and left." Deb stepped forward and sat next to Katie in the grass. "She's really concerned about you. She'd been crying. Her eyes were all puffy and her face was streaked." Deb stared at her for a minute. "She wanted to come with me, but I talked her out of it."

Katie nodded and picked at the grass in front of her.

"You know, I was lucky I found you here. I kept trying to think of all the places you would go. I was totally wracking my brain. Then I thought you probably needed to go somewhere you could be alone." She glanced around the cemetery. "It doesn't get much lonelier than this."

Katie squinted at the horizon. Deb could be so intuitive when she wanted to be. Katie also knew that Deb wasn't going to leave until Katie told her what was going on. Deb was persistent like that. Normally, Katie enjoyed that about Deb; it made her easy to talk to. But those conversations usually centered around what a jerk Wes was, and then the rest of the school knew what a jerk he was, but three-fourths of them didn't realize he went to their high school. Could she tell Deb the truth? Would Deb believe her or think she had totally lost her mind? Would the rest of the school be talking about it on Monday and think she was an escaped mental patient? At that point, did Katie really care or did she just need to get the story off her chest?

Deb took a deep breath, her forehead wrinkled with seriousness. "Katie, look, I know you've been going through a lot lately. Exactly what is still a mystery. But I want you to know I'm here for you." She reached out and grabbed Katie's hand. "You can tell me anything. You know that, right?"

Katie grabbed Deb's hand and laid back in the grass. She was thankful her friend was there. Deb made her feel safe. Despite her quirks, she was the one person who had always been there for Katie.

"What did they say about me at the reservoir?"

"Oh, my God, Katie! It was insane!" Deb laid down next to her. "After we went down to the docks, we got on the boat and Stan's cousin went to start the engine. The thing wouldn't start. He forgot to put gas in it. Can you believe it? Who takes a boat to the lake without any gas? Then, he tried to tell all of us that if we wanted to ski, it would cost twenty bucks. Forget that! The boat was a mess. Beer cans littered the ground, fish hooks were everywhere. Seriously, I almost stepped on a rusty one. I wasn't expecting a luxury liner, but this was more like a log with an engine on it. I wasn't going to waste my money on that. I went back to the beach and noticed the crowd. Not wanting to be out of the loop," she squeezed Katie's hand, "I immediately ran to find out what happened. That's when I heard about the fight between Wes and Josh."

Katie listened patiently. Deb was never one to make a long story short. Every detail was important, especially the details that involved her.

"I had just missed it. Josh was in the middle of the crowd, bleeding. Oh, he looked awful. His right eye was starting to swell shut, his lip was swollen, blood was crusted around his nostrils, and he kept spitting blood on the ground. I thought I was going to puke. It scared the crap out of me. I asked him if he was all right, and he smiled at me and said, 'Of course.' Like it was totally normal for him to be in a fight. Then I asked where you were and he said he didn't know. He was really worried though. Then Mandy Parsons told me she saw you run off for the bathrooms. Josh and I went to find you, but you were gone. Josh was pissed. He was sure Wes had taken you somewhere. He ran off to find you. I decided to go to the car and head home, thinking Wes brought you back to town." She turned her head to look at Katie. "Where did you go?"

Katie ignored the question. "Did anyone else say anything? Talk about what an awful person I am?"

"No. Why would anyone say that?"

Katie shrugged. "Zack told Wes and Josh I wasn't worth fighting over. You should have seen the looks everyone gave me."

Deb clicked her tongue. "I don't think Zack thinks any woman is worth fighting over. He's a jerk. No one listens to Zack."

"He's the freaking quarterback! The most popular guy in school. Isn't his word like gospel?"

"Do you live in a high school movie? People know him, yeah, and he's popular, but he's also the most conceited jerk in the whole school. He couldn't get a date with a member of the chess club. Everyone pretends to like him, but no one really does, and no one listens to what he has to say."

Katie found that surprising. She'd always equated popularity with likeability, but as she thought about it, it made sense. Hitler was popular and not well liked. She really needed to break out of her self-absorbed shell and pay attention to what was going on in her school.

"Still," Katie commented. "Everyone must think I'm such a witch."

Deb squeezed her hand again. "Are you kidding me? At this moment, you're probably the most popular girl in school! Everyone wants to know who you are and what is so special about you that you have boys fighting over you." Deb snorted. "Not that anybody cares about Wes. No one knows who he is. But still. Everyone is talking."

Katie grimaced. Earlier in the day, she had found the attention flattering. After seeing what Josh was capable of—what he was—she didn't want to be in the limelight anymore. She wanted to fade back into obscurity. She didn't want things to go back the way they were because she didn't want to have to deal with Wes and the heartache, but she didn't want her classmates scrutinizing her every move either.

Deb rolled over onto her side and placed her arm under her head. "Is that why you've been so weirded out lately? Because Josh and Wes have been fighting over you? If you ask me, Josh is the clear choice. He's smart, has an amazing body, and a smile to die for. Now, Wes isn't exactly ugly, but his past actions speak volumes. How many times has he hurt you? You don't want him to continue to do that to you."

Katie's gaze drifted toward the leaves. It would be so nice if the situation was that simple. Of course Josh was the obvious choice. Katie would have gone for it in a heartbeat if it was a normal situation. Deb had to know the truth. Otherwise she would be mad and think Katie was super picky when it came to boys, and then the school would get wind of it and she'd probably never date again. She turned to face Deb.

"Things are a little more complicated than that."

Deb's face crunched in confusion and disbelief. "I know you have a long history with Wes and change can be scary, but come on! You deserve better! And I can't believe you let Wes bring you home."

Katie shook her head. "Deb, seriously, this goes way beyond feelings I've had since kindergarten. Besides, I don't think Wes will ever talk to me again. We had a huge argument."

Deb rolled her eyes. "How many times have I heard that before? You and Wes are always fighting. He's always doing something to hurt you or upset you. There have been numerous calls where you've been crying and distraught because of something he did. Normally I just sit back and listen, but I'm done, Katie. I'm done listening to how much that boy has hurt you. I'm going to say it flat out. Wes is no good for you. You need to move on, otherwise, he will be the death of you."

Katie couldn't agree more with Deb's statement. It was just a shame Deb didn't know how true her words were. And Deb was right. She normally sat back and listened to Katie, was a shoulder for her to cry on, rarely ever telling Katie she was an idiot for liking Wes. Katie wasn't stupid enough to think Deb liked Wes. Just because she kept her mouth shut and didn't say much about him didn't mean she didn't think ill of him. Katie could tell by the way Deb's jaw set when Wes's name was mentioned or how she narrowed her eyes at him when he passed in the hall. Katie appreciated that Deb kept her opinions about him to herself, especially when Katie thought she still liked him, but apparently Deb had her breaking point, and this was it.

"Deb, this time I'm serious. I made some comments about his family. Things I probably shouldn't have said, but it's too late now. I can't take them back. I really hurt him."

Deb's eyes lit up. "Don't beat yourself up for saying those things to Wes. They probably needed to be said. He probably needed to be hurt as badly as he hurt you. So then there's no issue. You and Josh can hook up and everything will be all right with the world."

"Not exactly." Katie took a deep breath and prepared herself for what she was going to say next. "Josh is a demon."

Perplexity crossed Deb's face. "Like in the sack?" Shock replaced the confusion and she smacked Katie's arm. "Katie! I can't believe you slept with him!"

Once again, Katie shook her head. "No, Deb. That's not what I meant. I mean he's an actual evil-from-Hell demon that takes people's souls."

Deb forced out a laugh but stopped abruptly when Katie didn't join her. "Why aren't you laughing? That was actually a good joke."

Katie closed her eyes. "You have no idea how much I wish that was a joke. I know how crazy it sounds, but please hear me out. I really need to talk to someone." She opened her eyes and stared at her friend.

At one point, Deb's family had been extremely religious; they went to church every Sunday. Katie had joined them on a few occasions. Deb's parents and siblings still attended service, but Deb had stopped going. Katie asked her about it once, but Deb had just shrugged and said she was trying to figure things out. Katie didn't push her. Deb would talk about it when she was ready to.

Deb's eyes were wide and she nodded in quick, jerky movements.

"The next thing I'm going to tell you, you have to swear not to tell anyone else." She held up her pinky.

Deb wrapped her finger around Katie's. "I swear."

"The reason Wes and Josh are fighting is because Wes is a Praesul."

Katie told Deb everything that had happened in the last few days. Deb listened silently, her mouth pressed into a line, her head bobbing every now and then to indicate she was still listening.

Katie felt a weight lift off her as she spoke. It might not have been the best idea to reveal that Wes was a Praesul, but Deb needed to know the whole story. Besides, Deb pinky swore she wouldn't tell anyone, and Katie knew she wouldn't. Deb didn't like Wes, and the school knew that, but even if she told everyone what Katie just told her, no one would believe the story anyway. No way would Deb risk her popularity on craziness like this. Her mouth would stay shut.

"Now you understand why I've been weirded out lately and why things are so complicated."

Deb stared at her friend for several long moments. "So a Hell Hound tore up your arm, not a stray dog?"

Katie nodded.

"And you were in the warehouse as bait because Josh took you there. You didn't actually skip school to make out with Wes."

Katie pushed her eyebrows together. "I never said we went there to make out. I said we went there to talk."

Deb waved her hand through the air. "Whatever." She took a deep breath. "Now I have something to tell you. Something I've wanted to tell you forever but didn't think I could."

Katie's confusion deepened. "What?"

"My great-uncle, my grandpa's brother, was a Praesul too."

CHAPTER 18

KATIE SAT UP AND STARED AT DEB, searching her face for…what? Deb wasn't one to lie to Katie. She had never done it before. And no one would make up knowing a Praesul. They kept themselves a secret; they didn't want the world to know about them. Katie shouldn't have been surprised, especially with how religious Deb's family was, but they weren't the type of people to shove their beliefs down others' throats. Come to think of it, neither were Wes and Randy. In fact, she couldn't remember a time when Wes had gone to church. Perhaps it wasn't important that the Praesul went to a church and worship but that they just believed in God. Katie would have to ask someone about that.

Deb sat up next to her and held out her hands. "I know, you think I'm making this up, but I swear to you I'm not. He's really truly a God's chosen protector."

"A few days ago I would have thought you were crazy. Now, absolutely anything is possible." Katie took a deep breath. "So what do we do now?"

Deb reached out and put her hand on Katie's shoulder. "I don't know." Her gaze drifted over Katie's shoulder and she was lost in thought for several moments. "Now that you explain that about Wes, his actions make sense. I should have put two and two together."

Katie grimaced. "Oh, so now his actions are excusable?"

Deb focused back on Katie's face. "That's not what I meant. It doesn't excuse what he's done, just explains his actions. He's still a total jerk, but at least he has an explanation for why he did it."

"Did your great-uncle act the same way?"

Deb waggled her head side to side and pursed her lips. "Possibly. He wasn't around much. I never really knew him."

"Then how do you know he was a Praesul?"

"My grandma told me. And I've read the letters he's written her." She smiled slightly and got a faraway look in her eyes. "I found them after my grandpa died. I don't think I was supposed to, though. They were buried at the back of her closet. I was just trying to help her clean out Papa's stuff." Her gaze flicked to the ground, moist with tears.

"What did the letters say?"

Deb shook her head. "Not a lot. They mainly talked about the places in the world he was visiting. The amazing sites. How much he missed her." Deb smiled. "I think I caught my grandmother in a moment of weakness. She had been crying about my grandpa for days, but when I asked her about the letters, she smiled. She told me everything about Uncle Edgar. He sounds like an amazing man. If he has one fault, it's his inability to have a relationship."

"Sounds? So he's still alive?"

Deb shrugged. "As far as I know. It's been a few months since Gram has gotten a letter."

Hope surged through Katie. This was exactly what she needed: an outside person she could talk with to get answers to her questions. Yeah, she knew Deb's grandma, had gone to some family dinners with her and talked to her, but she wouldn't say they knew each other well. Deb's grandma was the perfect person to give her advice. And if the worst came to pass, maybe Deb could contact her great uncle to make everything all right. Katie leaned forward.

"Do you think I could talk to your Gram? Maybe she has some answers to what is going on."

Deb's shoulders slouched. "I don't know, Katie. She's pretty mad at me for becoming agnostic. She might really lose it if she knew I told you about Edgar. She swore me to secrecy."

"Please, Deb. I really need some help. You can tell her about my situation if it will make things easier."

Deb frowned. "I'll see what I can do. Feel out the situation, but I can't promise anything."

It wasn't what Katie wanted to hear, but it was going to have to do. No one wanted to risk their lives or the lives of their families, especially when a demon was involved. Maybe it was foolish to get Deb involved. What if Katie just endangered Deb's life by telling her about Josh and Wes? She would never forgive herself if something happened. A knot developed in her stomach. Was this how Wes felt every day? No wonder he was always stressed out. It also became painfully clear why he never fulfilled his promises. Katie fought back the urge to leave Deb sitting on the grass. If a demon attempted to find her and wanted to force her to do something, threatening Deb would be a fairly convincing argument. Katie probably wouldn't say no.

Logically, though, that thought process was flawed. Josh knew Deb and Katie were friends. He knew Katie had a family. Whether Deb knew he was a demon or not, if he wanted to use Deb to hurt Katie, he would. Any demon would. Humans were very social creatures and had lots of connections. It wouldn't take much for a demon to exploit any of them. Katie's presence could possible endanger her friends and family, but it also might save them.

Katie sympathized with Wes, but she found his actions reprehensible. Maybe now that Deb knew the truth she would be more cautious of Josh, watch and scrutinize his every move. If Wes had warned Katie, she would have avoided Josh all together. Knowledge was never a bad thing, and this information could potentially save Deb's life.

"We should head back now." Deb glanced around. "It's getting late."

Katie wasn't quite ready to head back yet; she had some more thinking she needed to do. But she knew Deb was right. Her mom would freak out even more if Katie didn't head home. She figured she'd made Mom suffer enough, especially if Deb was correct about her emotional state. Even though Katie was still upset, there was no sense prolonging the inevitable. She had to go home sometime. She sighed and stood. Deb followed her lead, brushing off the back of her shorts. They headed for the parking lot, and Deb put her arm around Katie's shoulders.

"Everything is going to be all right." She gave Katie a squeeze "By Monday, I bet most of the people forget what Zack said. But you'll still be a celebrity."

Katie snorted. "Yeah, because that's what I'm most concerned about at this point in my life."

Deb clicked her tongue. "Okay. Since you're being pursued and used by a demon, I'll talk to Gram. We'll figure this out together so we can worry about getting dates for prom."

Katie laid her head on her friend's shoulder. "Thank you."

Not that she cared about prom, but given the option of worrying about that or if she was going to lose her soul, she'd take prom.

*   *   *

Katie sat in the driveway and stared at her house. She felt a little better after being in the cemetery. She at least felt like she had a chance to breathe and think. It relieved her that Deb knew what was going on too. That way, if anything happened to Katie, like Josh taking her back to Hell permanently, someone would know where to look. Even though people wouldn't believe her at first, Deb had a way of making people listen. She wouldn't give up until someone did something. Besides, Deb had connections. She could get a hold of her great-uncle if worse came to worse.

As Katie sat in the car, she contemplated driving to Deb's grandma's house. She'd been there a few times, and she was sure she could find it again. It wasn't that she didn't trust Deb– she knew Deb would talk to her grandma like she said she would–but Katie would feel so much better acting instead of sitting around waiting. What if Deb was right? What if her grandma refused to help because she was upset with Deb's actions? What would Katie do then? Perhaps if Katie asked for help personally, Gram would be more willing to assist.

Katie was half a second away from starting the car when she noticed her mom glance out the window. There was no chance of leaving now. Mom had let things slide for a while, given Katie the space she needed, but Katie shouldn't push too far. She didn't need her mom calling the cops and winding up in the hospital again. No doubt her mom still wasn't convinced Katie was all right. With a sigh, she pushed open the door and headed into the house.

The foyer was bright and inviting, and the soft orange lights illuminated the small room. The scent of chicken and potatoes hit her nostrils, causing her stomach to growl. Her mouth watered and a weakness took over her body. When was the last time she had eaten? If she couldn't remember, it had probably been too long. She headed for the kitchen, trying to figure out what she was going to say to her mom. Maybe she would wait until her mom spoke first and respond accordingly. That was probably the safest approach.

Katie stepped onto the linoleum floor, her base desires driving her to eat, and stopped in her tracks. Her mom stood at the kitchen sink staring at her, and Wes and Randy sat at the kitchen table. Her first inclination was to turn around and walk out of the house. It didn't matter where she went, she just wanted to get away. But what would be the point? Wes and Randy could stop her if they really wanted or hunt her down. Her mom would commit her to an asylum until she was convinced Katie was mentally stable. No, the best course of action was to convince everyone she was fine so they would leave her alone.

She was genuinely surprised to see Wes in her house. After the confrontation on the mountain, she thought for sure she would never see him again. And that really didn't bother her. It didn't escape her notice that Wes refused to look at her. His gaze was focused on the table, the muscles in his jaw were tight. He probably wanted to be there even less than she did.

"I like that tankini." Her mom's voice drew her attention away from Wes. "You borrow that from Deb?"

Katie glanced down at herself. "Yeah. We went to the reservoir instead of shopping today."

Mom forced a smile. "I heard. Did you have a nice day?"

Katie folded her arms across her chest. "Not really." She shot a glare toward Wes.

Mom nodded and opened the oven door. Pulling out the pan, she set it on the stove. The scent of chicken was overwhelming and Katie's stomach growled audibly. She needed to eat or she was going to pass out. Barely feeling her feet beneath her, she went to the table and sat down. Mom had already set the table and Katie couldn't wait to fill her plate.

The tension in the air was palpable. Wes's hands balled into fists before he pulled them from the table into his lap. Katie fought back the urge to scream at him and tell him what a jerk he was. Sadness and anger mixed throughout her body. She shouldn't have said some of the things she said, but Wes shouldn't have said or done certain things either. She really didn't want him in her house, let alone directly across from her. The hollowness in her chest grew more apparent, making her feel even more irritated with his presence. She glanced at Randy. He stared back at her, tapping his finger on the table, and nodded once. The urge to stick out her tongue at him overwhelmed her, but she refrained. Why were they here if they didn't want to save Katie? They'd made it very clear she was untrustworthy and needed to be sacrificed for the greater good. She grabbed her napkin and placed it in her lap. Mom placed the pan of cheesy chicken and potatoes in the center of the table and took a seat. Katie waited impatiently for the "guests" to be served first, then spooned a huge helping onto her plate.

"So what's the special occasion that Wes and Randy honor us with their presence?" Katie was tired of playing nice. She didn't care how snarky the comment came out. She wanted to know what was going on.

"Katie." her mom huffed. "That's no way to talk about guests."

Katie shoved a forkful of food in her mouth to keep from telling her mom she was an idiot for thinking Wes and Randy were fine upstanding human beings.

"They're here because they are concerned about you." Mom folded her arms on the table and leaned forward. "They think you might have fallen in with a bad crowd."

Katie stopped chewing and glanced from her mom to the guys sitting across from her. Was this some kind of joke? Had they really come over to her house to control her life? Did they really think tattling on her was going to change things?

Her mom cleared her throat. "I heard about the fight today at the reservoir, Katie. I've also been told about Josh. Were you ever going to tell me about him?"

Katie swallowed the bite in her mouth. She hadn't chewed properly, so it took a while for it to go down. How much did her mom know? Did Wes and Randy reveal to her mom what Josh was? Katie scoffed inwardly. No, that wouldn't happen. They wouldn't even tell the truth in the hospital, no way were they revealing anything now. She narrowed her eyes to slits and stared at Randy and Wes.

"Oh, they did. And what did they tell you about Josh?"

"They said he's bad news. That he has a record. Deals drugs." Mom straightened up in her chair. "I don't want you hanging out with people like that, Katie."

Katie couldn't help but laugh. The seriousness in the room was overwhelming; the lies were unbearable. Was this really how Wes and Randy were going to sway Katie to the good side? They were going to sic her mom on her? Katie would have entertained the notion of not seeing Josh anymore if someone asked her nicely not to. She'd been to Hell, she'd seen what he could do; he was bad news. There was no denying that. Now, however, she wanted to do something to spite her mom and the guys who were supposedly looking out for her safety. She knew they really didn't care about here. This was just their way of getting back at Josh.

Mom stared at Katie wide-eyed. It took a few moments before Katie was able to regain control of herself.

"Is that really what these two told you?" Katie pointed across the table. "Yes."

"And you believed them?"

Mom hesitated, glancing from Katie to the guys and back to Katie. "Why would they lie? We've known them for years."

"Known them?" Katie almost choked on the words. "You told me you haven't spoken to Randy for years. You told me that after his wife died," the word came out full of spite, "he isolated himself from you. I'm betting the first time you actually talked to Randy in a long time was the other night when he showed up at the house looking for me." She raised her eyebrows questioningly.

"That's not the point, Katie. Wes and Randy only want what is best for you. They want you to be safe. So do I. Look at what Josh did to Wes."

For the first time, Wes raised his head and Katie was able to see the bruises and cuts. Anger flared across his eyes as their gaze met, and his lips pressed into a thin line. Katie clenched her jaw.

"You should see what Wes did to Josh! He started it! Wes whacked Josh in the back of the head with a log!"

"Are you actually defending him?" Wes growled between gritted teeth. His voice was barely audible.

Katie snarled. "Are you actually sitting in my house, eating my food, and telling my mother lies? Don't you dare get holier-than-thou on me!"

Randy held up his hand. "Katie, there's no need to get upset. Let's just have a civilized discussion here."

Katie slammed her hands down on the table. "No need to get upset? Are you kidding me? You've destroyed my life! You put me in the middle of a war that I shouldn't be in, then come in here and make it sound like everything is my fault. I didn't ask Josh to come here. I didn't make him attack Wes at school, and I sure as hell didn't want to be taken to that warehouse." She pointed a finger at Wes. "If it weren't for me, you would already be dead! Do NOT come into my house and dictate who I should or should not hang out with. YOU brought this on me."

Wes stood from his chair with such force it toppled over backward. "Do you really think I'm trying to harm you? I never wanted any of this! I wanted you to be safe, but you keep putting yourself in harm's way!"

Randy placed a hand on his son's arm, trying to get him to calm down. Mom's eyes had gone wide; her mouth was pressed shut and confusion covered her face. Katie felt slightly bad for dragging her into the situation, but that was all on Wes and Randy. They could have left her out of it. They could have left Katie out of it. They should have just walked away. Wes should have left her alone after the mountain. It would have made things so much easier and her mom wouldn't have gotten involved. What were Randy and Wes trying to accomplish? What was their end game?

Wes panted, his face red with anger and exertion. Eventually, he stormed out of the house, slamming the door behind him as he did. Randy rose slowly from his chair. Katie couldn't tell if it was because of his injuries or hesitation. As he walked past her mom, he placed a hand on her shoulder.

"I'm sorry about all this. I'll call you later."

She nodded, and Randy left the house. Katie leaned back in her seat, her appetite completely gone.

"Would you mind explaining to me exactly what that was about?" Mom's voice had an accusatory edge to it.

Katie scoffed. "Really? You're going to make this my fault?"

Mom waved her hand through the air. "That's not what I'm doing, Katie. I'm just trying to figure out what is going on."

"Your tone says differently."

"Well, your tone isn't exactly friendly," Mom snapped.

Katie stood from her seat. "I can't believe you were willing to listen and believe Wes and Randy without even talking to me first. It's just like what happened the other day when you took me to the hospital. Why don't you listen to me anymore?"

Mom cocked her head to the side, her mood softening. "I'm listening, Katie. Tell me what's going on."

Katie rolled her eyes. "It's a little late for that now, Mom." She left the kitchen and stomped up to her room.

CHAPTER 19

KATIE LOCKED THE DOOR TO HER ROOM and cranked up her music. She figured Mom would be up in a few minutes, coaxing her to talk through the door. How could her mom listen to Wes and Randy without talking to her first? What had they told her that was so convincing that she wouldn't believe her own daughter? What had she done that made her mom turn away from her?

Katie threw herself on her bed and buried her face in her pillow. Anger, confusion, and sadness surged through her body. She didn't know how to react, so the emotions flooded out of her in a scream that was muffled in cotton. On one hand, she realized Wes and Randy were just looking out for her and attempting to keep her safe. After all, Josh was a demon. Katie'd caught a glimpse of his true self at the reservoir. The memory sent a chill down her spine. What bothered Katie the most about the situation was that Wes and Randy didn't seem to be acting in her best interest. If they wanted to protect her, why didn't they talk to her? Why didn't they let her help? She wasn't a child, and it irritated her to no end that they were treating her like one.

Katie rolled onto her back and stared at the ceiling. She wasn't sure if she wanted to scream again or cry. She didn't get the chance to do either. A light swirled in her room. Katie leapt from her bed toward the door. She wasn't going to exit just yet, but she couldn't risk opening the door and her mom seeing the anomaly—there was no telling how she would react—and she needed to calculate her odds of getting out if Wes stepped out of the portal. She glanced from the light to the door. It wasn't that far; with some running steps, she should be able to get out. Dang it! She locked the door to keep her mom out. It was going to slow her down unlocking the door, potentially giving Wes enough time to grab her and pull her through. He was the last person she wanted to talk to, and she thought he had felt the same way, but she had been wrong before—many times before.

The figure stepped out of the light. Katie relaxed. Josh's chiseled face and to-die-for smile was focused directly on her. Not that Josh was any better than Wes, but given a choice between the two, she would take the demon any day. He still wore his swimsuit, but his face was bruised and swollen from the fight. Katie almost felt sorry for him, but then she remembered what he was and what he did. Why couldn't he be a normal teenage boy? She folded her hands across her chest. As the blaring music hit Josh's ears, his smile faltered.

"Everything all right?" He had to yell to be heard.

She shook her head. Without saying anything, she stepped up to him and put her mouth close to his ear so she didn't have to yell. "Take me somewhere. I don't care where. Anywhere is better than here."

The smile once again grew on his lips and he wrapped his arms around Katie's shoulders. They stepped into the light. Katie knew she shouldn't be going with him; she knew what she was doing was dangerous, but a part of her really didn't care. A part of her wanted to show Wes, Randy, and her mom that she could take care of herself. She was a big girl, she didn't need them looking out for her. She was going to prove that Josh wasn't that dangerous. Yet, a small voice at the back of her brain told her she was getting in way over her head, and that made her stomach ache.

The pair stepped onto a sandy beach at sunset. Pinks, oranges, purples, and blue splattered the sky. A humid breeze tossed her hair, the smell of fish and salt entered her nostrils. Waves crashed against the sand in steady rhythm. Instantly, Katie felt relaxed, at peace. She glanced at Josh. He still had his arm around her shoulders.

"I figured we were still in our suits and didn't get a chance to enjoy the reservoir, so we should come some place tropical."

Katie couldn't stop the smile from spreading across her lips. She thought about asking where they were, then decided she really didn't care. As long as she was away from the issues at home, she was happy. He may have been a demon, but he was pretty good at figuring out just what Katie needed. Was that a good or bad thing? What did it say about Katie that she was willing to go with him wherever he led? Her stomach cramped further.

"What's going on now?" Josh asked. "What's all the drama, mama?"

Katie cringed. "I don't want to talk about it."

Josh shrugged. "Fine with me. Shall we enjoy the fine evening air?"

In response, Katie plopped down onto the sand. The warmth seeped through her shorts, the sand squeaked with her movements. Her gaze drifted to the horizon and she watched the colors swirl and change as the sun sank into the ocean. Sweat beaded on her skin. Or perhaps it was humidity. She couldn't tell, and she really didn't care. As long as it wasn't her cramped room, she was happy. Josh took a seat next to her and she looked at him out of the corner of her eye. He leaned back on his elbows, his feet extended out before him. The soft rays of fading light illuminated his muscular physique. His torso was perfectly defined with muscles, his skin evenly tanned. Aside from the bruises and cuts on his face, he was flawless, perfect. A little too perfect for a high school boy. Katie was able to see that now because she knew exactly what he was. He used his charm and played on other's perceptions and ideas of perfection to get them to do what he needed them to do. His looks were disarming. He appealed to both males and females because he portrayed the perfect human specimen. Katie had fallen for it; she wouldn't deny that. She was blinded by hormones and teenage naïveté. Even as she sat there, she couldn't deny how attractive Josh was. How much she wanted to be with him, to make a relationship work, to change him from being an evil demon. And he had picked her. Out of all the other girls in the school, he had his eyes set on her. It was flattering and disturbing all at the same time. So what if the motivation was to take down Wes? He was spending time with her, and she could turn his gaze and focus away from Wes, she was sure of it. Exactly how was still a mystery, but she was a smart girl; she'd figure it out.

Josh caught her sideways glance and smiled, reaching his hand out to take a hold of hers. Katie didn't fight it, but her skin crawled where he touched her. The vision of him taking Paul's soul played through her mind. His body was just a shell that housed something very dark and menacing beneath, something evil and dangerous. It scared her that it was his true form. The reminder that he wasn't human upset her. What disturbed her even more was the fact that she willingly and without question went with him whenever he commanded. Why did she do that? Was she wrong about the black mark on her soul? Was she really evil and destined to do horrible things? She dropped her gaze to her lap. Could she change her destiny?

The sun dropped into the sea and cast a gray hue over the world that quickly faded into black. The breeze continued to blow from the ocean, cooling slightly in the darkness. It dried the sweat on Katie's body into sticky streams. Josh squeezed her hand.

"Hey, I have an idea. You wanna go somewhere and have a little fun?"

She looked at him. "Like where?"

Honestly, Katie just wanted to sit on the beach and let her mind wander. She didn't want to be around other people and pretend like everything was all right with the world. Her desire was to replay the events from the day and figure out what she needed to do. She wanted to formulate a plan. But she also didn't want Josh to get bored. He might leave her if that happened. What would Katie do then? She was stuck without him, so she didn't want to anger him.

Josh stood from the beach and helped her to her feet. He stood in front of her, his body right next to hers, and ran a hand through her hair. A slight smile played on his lips. A look of affection crossed his face as he took in her features. Katie tried not to let the confusion show on her face, but the gesture was awfully gentle, almost human. Was it another of Josh's ploys to suck her deeper into his world and to make her believe he could be more than a demon? Her limbs tingled, and her heart rate increased. Josh leaned forward and pressed his lips delicately against hers. His lips were soft and smelled faintly of mint. Despite everything she knew about him, she kissed him back, losing herself in his embrace and warmth.

After several moments, he pulled his lips away and rested his forehead against hers. Again, he ran his hands through her hair and down her back. His touch caused goosebumps to form on her flesh. Her breath hitched; she felt dizzy. The world melted away, and the only thing that existed was Josh. His warmth, his smell, his gaze were the only things that Katie could see, the only thing that mattered. Butterflies entered her stomach. She didn't want the moment to end. She didn't want to be without his presence. Memories of what he was vanished. Katie didn't care. All that mattered was that he could appear to be human, mimic their emotions and mannerisms, and Katie was willing to take that.

"You ready to go?" His voice broke the spell.

Katie nodded, still feeling weak from his embrace.

He grabbed her hand and led her down the beach. She obediently followed.

After a short while, Katie found herself on a paved road surrounded by buildings and people. Lights flashed all around them, and music pulsed into the streets. Her eyes grew wide. How could that much activity be going on and she didn't notice while on the beach? They weren't that far from the city, and yet she thought they were isolated from people. Josh led her though the crowds to a club in the middle of the block. It rose three stories and boomed with bass. A line snaked around the front of the building and into an alley. Katie tightened her grip on Josh's hand. He looked at her, reassurance on his face, and gently brushed his fingertips across her cheek. She forced a smile, but her stomach was in knots. It felt like she was going to throw up.

Josh bypassed the line and headed straight for the bouncer. Katie had no idea how they were going to get in. She didn't have any money or an ID. She was fairly certain Josh didn't either. The man nodded at them and opened the velvet rope for them to enter. Shock flowed through Katie. A few people standing in the line glared at them as they entered. They had probably been in line for a long time. As they stepped into the building, the music thudded in Katie's ears, thumped in her chest. Smoke surrounded her; the smell of cigarettes, alcohol, and sweat gagged her. Bodies gyrated and moved on the dance floor. Lights barely pierced the hazy air. Katie's flip-flops stuck to the floor. Josh directed her to the bar and let her have the only empty seat.

"You want anything to drink?" he yelled over the melee.

Katie shook her head. Her mouth had gone dry as they entered the establishment, but she was too afraid to put anything in her body. First of all, she didn't know where she was. Secondly, her stomach was so upset she was afraid she would throw up. She slouched in her chair and tried to make herself as small as possible. The bartender approached and asked what Josh wanted. She spoke Spanish. Josh responded in kind. Katie mentally kicked herself for taking French in school. The woman placed a mug of beer on the counter and nodded at Josh before heading off to take care of other customers.

"Don't you have to pay for that?" Katie spoke as loudly as possible and pointed to the beer.

Josh smiled and took a long drink. "I don't have to pay for anything here." He raised his eyebrows and finished off the liquid.

Katie didn't understand what he meant, but it was too hard to carry on a conversation. She'd have to ask him later when it was quieter what he was talking about. He set the empty glass on the bar and bopped to the music. Katie glanced around the room, trying to get an idea of where she was at or a name of the club. If nothing else, she could look it up on the internet later.

Just then, she realized she'd forgotten her phone. She patted her pockets just in case, but she didn't feel it in her shorts. Nervousness tingled through her. What was she going to do if she got into trouble and needed to call someone? She glanced desperately at Josh. She couldn't let him out of her sight. He was her only chance at getting home. Was that part of his plan? Was he trying to isolate her from her family and friends? If so, she'd fallen right into it. He glanced down at her and pushed his eyebrows together.

"You all right?"

Katie shook her head. "I think I should probably go home."

"If that's what you wish." Josh leaned forward and kissed the top of her head. "Give me just a minute. There's something I need to do." Without another word, he disappeared into the crowd.

Katie felt her heart sink as he vanished, and she scanned the crowd desperately trying to find him. Her palms started to sweat, and her chest felt tight. The urge to go to the bathroom overtook her, but she was too afraid to get out of her seat. A hand gently touched her arm. She spun around in her chair, hoping Josh had come back. A young man dressed in khaki shorts and a pink button up shirt stood before her. His hair was slicked back with gel, and his brown eyes were red and glassy. He sucked his drink through a straw for several moments before smiling at her.

"Americano?" he asked. His voice was rich and full of bass.

Katie nodded.

"Hablas español?"

Katie didn't speak Spanish, but she knew enough to know what the young man was asking. She shook her head, then glanced anxiously around the room to see if Josh was heading back.

The man moved closer. His body touched her arm. Katie tried to shrink away, but there was nowhere for her to go. The bar was behind her and other patrons sat next to her.

"You want to go somewhere more quiet?" The man's voice was thick with an accent, his breath reeked of alcohol. He was so close to Katie, the smell burned her nostrils.

She plastered on a smile and tried to be as nice as possible. "No, thank you. I'm waiting for someone."

The man took another long sip of his drink. He had to move back from Katie to accomplish the task, and she was thankful to get away from him. He swayed slightly as he finished the liquid and leaned forward to put the glass on the bar.

"I can be your friend." He smiled slyly and his eyes glazed over.

Katie's discomfort grew deeper. She had no experience rejecting guys in bars, and this one was obviously incredibly drunk. She didn't want to offend him and cause him to become belligerent, but she also wanted him to go away. Where was Josh? She really needed his help.

The guy grabbed her hand. "C'mon. We go someplace quiet." He pulled her with such force, she slid out of the seat.

Katie tried to jerk out of his grasp, but he held on too tightly. She attempted to plant her feet onto the ground and pull away, but he was too strong. He jerked her forward, and she had to take a step to keep from falling on her face. The momentum was all he needed to get her moving forward. Katie fought as best as she could, but she couldn't get out of his grasp. Her eyes darted around the room, desperately looking for someone to help, even if it wasn't Josh. They had to notice that she was being dragged off against her will. Maybe she should scream, maybe that would get him to let her go. Then again, maybe no one would hear her. The club was incredibly loud. Using her free hand, she clawed at the man's fingers, trying to get him to let her go. He ignored her gestures and tightened his grip on her wrist. Pain radiated up her arm. He had a hold of the arm that had the stitches in it.

They snaked through the crowd toward the back of the club. Where was he taking her? Even if she could get away, where was she going to go? The crowd would be impossible to get through, and if she got onto the street, she had no idea where to run. She looked for a bouncer or some type of club security. Perhaps they could help her. What did they look like? She envisioned that they would have dark suit coats and things in their ears, but she didn't notice anyone that matched the description. Her heart leapt into her throat. How was Josh going to find her?

The crowd thinned and the thump of the music lessened. Katie noticed they were in a hall, surrounded by neon lights that cast an eerie blue and red hue on the people standing around there. Doors lined either side of the hall. Where was she? Her imagination ran wild, and all she could think was that something sinister was behind those doors. Beds or torture chambers. She'd watched TV shows where cops investigated murders in clubs like this, and inevitably behind the doors was a sadomasochism chamber. Katie didn't want to go in there. She wanted to be back home, safe in her room. She was sure she would never see it again. This guy was going to chain her up, have his way with her, and kill her. She made one last desperate tug to get away, but it was fruitless. He wasn't going to let her go anywhere.

He stopped at a door on the right and turned to Katie. His lips curled into a sneer, and he reached for the handle. Katie squeezed her eyes shut and said a silent plea in her head. She apologized to Wes, Randy, and her mom in her thoughts, wishing she could be there in person to let them know she had been a fool.

"What do you think you're doing?" The voice was familiar, and Katie's eyes shot open. Josh stood next to her, his hands on his hips, anger shrouding his face.

The man dropped her hand and stepped backward. Katie positioned herself behind Josh.

"Nothing, man. I didn't realize she was here with someone."

"Well, she is." Josh snarled. "And if you want to party with her, you have to pay."

Katie's jaw fell open. What did Josh say? Was he pimping her out? Surely she misunderstood. Her ears were ringing from the music, so she didn't hear correctly.

The man straightened up;, the look of fear vanished from his face. He looked Katie up and down, licking his lips.

"How much?"

Josh gestured toward the room. "Shall we talk inside?"

The man responded by opening the door and stepping inside. Josh followed behind. Katie didn't want to go in, but she also didn't want to be left out in the hall alone. Who knew what was going to happen out there? She grabbed Josh's arm and stayed behind him. The room was decorated with a couch and a bar. The music from the club played overhead, but it wasn't deafening. Katie's heart thudded in her ears, bile rose in her throat.

Josh turned to Katie and gestured toward her with an open palm. "Te gusta lo que ves?"

Once again, the man's eyes drifted up and down Katie. She felt exposed, dirty. Her skin crawled as his gaze took her in. She wanted to cover herself, crawl into a ball. What was Josh doing? Why was he putting her in this situation? The man nodded.

"Cuánto?"

Josh rubbed his hands together. "Tu alma."

The man blinked several times and stared at Josh. "My soul? Is this some kind of joke?"

Josh shook his head. "You want her, you give me your soul."

He laughed and pointed a finger at Josh. "You Americans. Such jokesters."

Josh set his mouth in a firm line. "I'm not kidding."

The man held his hands out to his sides, the amusement still on his face. "Fine. Take my soul. If that's all it takes."

Josh stepped forward, his hand raised in front of him.

Katie shook herself out of her stupor. She grabbed Josh's arm and spun him around. Anger coursed through her veins; heat rose to her face. She spoke between clenched jaws. "Just what do you think you're doing?"

"Don't worry. He's so drunk he'll pass out as soon as I take his soul. You won't have to do anything." He winked at her.

"Take me home. Now."

"In just a sec. I have something to collect first." Josh approached the man and placed his hand on his chest.

Katie turned away as he collected the soul, only turning back around when she heard something thump onto the floor. The man lay in a heap, breathing heavily. Smiling a self-satisfied smile, Josh opened a portal on the other side of the room. Katie stomped toward it and stepped through with a huff.

CHAPTER 20

THE MUSIC STILL BLARED as Katie stepped into her room. The first thing she did was turn it down. Her ears couldn't take any more obnoxiously loud music. Josh stepped into the room behind her. She folded her arms across her chest and faced him, her lips pursed and eyes narrowed. He plopped onto her bed and stared at her.

"What?"

Katie's jaw threatened to fall open; her eyes wanted to grow wide, but she wouldn't let her surprise overtake her anger. Did he really not know why she was mad at him? The half-smile on his face told her he was playing dumb, which irritated her even more.

"What would have happened if he wasn't so drunk he passed out? What did you expect me to do?" Katie had a hard time keeping her voice under control, but she didn't want to alert her mom that something was going on. "He could have raped me."

Josh shrugged a shoulder. "You had nothing to worry about. I had eyes on you the whole time." He laid back on the bed, propping himself up on one of his elbows. "Honestly, I thought Wes would show up to rescue you. I was kind of counting on it."

Katie smashed her teeth together so hard her jaw ached. The bastard! Once again, he was just using her to get what he wanted. He didn't care about her. He was only concerned with furthering his own needs, getting what he wanted. The scene on the beach, right before he kissed her, was another of his lies to make her feel needed and wanted. She was such a fool. She balled her hands into fists. She had obviously miscalculated her ability to draw his focus away from Wes.

Josh smirked. "You wouldn't have had to do anything with him. I would have protected you. I did protect you."

"You put me in that situation. You left me at the bar while you traipsed off to do God knows what. I didn't even know where I was!"

An evil smile crossed Josh's lips. "Not even God knows what I went off to do." He turned his gaze to the bed and picked at a string. "Like I said, there was nothing to worry about. I had you in my sights the whole time. I knew what I was doing."

"So you purposely left me there as bait. You knew that guy was going to do that to me."

"Hey, you do what you gotta do to get a soul. It was worth it. One less heathen soul on planet Earth."

Katie's knees felt weak and she sunk to the floor. Was Josh really being that callous? Katie knew she shouldn't dwell on the what-ifs, but she was still shaken by the experience. So many horrible things could have happened to her. Yes, Josh stopped them from happening, but she wouldn't have been in the situation if it wasn't for him. Her throat constricted, and breathing became difficult.

"But wasn't it a rush?" He leaned forward on the bed. "Didn't the excitement make you feel alive?"

Katie stared at him. Was this guy for real? How was that exciting? Perhaps as a demon there was little that got his adrenaline pumping, but being scared half to death was not Katie's idea of a good time. She didn't answer his question. The smile fell off his face.

"You're going to have to get used to it, Katie. If you're going to help me gather souls, you're going to have to get your hands dirty."

Katie swallowed thickly. "Help you gather souls?" The words barely left her mouth.

Josh slid off the bed and sat next to her on the floor. He draped his arm across her lap and laid his head on her shoulder. "It's pretty obvious which one of us you've chosen. There are duties involved with picking a side." His voice was barely over a whisper, his breath tickled her earlobe.

Katie's stomach lurched. Inadvertently, she had chosen a side. She hadn't realized that was what was happening at the time. She thought she was gathering information, figuring out what was going on, but it was more than that. She'd gotten into a huge fight with

Wes, and left him to go with Josh. His words were so convincing, and he seemed so sincere. Katie was able to overlook his evil tendencies because of his truthfulness. He made her feel important, like she mattered. Had Katie known this was something she was going to have to do, she would have avoided Josh all together. She would have told him to stay in Hell. Or would she?

At the reservoir, she knew Josh was going to take Paul's soul. Same thing in the club. And she did nothing to stop him either time. She could have intervened, told them to run away, told Josh to find someone else, but she stood back, shocked at first and then so angry she couldn't bear to watch. In both cases, she'd done nothing to stop it, as if the act of taking a soul was an everyday occurrence, normal.

Katie probably should have felt bad for the two guys, but she didn't. Yeah, Paul may have been able to get some help and kick his pill habit, turned into a decent human being, but maybe he wouldn't. Maybe he would turn into a junkie and start robbing and killing people for money to get drugs. Katie didn't know what his future held. The same thing could be said about the guy in the club. Katie had been afraid for her life; she had no idea what the man's intentions were. She could probably guess that he wouldn't relent until he got what he wanted. Her attempts to get away had been futile and he hadn't minded putting her in pain to get what he wanted. That was obvious in how tightly he'd held onto Katie's wrist. Perhaps he was also destined for something far worse. Maybe he had already done something horrible. For all she knew, Josh did the world a favor by harvesting their souls. Although she wasn't really sure what happened to them after he swallowed them. Both men obviously weren't dead. Did they continue to live their lives doing evil deeds until they died? That was something Katie was going to have to find out.

If Katie picked Wes's side—if he had given her a reason to pick his side—there was no doubt in her mind she would have to help him defeat Josh. From the story Randy told her, she would be expected to kill. Sure, it would have been demons that she destroyed, but murder was still murder. Maybe Wes and his dad justified it as self-defense, but how would Katie sleep at night knowing she had taken a life? Both sides had their unsavory aspects.

As much as she wanted to be a neutral party, she no longer was. That had been taken away from her when she walked out of the warehouse alive.

"Now, I can't promise you every time will go as smoothly as tonight did," Josh whispered into her ear. "There may be times you need to take things a little further, push the person deeper into sin. But I can promise you I won't let them harm you."

Katie huffed and placed her hand on the bandage on her arm.

He wrapped his arm tighter around her waist and pulled her into his body. His lips brushed gently against her neck. "I'll train you. Show you ways to make sure you stay safe. But there is another alternative. A way to ensure that no harm will ever come to you."

Katie craned her head to look at him. "How?"

"You become a demon."

The breath left her body for a brief second. "What?"

His lips touched her neck again, moving slowly toward her earlobe. "It's really simple. You just have to give me your soul, then be reborn into darkness."

Katie's heart fluttered in her chest, her hands became clammy. Had this been Josh's plan all along? Once he figured out he couldn't—or wouldn't—kill her, he was going to change her into what he was? She didn't want to die, she knew that. She was only seventeen; she had her entire life ahead of her. Her head spun, and black dots appeared in front of her eyes. She forced herself to take deep breaths to keep from passing out.

Josh straightened up beside her. "It's a lot to take in. I understand your hesitation. I'll give you some time to think about it."

Katie didn't know what to say. Everything seemed to be spinning out of control. Nothing made sense. Why couldn't she tell him she didn't want to be a demon? She didn't, did she? No, that wasn't who she was, was it? Her head ached. Squeezing her eyes shut, she attempted to clear her mind.

"I will tell you this, though." Josh moved some hair behind her ear. "The next time Wes comes around to interfere with our plans, we're going to take him down."

Katie stared down at her lap. "Wes won't be an issue any more. You don't have to worry about him."

Josh cocked his head to the right. "What do you mean?"

Katie's shoulders slouched and she looked Josh in the eye. "We had a falling out. A fight. I'm fairly certain he doesn't like me anymore. I doubt he'll come to my rescue again."

Josh cocked his right eyebrow upward. "I guess we'll just have to wait and see about that, won't we?"

Katie shrugged. "I guess."

There was no sense trying to convince Josh what had happened. He had to see for himself and she was too tired.

Josh cupped her cheek in his hand and smiled. He pulled her face close to his and kissed her lips gently. "I'll see you tomorrow. Perhaps we can find another soul to take."

Katie forced a smile. "Perhaps."

She said it so he would leave. The thought of finding another soul turned her stomach. She didn't want to be used like that again.

Josh kissed her quickly one last time before standing from the floor. He opened a portal and stepped through, keeping his gaze on Katie until he disappeared.

Katie leapt from the floor and headed for the bathroom, jumping in the shower, hoping the hot water would wash away all of the ickiness that clung to her. Visions of the day's events ran through her mind, causing her to gag. Why hadn't she done more? Was there more she could have done? Surely she could have handled the situation with Wes better. She didn't need to get so angry with him and push him so far away. Her thoughts drifted to the numerous times he had left her hanging after promising to be there. The images of crying herself to sleep or staring longingly out the window awaiting his approach flooded her mind. She admitted she probably hadn't handled the situation with Wes the best she could have, but cutting ties with him was the best possible outcome. She couldn't stand the heartache anymore. Was taking Josh's side a better alternative? Probably not. It had its share of heartaches and headaches, but at least Josh was right next to her. Sure he put her in danger and could have gotten her killed, but it hadn't happened. He had saved her before it happened. He was there.

That thought wasn't comforting. Nothing about what had just transpired made her feel good. She wanted to have a relationship with a boy that didn't result in her being abandoned or used as bait to lure in sinners. Was there middle ground? She didn't think so. Even Deb had relationships that were hard work and inevitably ended in hard feelings. And Deb was liked by pretty much everyone. There seemed to be good times, moments when nothing else mattered but being with the other person, looking into their eyes and feeling comfort in their arms. At least Katie thought—hoped—those moments existed. With Deb, they usually occurred at the beginning of the relationship. Katie had never experienced them for herself. Well, she thought she'd experienced a version of them with Josh, but there was the underlying issue of him being a demon. Still, she couldn't get the look he gave her on the beach out of her mind. For a brief moment, she'd thought she had seen real emotion, real caring in his face. Maybe she was trying to justify things in her mind, but if he didn't care, would he really have saved her from that guy at the club? Probably, since he was after the guy's soul. He shouldn't have put her in that situation in the first place.

It wasn't too late. There was still a chance she could tell Josh where to go. She didn't have to be on a side. If both Josh and Wes were out of the picture, she could truly be on neutral ground again. That's where she really wanted to be. But if that happened, she'd never be able to see if Josh could be saved. There was a chance, she knew it. She had seen it in his eyes on the beach. Yeah, he had put her in danger, but he'd also saved her. He was a demon, but he could be so much more, and maybe Katie was the one to save him.

She stamped her foot on the floor of the tub and shoved her face under the water. She was so tired of thinking about these things and trying to figure out what was going on. She needed someone to talk to, someone who had experience with this kind of stuff. Mentally she crossed her fingers that Deb's grandmother would be willing to talk to her. If not, she'd have to go with Plan B, and that was talking to a priest. She hadn't been to church since she was little, before her dad died. Afterward, Mom had said it made her too sad to walk through the doors and had stopped going.

Katie wasn't opposed to talking to a priest; she just wasn't sure exactly what she wanted to say. She didn't want to be judged for straying and taking the side of evil. Oh, God! What if Deb's grandmother refused to talk to her because of her indiscretions? Katie felt bad for the things that had happened, but she didn't feel horrible. Did that make her a bad person? Would no one help her because of her choices? She leaned her head against the tiles in the shower. There was one person who would be able to help her with this issue, one person who, when he was around was a great listener, but Wes was out of the picture. The emptiness in her chest felt larger.

Despite the multitude of Wes's failings, he was a superb listener. When he was around, Katie could tell him anything. He always had the best advice, too. If Katie missed anything about him, it was that. She hadn't realized how much she'd relied on him until he was gone. If she really wanted, she could suck up her pride and apologize. She could tell him that she knew he was only acting in her best interest and she was being stubborn. But why should she? That would put her right back into the same situation she had been in before where Wes would feel free to break her heart and treat her like crap. He told her he didn't trust her, and she no longer trusted him. How could they be anything without that? She wasn't going to be sucked back in to Wes's game. For her sanity, she couldn't be. This was her one chance to get out. She had to take it.

She shut off the water and grabbed a towel. Stepping out of the shower, she stared at herself in the mirror. The steam had fogged it up, so she couldn't see herself clearly, only her outline. Dark spots indicated where the features on her face were, but otherwise her reflection looked like a faceless shell. Was that how Josh saw himself? Just an empty husk that he dropped his true form into? From there he molded it into what he wanted it to look like. Would Katie do that if she took Josh up on his offer? She wiped the condensation away and stared at herself.

Why was she even contemplating taking him up on his offer? She didn't want to steal souls or become a demon. She didn't want to push people into sin. She didn't even know what college she wanted to go to. Her whole life lay ahead of her, and she wanted to explore the different possibilities that existed. Part of that exploration was getting involved with boys and figuring out how relationships worked. Was it her fault that a demon happened to be the first one besides Wes that paid her any attention? She was curious about that world, she could freely admit that, and she was happy to have the chance to explore it. If Wes stopped being a jerk long enough to let her in, she would gladly explore his side of the world too. But curiosity was as far as it went. She'd seen enough and experienced enough to know it could only get darker, the sins more horrific. After going to Hell with Josh and seeing a few of the things he did, she didn't want to see more. She could only imagine what Wes saw while fighting evil. Katie had her experiences, and now she was happy to take the knowledge and move on. She'd learned a lot in the process, but she didn't want to stay there forever. Unfortunately, Katie didn't think she had a choice in the matter. She highly doubted Josh was going to let her walk away.

Katie dried off and pulled on her pajamas. She headed back to her room and climbed into bed. The house was dark, quiet, so she glanced at the clock. 3:00 a.m. Wow. She was shocked it was that late. How had time flown so fast? How long had they been at the club? She wasn't tired at all, but she figured she should try to get some rest. Sunday was going to be a long day, especially if she had to devise a plan to get out of Josh's grip. She pulled the covers to her chin and stared at the ceiling.

Why wouldn't Josh let her go? There was nothing she could do or say that would hurt him. They could part ways and he could continue sucking souls from the world and she could finish high school and move on with her life. Neither one of them would lose anything. It would be beneficial to both of them. And the best part would be that Katie wouldn't have to lose her soul to Hell. As much as she didn't want to be a demon or involved with demons, she found it hard to resist Josh's charms. He was so attractive and he seemed to know exactly what Katie needed. He'd told her the truth about what he did and genuinely seemed to like her. But on the other side of that coin was the sinister. He'd used her and put her in harm's way. He could literally be the death of her if she wasn't careful.

Katie rolled on her side and placed her arm under her pillow. She had to cut things off with Josh. It was a simple as that. She would take the direct approach, tell him flat out that she was done. If that didn't work, she'd figure out a harsher method, maybe drive him away like she'd driven Wes away. It was in her best interest to cut all ties with both of them. After that, she would figure out a way to stop falling for boys that were bad for her soul.

Closing her eyes, she pushed the thoughts from her head and attempted to fall asleep. She would deal with the mess in the morning.

*   *   *

Sun pierced through the shades and hit Katie right in the face. Squinting and moaning, she rolled over and placed the pillow over her head. Why hadn't she closed the blinds the night before? Her head pounded, and her body was heavy with exhaustion. She didn't want to get out of bed. The clinking of dishes from the kitchen sounded through her door, and the scent of coffee drifted to her nostrils. With a huff, she pulled her head from under the pillow and stared at the clock. 10:05. It wasn't horrifically late or early, but Katie certainly didn't want to get out of bed yet. Her mom's voice drifted into her ears. Due to the distance and the fact that her door was closed, Katie couldn't tell what she said, but she found it odd her mom was talking. Who would she be talking to? A gruff male voice responded. Gritting her teeth, Katie threw off her covers and stomped downstairs. She had a pretty good idea who was in her house. What did he want? Was he coming to spread more lies about her and sway her mom to their side? Not this time. Katie was going to stop it before it got out of hand.

She stood in the doorway of the kitchen and folded her arms across her chest. Randy sipped his coffee and stared at her over the rim of his mug. His eyes were bloodshot and dark circles shadowed his cheeks. His hand shook as he drank. A sinking feeling entered Katie's stomach. Something had happened. She sensed it. Her mom walked across the kitchen and embraced her in a hug. It felt great to be in her arms, but there wasn't time for this. What was going on?

"What's he doing here?" she asked her mom softly.

Mom pulled away and stared at Katie. "He's hoping you know where Wes is."

CHAPTER 21

KATIE'S STOMACH KNOTTED and her eyebrows pushed together. Randy took another sip of his coffee and continued to stare at her. What was he trying to do? Make her feel guilty for being so mean to Wes? It wasn't going to work. Wes had put her through hell since kindergarten. Once she had the courage to stand up to him and this was how they treated her? Like a criminal. She hadn't done anything wrong! If Wes ran off, that was his problem, not Katie's. It wasn't her fault he couldn't handle rejection.

"Why would I know where Wes was?" She tried to keep her voice calm. Anger seethed just below the surface.

Mom moved some hair behind her shoulder and patted her arm. "We thought maybe he contacted you and let you know where he was going."

Her gaze turned to her mom, her mouth fell open in surprise. "Did you not see what happened in this kitchen last night? Do you really think Wes is going to talk to me after that?" She gestured toward Randy. "Why didn't he tell his dad where he was going?"

With an unsteady hand, Randy set his mug on the counter. "After leaving here, he said he needed to get some air. He wanted to cool off. He never came home."

"So then why do you think he came and told me where he went?"

"He sensed a...um...disturbance. And came back to investigate." Randy raised his eyebrows, as if Katie was supposed to pick up on his hidden meaning.

Katie realized he referred to the portal. Randy must have thought he'd followed her and Josh to their destination. He could have; Katie didn't know. She hadn't seen him anywhere, but that didn't mean he wasn't lurking in the shadows. Maybe one of the locals found him and did something with him. If Katie had known where Josh took her, she could inform Randy and he could conduct his own investigation. Or if he really wanted to know, he could head through the portal and figure it out himself. He had more options at his fingertips than asking Katie what was going on, especially since she really didn't know.

Mom placed her hand on the middle of Katie's back. "See, honey, he still cares about you. Wes came back to make sure you were all right."

Katie rolled her eyes and continued to stare at Randy. "I didn't see him last night. I honestly don't expect to ever see him again. I'm fairly certain our friendship is over."

Randy averted his eyes to his coffee cup. "That could very well be. He hasn't spoken to me about what's been going on." He raised his head and met Katie's gaze. "But this isn't like him. Even with how angry he was. Something has happened to him."

Katie threw her hands out to her sides. "What do you want me to do about it? Can't you use your divine influence to find him? I know you can track where we went. Just do that and see if Wes was there."

"Went, Katie? What are you talking about?" The confusion was apparent in Mom's tone.

Katie huffed and turned to her mom. "Josh and I went out last night, Mom."

"Where did you go?"

Katie shrugged. "I don't know. Some club."

"But how could that be? You were in your room, listening to music. No one came to the house." Mom's eyes searched Katie's face, as if the answer would be written there.

Katie really wanted to tell her mom what had happened with Josh, but she couldn't. Mom wouldn't believe her. It was best to leave things as they were, to let Mom's mind make up any story it wanted to explain Katie's disappearance. In the end, it would make things so much easier than trying to get her to believe the truth.

She tightened her grip on Katie's arm and turned her to face her straight on. "Why are you still seeing that boy? I thought I told you to stay away from him."

Katie tried to wiggle out of her mom's grasp, but she held on too tightly. Her nails dug into Katie's flesh. She grabbed at her mom's fingers to lessen the grip. "Ow! You're hurting me."

Suddenly, her mom released her grip and laughed. Had she completely lost her mind? She tossed her head back and let the maniacal sound shake her entire body. Katie stepped back, wondering what in the world was going on. She glanced at Randy. His eyes widened. He stepped forward, reaching into his back pocket as he did. He wasn't fast enough. With lightning quick speed, Mom was across the kitchen and had her hand around Randy's neck. She slammed him into the counter.

"Mom!" Katie would have run forward to do something, but her legs wouldn't obey her commands. All she could do was stare in horror as the scene unfolded in front of her.

Randy grabbed the mug from the counter and slammed it into Mom's head. Pieces clattered onto the kitchen floor; her mom stumbled backward slightly, lowering Randy so he could get his toes on the linoleum. He clawed at Mom's hand, trying to get her to release her grip. Katie felt the urge to punch Randy in the face. How could he whack her in the head like that? But she still couldn't move. And something really wasn't right. Randy wasn't Katie's favorite person; she would like to attack him too, but where did her mom get that kind of strength? She had just lifted a full grown man off the floor and carried him several feet. That wasn't natural. Katie glanced around the room, looking for a weapon. She didn't want to hurt Mom, but she needed to get her away from Randy.

Mom recovered from the blow to the head and slammed Randy into the counter again. He grunted in pain, and the clawing at her hand weakened. Mom smiled, then tossed him across the room into the fridge. He hit, then slid to the floor. His head shot up immediately, but he had trouble pushing his weight up on shaky arms. Katie intervened. She placed herself between Randy and her mom, holding her hands out to her sides to make herself appear larger.

"Leave him alone!" Katie yelled.

Mom snarled and continued to move forward. She grabbed Katie around the neck and lifted her from the ground.

The air left Katie's lungs, and pain radiated through her neck. Feebly, she kicked at her mother's chest. She landed a few, but they were in vain. The grip tightened. From somewhere behind her, a low, growly bark sounded. Black dots danced in front of Katie's eyes, but she was able to see Mom snarl once again before Katie was dropped to the floor. Sucking in deep breaths, Katie couldn't get oxygen into her body fast enough, and it felt like broken glass tore at her throat. Her vision returned, and she watched Mom walk across the floor toward Randy. He had gotten himself to his knees, using the fridge as support.

Mom grabbed the back of his hair and helped him up. Once again, Katie glanced around the kitchen for a weapon. Irritation and panic gripped her chest. How many knives did they have in that house? And she couldn't find one of them. Her back was against a cupboard, so she threw it open, planning to use whatever she could find. Inwardly, she hoped she wasn't against the cupboard that held the grocery bags and dish soap. Those probably wouldn't be much help. She reached in and grabbed the first thing she felt. Leaping to her feet, she raised the frying pan over her shoulder and swung with all her might. A dull thud sounded as the metal contacted the side of her mom's head, causing her eyes to roll in their sockets. Mom's grip loosened on Randy and she stumbled slightly but didn't go down. Thank goodness it wasn't a bottle of soap.

Randy used the momentum shift to his advantage. He slammed his shoulder into her chest and shoved. Mom lost the rest of her balance and splatted onto the linoleum. Randy scrambled on top of her, reaching for her flailing arms as she punched and scratched at his face. Without thinking, Katie stepped forward and grabbed her mom's right arm, pinning it to the floor while Randy finally got a hold of the left. Mom attempted to rear up and bite, but Randy was planted firmly on her chest. Mom howled. The sound rattled Katie's skull, threatening to explode her eardrums. She desperately wanted to cover her ears, but she knew she couldn't let the arm go. She gritted her teeth. The frying pan was right next to her. If she could get a hold of it and smash it into her mom's face, that would stop the sensory onslaught. Katie adjusted herself so her knees were on her mom's arm and one hand was free. As she reached for the pan, something slammed into her back and knocked her over.

Mom jerked out of her grasp, sending Katie sprawling on the floor, a weight perched on her back. She glanced over her shoulder. Her gaze was met with white pointy teeth dripping with drool. Hell Hound! Katie rolled quickly to her side, throwing the dog onto the floor, and reached for the pan. Still on her back, she readied to whack the Hound if it came after her. It scrambled to its feet but didn't attack. Mom was in a sitting position, her arms once again grabbing for Randy's neck, but they weren't reaching their target. Plunged into Mom's chest, up to the hilt, was a gold knife with a cross-shaped handle. A gurgling sound escaped her lips, and black ooze flowed from the wound. The Hound at Katie's side growled and lunged forward. Just as it was about to sink its teeth into Randy's arm, Katie brought the pan down on its head. With a whimper, it sprawled onto the floor, legs sticking out at its sides. With a quickness Katie didn't think possible, Randy reached into his pocket and pulled out a vial of water. The droplets hit the dog and smoke appeared. The creature squealed, then exploded.

Outside came the sounds of baying dogs. Randy glanced around, wide-eyed. Katie pushed herself into a sitting position. Leaping to his feet, Randy grabbed Katie's arm and pulled her to the door. Cracking it open, he stared out.

"We're not going to be able to make it on foot." He closed the door and turned to Katie. "Do you know where your mom's keys are?"

Katie turned to the table behind her and grabbed them. She held them up for Randy to see. With a nod, he pushed past her and grabbed for the handle on the garage door. Once again, he cracked it open and peered inside. Growling sounded. Randy slammed it shut. Barking and scratching resounded from the other side. Randy turned to Katie, his face red with exertion.

"There's only one that I can see." He moved away from the door and indicated toward it with his head. "You throw it open, I'll hit it with the Holy Water."

Katie grabbed the handle. The door shook and vibrated beneath her grasp as the Hell Hound attempted to get through. Her eyes stayed on Randy. He pulled the lid off the vial and positioned himself near the door. He nodded, and Katie opened the door a crack. The dog's snout exploded through, followed by the head. Using all of her weight, Katie pushed against the door, stopping the Hound from getting farther into the house. Randy wasted no time and splashed the water into the dog's nose. It yelped, then backed into the garage. A pop sounded as the creature exploded.

Katie threw open the door and rushed into the garage. Randy hobbled behind her. She climbed in the front seat and turned the car on. Randy barely had his door closed before Katie put the vehicle in reverse. She tapped her hand impatiently on the steering wheel, waiting for the door to lift fully.

"Head to my house," Randy instructed. "We'll be safe there."

Katie squealed the tires as soon as she was clear. She didn't even take the car out of reverse and angled it toward Randy's house. His car and Wes's truck were in the driveway, so she pointed the car at the lawn. She tried to avoid the mailbox, but she wasn't that lucky. More baying and barking sounded throughout the neighborhood. When she had a chance, she glanced out the windshield. Hundreds of dogs had converged on their position, their jaws snapping open and shut, drool flying from their mouths. They all looked like the dog Katie had seen earlier – black and brown German shepherds. Katie threw the car into park and pulled the key out of the ignition. Throwing her shoulder into the door, she pushed it open then ran for the house. Somehow, Randy was already on the porch with the door open, waving for Katie to get inside. She barreled through the opening and slid on the tiles in the foyer. The door slammed behind her.

Panting, Katie turned to Randy. "Why didn't you just use a portal?"

Randy walked past her and headed for the living room. He flopped onto the couch, a grimace covered his face. Katie stood before him, her hands on her hips.

"I couldn't. I couldn't risk another demon coming through. They knew where I was. It was a planned attack."

Katie didn't know if that was true or not, she knew so little about portals. She figured they could be used whenever, wherever. It was yet another question to put on her list.

Randy leaned forward, his eyes squeezed shut. Pain pinched his face. Katie wasn't overly fond of the guy, but she also didn't want to see anyone in that much pain. She knelt down in front of him.

"Can I get you something?"

He shook his head and held his arm out in front. A portal opened in the living room. Katie stared at it for a moment. How come he could open one here? He grabbed Katie's arm and attempted to pull himself up. Katie wrapped her arms around his shoulders and lifted him to his feet.

"Get me into the light," he wheezed. "But I'll need you to stay here."

Katie did as he instructed, and the light vanished behind him. She glanced around the room nervously. How long was he going to be gone? Where had he gone? What should Katie do until he got back? A howling dog drew her attention to the window. She glanced out onto the street. The dogs lined the sidewalk and the neighbor's yards, just outside the boundary of Wes and Randy's property. Some paced back and forth, their tongues hanging out of their mouths, their eyes locked on the house. They may have looked like regular dogs, but Katie knew they weren't. Right behind the eyes she saw the whiteness that indicated they were Hell Hounds. She shivered. It all became clear what Randy was talking about when he said they were going to be overrun with strays. Josh must have brought them as sentinels to keep an eye on things. They could travel anywhere and no one would pay them any attention. Even now if someone called Animal Control, what were they going to do? The dogs vastly outnumbered them and probably wouldn't think twice about tearing them to shreds.

Wes and Randy's property must have been holy ground. That would be the only explanation of why the dogs weren't attempting to get into the house. It made sense, given that they were Praesuls. They would need somewhere safe to sleep at night. That might also explain why Randy was able to open a portal here. Demons couldn't come through onto holy ground. She chewed on her thumbnail as she stared at the dogs. What were they going to do?

A light flashed behind her and Randy stepped into the room. His shoulders were back, his head was held high. The bruises were gone from his face, the cuts faded into scars. Katie sucked in a sharp breath. The light faded behind Randy, and he placed his hands on his hips.

"How many are out there?" He indicated toward the window.

"More than you can handle." Katie folded her hands over her chest. "Where's my mom? Is she..." Katie couldn't bring herself to say the word.

Randy shook his head. "No. I'm guessing she's in the same place as Wes. And I guarantee you Josh took them both."

Disbelief surged through Katie. "Why would he do that? He promised me he wouldn't hurt my mom."

Randy shrugged. "And I'm sure he fulfilled that part of his promise. The next time you see him, I'm sure he'll tell you no harm came to your mother. But he needed her out of the way so he could replace her with a demon and go after me."

"How do you know he was going after you?"

Randy dropped his hands to his sides. "He won't do anything to hurt you. He thinks you're on his side. He wants to stop me from turning you against him."

"Is he going to give her back?"

Randy shrugged. "I honestly don't know. He'll keep her for as long as he needs to get what he wants. If he feels he's losing you, he might use her to sway you back to his side."

Katie's chest felt tight; it was hard to breathe. Her knees felt weak and she sunk to the floor. Her head spun. This wasn't how this was supposed to go. Josh wasn't supposed to go after her family, especially her mom. Mom didn't know what was going on; she had no way to defend herself. This was all Katie's fault. She should have never gotten involved with him. She should have listened to Wes and Randy, and then her mom would be safe. She had to make this right. Taking a deep breath, she climbed back to her feet.

"Where did he take them?" Katie didn't even try to keep the anger out of her voice.

"I don't know. There's only one person who does know, and you need to contact him."

"How? I don't have my phone."

"Where is it?"

Katie pointed out the window. "At my house."

"You'll need to get it."

Katie huffed. "Right. With all those dogs out there? You're crazy."

"They won't hurt you."

"How do you know?"

"Because Josh won't let them. Me, they would tear apart in a second. But they are there to watch over you, to keep you safe."

Katie stared at him for a moment, unbelieving of what he told her. "Then why did the one knock me over in the kitchen at my house?"

"You were interfering, so it had to stop you. But notice it didn't actually attack you. It just moved you out of the way."

Katie glanced back out the window. Could she believe what Randy told her? Could she walk outside and not be attacked? Wasn't there a better way to get Josh's attention? She tapped her foot on the ground, trying to figure out what to do. If it had just been Wes that was missing, she probably would have told Randy to go after his son himself. Her mom was a different story. She needed to get her back. She unfolded her arms from her chest with force and stomped her foot on the ground.

"Fine. I'll get my phone. I just really hope you're right about this."

A small smile crossed Randy's lips. "Don't worry. Have faith."

On shaky legs, Katie headed for the front door. She opened it slowly and stepped onto the porch tentatively. Several of the dogs saw her approach and sat down. She stepped on the driveway. More and more dogs took a seat and stared at her, panting. If Katie didn't know better, she would have thought they wanted to play. As she got to the street, the dogs separated, opening up a path to her house. Without hesitation, Katie ran. She went into her room and grabbed her phone, then headed back to Randy's house. As soon as the door was closed behind her, she went to the window and stared out. The dogs paced and growled once again. Katie leaned against the wall and sighed. They could do whatever they wanted now that she was in the house. Thank goodness Randy had been right. She looked at him.

"Now what?"

"Send him a text. Tell him you want your mom back."

Katie typed the words into her phone, inwardly hoping this plan actually worked.

CHAPTER 22

SECONDS AFTER SENDING THE TEXT, Katie's phone rang. Josh's number flashed on the screen. Katie couldn't answer fast enough.

"What did you do with my mom?" Katie had no time for pleasantries.

Josh laughed. "She's safe. Don't worry. I promised you no harm would come to her and I meant that."

Katie glanced at Randy. He had been right about what Josh would say. Still, that didn't change the fact that he took her mom in the first place.

"I want her back. Now."

"You'll get her back, Katie. Don't worry. But we have some other things to discuss first. I assume you're with Wes's father."

"Yes."

"Good. I need you two to meet me. Remember the warehouse I tried to kill Wes in?"

Katie's throat constricted. "Sort of."

"Randy will know how to get here. Meet me in an hour." The phone went dead.

Katie stared at Randy. "He wants us to meet him in an hour."

"Where?"

"The warehouse."

Randy nodded. "Of course he'd want to meet there." He paced around the room. "He's trying to make a point."

"He's not going to hurt my mom, is he?"

Randy looked at her, his eyes turned down with sorrow. He took a deep breath. "He shouldn't. He likes you, wants you to be with him, so unless he feels threatened, she should be just fine."

Katie swallowed thickly. "What would make him feel threatened?"

"It's hard to say. Basically, if he thinks he's going to lose you, he'll bend you to his will by threatening your mother." Randy stepped forward and placed his hands on her shoulders. "I can guarantee her safety, but I have to know what I'm dealing with first. I know you probably don't know everything, but tell me what you do know."

Katie nodded absently, then took a seat on the couch. She rubbed her hands together. "Where should I start?"

Randy sat next to her. "From when you first met Josh and what he did."

Katie took a deep breath, then told Randy everything. In any other situation, she would have told Randy to leave her alone. Her relationship with Josh was none of his business, but her mom was involved. Katie may have been upset that her mom had hospitalized her and wouldn't listen to her, but it was still her mom. They had their ups and downs and arguments all the time, but Katie couldn't imagine being without her. Mom was all the family she had left. It would kill Katie if something happened to Mom and she never had the chance to work things out.

When Katie finished telling her story, she lowered her head and stared at her hands. Guilt coursed through her body. All of this was her fault. If she hadn't gotten involved with Josh, everyone would be safe. Still, she couldn't change any of it. Her only option was to fix it. How was she going to do that? It was one thing when her safety was compromised, but to have two other people depending on her? There was no way she was going to get her mom back.

Randy placed his hands over hers. "If Josh had wanted them dead, he would have already killed them. Since he didn't, he's after something else. We just have to find out what that is."

Katie looked at him. "What if that something else is me? You gonna hand me over?"

Randy squeezed her fingers. "We already know he wants you. He's done a pretty good job of tempting you to his side. You're the only one who can decide if you're going to stay with him. No, there has to be something else." His gaze drifted out the window as he lost himself in thought.

Not only did Katie feel horrible, now she felt like a failure. Randy didn't sound like he was accusing her of anything by being tempted by Josh, but the way he said it made her feel ten times worse. It was obvious she'd made the wrong decision. Did he really feel like he needed to rub it in? She pulled her hands out from under his. She couldn't stand to be touched by him. It only reinforced what a horrible person she had become. Randy turned his gaze from the window to her.

"You're not the first person to fall for a demon's temptations, and you won't be the last. Those last words came out pretty harsh, but that's not how I meant them. I'm not angry with you. I don't blame you. And the fact that you're willing to help get Wes and your mom back says a lot. I, personally, won't hand you over to Josh. But I can't make your decisions for you."

Katie nodded. That made her feel a little better, but not much. At least she didn't have to worry about him selling her out to Hell, but could she trust herself to make the right decision? What was the right decision? She'd have to wait to see how the situation presented itself and decide from there. That thought made her stomach queasy and her palms sweat. Her breathing came in rasps and she felt like she was going to pass out. How was she ever going to do this?

"We should head to the warehouse. I want to know exactly what I'm dealing with."

Katie nodded mechanically.

Randy opened a portal. Katie stood from the couch and stared at the light for a moment. It's for Mom, she reminded herself, then stepped through.

The warehouse looked exactly as she remembered it. Sunlight shone through the high windows, illuminating the dust and debris. Pools of dried blood stained the floor, and Katie shivered as she stared at them. It had only been a few days since she was last there, but with everything that had happened, it seemed like an entire lifetime had passed. Her stomach knotted, her hands were sweating profusely, and the desire to run out of the building coursed through her. She entered the space alone. Randy was convinced that Josh himself or his spies would be there, so he had taken a less conspicuous portal. Katie didn't see what the point was. Josh knew of Randy's existence, so why wouldn't he expect him to show up? Besides, it wasn't like they were that early. They had procrastinated a good forty-five minutes before heading to the warehouse.

Her limbs shook with nervousness and anticipation. She clenched her fists and took deep breaths to get herself under control. She wasn't afraid for herself. Josh wasn't going to do anything to hurt her. He'd had plenty of opportunities to do so and he didn't take them. She was scared to death for her mom, though. What would happen to her? The demons could do anything they wanted to her. A Tormentor could attach itself to her and force her to do horrible things. How was Katie supposed to stop that?

If she were honest with herself, she would admit she was afraid for Wes too. After all, he was the one Josh was after, and Josh probably wasn't going to let Wes leave alive. She had told herself many times that things would be so much easier if Wes wasn't around, but she didn't mean dead. Well, a few times she thought that would be the best solution, but now that she was witnessing it, she wasn't sure that's what she wanted. Her insides felt like they were being shredded. This was too much for her to handle, but she had to face it to save those she loved.

She paced around the open space, chewing on her nails, waiting for Josh's arrival. The pipe she had originally used against Josh still lay on the floor where she had dropped it. Her eyes drifted over it and she contemplated picking it up, but she didn't want to appear threatening. Who knew what would happen to her mom if Josh thought she was being defensive. No, the best way to deal with it was to see what Josh wanted first. She could stay close to the pipe, within a few arm's lengths, just in case she needed it.

Growling echoed through the space. Katie stiffened. Footsteps sounded all around her, and into the light walked Hell Hounds. They looked the same way they had the first time she saw them, skin and bones, not covered with their disguise to make them look like regular dogs. Several of them formed a circle around her. She spun to take them all in, inwardly wishing she had the pipe in her hand.

"You seem nervous, Katie."

Josh's voice caused Katie to spin abruptly, her breath catching in her throat. When had he gotten in the room? She didn't see a portal open. He smiled and held his arms out to embrace her. Katie remained where she stood. He pushed his bottom lip out in a pout.

"You aren't happy to see me?" He closed the distance between them and wrapped his arms around her. Her skin crawled. "I'm happy to see you."

Katie pushed him away. "Where's my mom?"

A pained look crossed his face. "She's fine. Just like I said she was."

"I want to see her."

Josh snapped his fingers and a portal appeared before them. A towering demon, close to eight feet tall, completely black, with large wings, shockingly white fangs, and piercing red eyes stepped through. In his arms was Katie's mom, dressed in her pajamas and limp, with eyes closed. Katie's heart leapt into her throat.

"Mom!" She tried to rush forward, but Josh grabbed her arm. Katie glared at him.

"She's just sleeping, Katie. No need to worry."

The demon set Mom down on the ground and crouched over her protectively. To Katie's confusion, the portal remained open. She turned a questioning gaze toward Josh.

"I assumed Randy would want to know how his son was doing." He glanced around the room. "Where is the man, by the way?"

Katie shrugged and shook her head.

"I know he came with you, Katie. Where is he?"

"I really don't know. My portal opened here, I don't know where his opened at." Her limbs tingled with nervousness. Something in Josh's tone told her things weren't going to be all right. It hinted at anger and irritation.

"Randy!" Josh's voice boomed off the warehouse walls. "Come out and join us!" He waited a few moments for a reply. When one didn't come, he continued. "If you want to see your son again, I suggest you come out and join us." He gestured toward the portal and another demon stepped out with Wes in his arms.

Wes wasn't unconscious like Katie's mom, but bound with black material that almost looked like cooled lava. He squirmed and writhed in the demon's arms. His mouth was covered with the black stuff to keep him from crying out. As soon as the demon was through, the portal closed. With a claw, the creature drew a line of blood from the side of Wes's skull. His face turned white, and a muffled cry barely broke through his gag.

"I'm here!" Randy called. "Stop hurting my son." He stepped out from the shadows on Katie's right, his hands up.

The Hell Hounds turned and curled their lips. They snapped as he walked by, but none of them attacked. Katie's heart thudded in her chest. What were they going to do now? Randy was supposed to be the backup if anything went wrong. With all of them captured, who was going to save them? As soon as he was next to Katie, the demon placed Wes on the ground and crouched over him like the first one. Josh nodded toward them.

"Why don't you join your son?"

Randy obeyed and stepped slowly across the room. When he was close, the demon grabbed his arms so he couldn't move.

Josh placed his arm around Katie's shoulders and turned so they both faced the prisoners. "I have to say, Katie, when you told me last night that Wes wasn't going to come to your rescue again, I thought you were lying to me. I didn't think there was any way Wes would give up on his beloved. Still, I was intrigued, so I decided to pay him a visit." Josh laughed. "I couldn't believe it, but he was broken!" He turned Katie to face him and ran his index finger over her cheek. "You did it, Katie. You broke him. When he lost you, he lost faith in everything." He leaned forward and kissed her gently on the lips. "And having a Praesul lose his faith is even better than having him killed."

Katie's entire body shook. Her stomach knotted. That hadn't been her intention. She didn't want Wes to lose everything. She just wanted him to know what it felt like to be abandoned by someone he loved. She wanted him to feel the pain and suffering she felt. Never once did she expect him to lose his faith.

Josh straightened up and stared at Katie harshly. "I have to say, though, I'm very disappointed you didn't tell me about his dad. It wasn't until last night when I went to check on Wes that I found out he was a Praesul too. That was kind of important information I needed to know."

Katie swallowed thickly. "I'm...uh...sorry. It never occurred to me that—"

Josh placed his finger on her lips. "It doesn't matter." He held his hand out toward them. "As you can see, I now have them both in my grasp. Besides, you can make it up to me later." He quickly kissed the tip of her nose and turned to the prisoners. Clapping his hands together, he stepped toward them. "Do you have any idea what I'm going to get for killing two Praesuls?" He glanced over his shoulder at Katie. "It's going to be amazing. Feel lucky to know me. It's been a long time since a demon has had this kind of success. We're going to be set for eternity!"

The world spun around Katie. Her chest was tight, and her limbs had gone numb. Unconsciousness threatened to take over. Her knees felt weak. There was nothing she could do. She was helpless. Her actions had gotten her mother kidnapped and was going to get two people killed. She mentally cursed herself for being weak and stupid. She wanted to curl into a ball and disappear. This was too much. Two huge demons stood before her, along with too many Hounds. She couldn't fight them all. Last time, she had barely been able to escape Josh's grasp, and Wes had been critically wounded. There was no getting out of this one.

"What about my mom?" The words croaked out of her mouth. If nothing else, she wanted to know that her mom was going to be safe. She was the innocent in all of this; she shouldn't pay for Katie's sins.

Josh glanced at the sleeping body. "She won't be hurt."

"Then let her go."

Josh clicked his tongue. "I can't do that. Not yet. She's still an insurance policy."

"For what?" Katie couldn't fight the weakness in her knees any longer. She sunk to the floor.

"To make sure you make the right decision."

Katie was pretty sure she knew the answer to her next question, but she wanted to hear it directly from Josh. "What's the right decision?"

He turned and cocked his head to the side, smiling. "That you stay with me forever."

Katie squeezed her eyes shut. That's what she thought he would say.

Josh stepped next to her and knelt down. He placed a hand on her shoulder, and Katie opened her eyes to look at him. "Don't you want to stay with me?" Sorrow covered his face.

Katie indicated toward her mom. "Not at the expense of my mother! If you really cared about me and wanted me to be with you, you wouldn't have to use threats against me. You would know I was going to make the right decision without being coerced into it."

Josh scrutinized her for a moment, then turned and looked at her mother. With a sigh, he nodded toward the demon. The creature lifted the limp body and opened a portal.

"Where are you taking her?"

"Back to her bed. She'll wake up and have no idea what happened."

The worry she felt for her mother lessened slightly. She wasn't exactly lying when she said she would stay with Josh. She enjoyed being in his company, as long as he wasn't using her to get what he wanted. He could be a really cool guy when he wanted to be. This gesture showed her that maybe she could change him down the road, help him see what it took to be more than a demon. A glimmer of hope sprung inside of her.

"I need you to do one thing for me. One tiny little thing. I showed you compassion by letting your mother go, now I need you to show me how much you really want to be with me."

"How?"

"I need you to kill Wes."

Katie's gaze drifted to the prisoners. They stared back at her. Katie would have assumed their eyes would be filled with pleading. They weren't. There wasn't even sadness or fear. If Katie had to describe the way they looked at her, she would say it was indifference.

CHAPTER 23

KATIE TURNED HER GAZE AWAY and stared at the ground. What else could she do? She had to ensure her mother's safety. Wes and Randy were Praesuls. They had to have a plan to get out of this. Surely it wasn't the first time they had faced such odds. Cracks ran through the concrete floor of the warehouse; an inch thick layer of reddish brown dirt covered the entire floor. Most of it was swirled and disturbed from the activity that had occurred in the area. Katie noticed she was right next to a large blood pool. It had been the place where she cradled Wes's head as he bled from his wounds and waited for the ambulance to arrive. He had faded in and out of consciousness. At the time, Katie hadn't been sure he was going to make it. She snorted. Where she sat was the place this whole mess had begun...and it was where it was going to end. Josh placed his hand under her chin and lifted her head so she looked him in the eye. Those beautiful blue eyes. If only she had known the evil they held. Still, something about them drew her in. There was adventure behind those eyes, experience, and she craved both of those.

"We don't have a lot of time," Josh said softly. "What's your decision?"

Katie's gaze didn't drift from the blue depths before her. "Untie him."

Confusion faded the smile on his face. "Why?"

"I'm not going to kill him while he's tied up. That's beyond cruel. He's not going to go anywhere. Your minions will make sure of that." She nodded around the room, indicating the Hell Hounds and winged demons.

Half of Josh's mouth pulled into a smile. "That's true." He stood and approached Wes.

Randy struggled against the demon's grasp as Josh got close. "Get away from him! Don't you dare touch him!"

Josh chuckled. "Or what? You're not in any kind of position to do anything."

Randy stopped moving and narrowed his eyes. "Trust me, demon, you don't want to know what will happen if you touch him."

Josh scoffed and fanned his hand at Randy. The big demon tightened his grip, squeezing some of the air out of Randy's lungs. Josh bent down and grabbed Wes's hair, pulling him into a sitting position. Wes struggled against Josh' grasp, but it was a fruitless endeavor.

"I highly suggest not even thinking about attempting to escape. My friends will tear you apart. And remember, she broke you, so it will be mercy for her to kill you." Josh grabbed the back of Wes's shirt and pulled him to his feet. When he was upright, he waved his hand over the bonds, which crumbled into dust and drifted to the floor.

Katie climbed to her feet. The room around her disappeared. Her vision focused on Wes and Josh. She stepped forward, attempting to walk with a confidence she didn't feel. What was she doing? How could she possibly conceive of killing another human being, especially Wes? Yeah, he had abandoned her and broke her heart multiple times, but it was Wes. She'd known him all her life. He was her first crush, her first kiss, her first everything, and she was going to end it for a demon she'd just met. Why was this happening? Shouldn't God do something to intervene? Why wasn't He protecting His chosen people?

The closer Katie got, the more she hoped lightning would strike through the roof and knock her dead. It would solve so many issues. Her eyes drifted upward and around the room. The sun shone harshly through the windows. Only the sounds of panting dogs and her footsteps filled her ears. Her gaze met Wes's. His face was still red, but Katie realized it wasn't from struggling against his bonds. Trails of tears lined his cheeks, his eyelids were puffy. Her heart skipped a beat.

"Don't do this." Randy said calmly, soothingly. "You have other choices. This isn't what you want."

Katie hesitated. He was right; this wasn't what she wanted. What she really wanted was to be in bed, sleeping, or at the mall with Deb. She wanted to be sitting on the couch watching TV with her mom. She wanted anything but to be stuck in a warehouse with demons and the possibility of death. At that moment, she would have taken being back in the hospital. But she couldn't change it. The option to turn around and walk out of the warehouse existed. She could turn her back and not take any side, go back to living a neutral life. But then she risked putting her mom's life in jeopardy. Josh already planned on using her against Katie, so he would more than likely do it again. Or go after Deb. Or any other of her friends and family. So what if Randy and Wes had to die? Didn't they say that sometimes the life of one was needed for the good of many? This was their chance to sacrifice themselves for the greater good. Katie hated that she had to be the one to do it. After that, she would find a way to get out of Josh's grasp. She would find other Praesuls, talk to priests, do whatever it took to free herself from evil. At least she hoped she would. Maybe she would enjoy what she was about to do. Perhaps the dark spot on her soul would take over her entire being. What if this was her destiny?

She regained her conviction and continued forward. When she was directly in front of Wes, he fell to his knees. His eyes never left her face. Tears flowed freely down his cheeks.

"Please, Katie." The words croaked out of him, coated in sorrow. "Show mercy and forgiveness. I'm sorry I hurt you. I never meant to. I only wanted what was best for you."

Katie reached forward and stroked Wes's hair. "I know." She spoke the words softly. "But it's too late to change things now."

Wes's gaze dropped to the floor.

The action should have brought some kind of emotion from Katie, but she found herself not feeling anything. Her whole body had gone numb, and she felt as if she was floating above the scene, watching it from a distance, not actively participating in it. She looked at Josh. A wide smile covered his face. He placed his hand on the back of Katie's head and kissed her passionately on the lips. Katie returned the gesture, wrapping her arms around his neck and losing herself in the moment. This was what her future held. It was best to enjoy and get used to it now.

When he released her, he reached behind his back and pulled something from his waist band. He held a matte black knife with a serpent handle out to her. She took it, aware that her limbs had stopped shaking. Was she so calm because this was what she was fated to be? Was her whole life leading up to this moment? Was it always ordained that she would betray her first love and turn to evil? Had there been any signs earlier in her life that would let her know what she was doing was right? Her mind drifted through her memories, trying to figure out when and where things had gone wrong. All she could think about was her mom. What would she say if she knew what Katie was doing? She would be so disappointed, so sad. Katie had failed her.

The knife shook in her hand. She gagged and turned away. She couldn't do it. No matter how much pain and suffering Wes caused, she couldn't take his life. Hadn't she done enough by breaking him? Surely he was putting himself through enough pain and suffering. Hands encircled her shoulders and her chest. Warm breath tickled her earlobe, and a sense of safety washed over her. She closed her eyes and allowed herself a brief moment of respite.

"You have to do this," Josh whispered. "You have to prove to me that you're all mine. One quick second and it will be done. If you want to be merciful, put the blade right in his heart. It will be quick and painless. End his suffering." He nuzzled against her neck.

She closed her eyes and pretended like all was right with the world. Her mind drifted back to the beach and the way Josh looked at her. The hope deep in her chest sparked.

Katie opened her eyes slowly and took a deep breath. "What if I can't?"

"Think of all the heartache he's caused. The lies. Focus on your anger and let it grow."

For once, Katie didn't want to. She was tired of thinking about the pain, tired of the tightness in her chest. She wanted it to end, but not like this. This wouldn't make the pain go away. This wouldn't undo years of tears and abandonment. It would possibly provide temporary relief, but in the long run, Katie was sure the guilt would consume her.

"If you need some motivation," Although Josh's voice was soft, it had an edge to it, "I can always have your mom brought back. I don't want to do that, Katie, so you had better prove you really want to be with me."

Katie's mouth went dry, her throat constricted. Visions of her mom lying in bed with a demon looming over her drifted through her mind. She had gotten her mom into this mess, so she had to get her out. Whatever Josh wanted, she would do, especially if it saved her mom.

"He's going to die either way. You decide if it's quick and painless or I torture him. And you will pay for deserting me. With your soul."

Katie turned and faced him. She placed her hand on his cheek. "I don't want to desert you. You need me."

Josh placed his hand over hers. "I do."

She turned her gaze from Josh to Wes. He had gained control of his emotions. His jaw muscles were tight, his eyes were hard. He climbed onto his feet and squared his shoulders.

"I'm not going to beg, Katie. And I'm done apologizing. I made my decisions and I can't change them. If I'm going to die in this warehouse, I want you to be the one to do it, not this beast." He spit the word at Josh.

Josh chuckled. "Valiant display of chivalry. It will serve you well in Heaven." He smirked. "And you'll be there momentarily." He nodded at Katie.

She tightened her grip on the knife and stepped forward. She was within an arm's length of Wes. It's for Mom, she told herself. Be brave. Be strong. She glanced again at Josh. He gave her an encouraging nod. Katie brought the knife back and stepped in close to Wes. She placed her hand on his shoulder for leverage. Clearing her mind, she tried not to think about what she was about to do. Her mom's face dominated her mind's eye. It was the only thing that would get her through what she needed to do. She brought her arm forward with all her might, but before the knife tip could penetrate his flesh, a blinding white light flashed through the room.

Katie was temporarily blinded, and the knife clanged onto the floor as she brought up her hands to rub her eyes. The sounds of growls and snarls echoed around the warehouse, followed by the scuffing of feet. She blinked and tried to clear her vision. A black blob floated in front of her, but the edges were clearing. She blinked a few more times. A dog rushed by her legs, catching her in the back of her knees and knocking her over. Her wrists and knees slammed into the concrete, and pain radiated through her body. Snarls and yips now sounded through the room. She turned to her left, where the sounds originated, and her vision cleared further. The demon who had had a hold of Randy wavered; his arms had been blown off, his chest and face oozed black liquid. Randy had a hold of his son, and the pair of them flicked water on the dogs around them. Explosions resounded.

"Don't let them escape!"

The knife! Katie needed to find the knife. It was unclear exactly what was going on, and with her eyesight slowly returning, it would be nice to have a little protection. On hands and knees, she felt around the floor, hoping her fingers would brush against the cool metal of the weapon.

Someone grabbed her arm and pulled her to her feet. The grip was soft but firm, so she figured it wasn't a demon. After several more blinks, her eyesight had almost completely returned. The person at the end of her arm came into focus. Wes pulled her across the room, and he had the knife in his hand. What was he planning on doing with that?

"NO!" Josh's voice rang through the warehouse.

To her left, Katie saw a portal open. Large black demons streamed through, followed by more Hounds. Josh charged toward Wes. He released his grip on Katie's arm and squared off to fight. Josh wrapped his arms around Wes's waist and drove him to the floor. Wes landed with a whump, the air left his lungs. Josh reared up to punch Wes in the head, but he never got the chance. As soon as his side was exposed, Wes jammed the knife into his flesh. Josh cried out and toppled to the side.

Katie watched the scene unfold as if it were happening in slow motion. Wes scrambled out from under the demon toward her. He made it a few steps before Josh reached out and grabbed his ankle. Wes went down to his knees and used his free foot to kick at Josh. Several Hounds jumped on Wes, grabbing his pant legs and arms.

Blood soaked through the material. The thought that Katie should help ran through her mind, but who was she going to help? All she could do was stand and stare. Josh pulled the knife from his side and raised it over his head. He was about to drive it into Wes's back when Randy appeared out of nowhere and kicked Josh in the face. He rolled to one side, blood leaking from his nose. His eyes rolled in his head as he attempted to regain his senses. Randy grabbed Wes under the arms and pulled him to his feet.

Katie wasn't sure who she wanted to win the fight between those two. Both Josh and Wes had their admirable qualities, and both of them had their reprehensible sides. The ideal situation would have been for them to mortally wound each other. Then Katie wouldn't have to decide which side she wanted to be on. It was a horrible thought, she knew that, but things would be so much simpler without them fighting over her. Perhaps things would go back to normal if both of them were gone. If nothing else, her mom and her would be safe.

And why was Wes fighting for her? She'd broken him, tried to kill him. Maybe she was confused about the situation. Maybe his hatred of Josh was so deep Wes would take any opportunity to go after him. Katie may have been completely out of the picture. That wouldn't surprise her.

Hissing and shrieks filled the room. Katie pulled her gaze from Wes and Josh to take in her surroundings. Wave upon wave of demons flooded into the warehouse, each with fangs bared and claws ready to fight. Fear gripped Katie's chest. She scanned the floor for her pipe, knowing the metal would do little to protect her against the evil army, but the weight would feel comfortable in her hands. The floor was a tangle of talons and dog paws. She couldn't see a thing.

"Wes!" Randy's voice rang out over the melee. "We have to go!"

Katie looked up to see where the man was. Her gaze fell on Wes, who once again raced toward her. What was he going to do? The look on his face was intense, focused. His eyes were locked on hers, determination covered his face. Was he going to kill her? He was surely angry that she had almost killed him, and after the fight and everything they had been through, it wouldn't surprise her if he had murder on his mind. Plus, she had chosen Josh's side. She was a threat to everything he believed and fought for. The last thing he needed was her running around threatening him and his family. No longer was he going to fight to save her. He was going to hunt her.

Her stomach tingled at the thought. If that was what Wes wanted to do, she wasn't exactly in a position to stop him. Her only hope was that a demon or a dog would intervene before he reached her. He was within a few arm's lengths and held out his hand, reaching for her. Katie stared at the limb as if it were radioactive. A few more steps and he would reach her. She braced for his touch. His fingertips brushed against her arm, but before he could grab her wrist, something grabbed her from behind. The grip was strong, forceful, but not threatening. Katie glanced down and saw the black flesh, the sharp claws, but she didn't cry out or struggle. She let the demon lift her from the ground and back away. Black wings closed around her, encapsulating her in a protective shell.

"Katie!" Wes's voice was full of anger and concern.

Hounds barked and lunged forward, demons' claws clattered against the floor. Katie peered through the crack in the demon's wings. Wes ran for her again, but was stopped by Randy. Wes struggled and fought against his father's grip, but Randy held tight.

Randy whispered something in Wes's ear, and he stopped fighting against his grip. Katie could only imagine what he told his son. No doubt it had something to do with her being an evil witch and making her choices. She imagined he convinced Wes there would be another chance to kill her. They lived across the street; opportunities would abound.

A portal opened behind them, and Randy ran through. Wes hesitated before stepping into the light, glancing over his shoulder. Katie felt a pang run through her chest. With lips pursed and demons closing in on his position, Wes stepped into the light and disappeared. A small, sad smile crossed her lips. Typical Wes, abandoning her when she needed him the most. At least this time, she had given him a reason to leave. At least she had driven him away by attempting to kill him. With him truly out of the picture, Katie could focus on what she needed to do next. She could figure out how to save herself.

MORE GREAT READS FROM BOOKTROPE

Billy Purgatory: I Am the Devil Bird **by Jesse James Freeman** (Fantasy) A sweet-talkin', bad-ass skateboarder battles devil birds, time zombies, and vampires while pursuing Anastasia, the girl of his dreams (and they aren't all nightmares).

Charis: Journey to Pandora's Jar **by Nicole Walters** (Young Adult - Fantasy) Thirteen-year-old Charis Parks has five days to face her fears against the darker forces of Hades and reverse the curse of Pandora's Jar to save mankind.

Forecast **by Elise Stephens** (Young Adult, Fantasy) When teenager Calvin finds a portal that will grant him the power of prophecy, he must battle the legacies of the past and the shadows of the future to protect what is most important: his family.

Of Stardust **by February Grace** (Fantasy) At the age of twenty-six single, geeky bookseller Till Nesbitt inherits the shock of a lifetime: a huge Victorian farmhouse filled with unique tenants, and the knowledge that there is a reason she's always been different. She's destined to become a fairy godmother, because the skills are written into her DNA.

Seducer Fey **by Cullyn Royson** (Fantasy) Book one of the Genetic Fey Series. When the fairies of Celtic mythology are combined with genetic engineering, youth and charisma can be sold.

… and many more!

Discover more books and learn about our new approach to publishing at:*www.booktrope.com*

CPSIA information can be obtained at www.ICGtesting.com
Printed in the USA
LVOW08s0853200114

370147LV00001B/15/P